THE RISE AND FALL OF A

ALSO BY SETH RUDETSKY

My Awesome/Awful Popularity Plan

THE RISE AND FALL
OF A

THEATER GEEK

SETH RUDETSKY

Random House New York

Text copyright © 2015 by Seth Rudetsky
Jacket art copyright © 2015 by Bruce Rolff

Visit us on the Web! randomhouseteens.com

Educators and librarians, for a variety of teaching tools, visit us at RHTeachersLibrarians.com

Library of Congress Cataloging-in-Publication Data
Rudetsky, Seth.
The rise and fall of a theater geek / Seth Rudetsky. — First edition.
pages cm.
Sequel to: My awesome/awful popularity plan.
Summary: Sixteen-year-old Justin Goldblatt lands a dream internship with his favorite Broadway actor, but the Big Apple comes with big trouble when his friends stop speaking to him and someone starts sabotaging his hero.
ISBN 978-0-449-81672-1 (trade pbk.) — ISBN 978-0-449-81671-4 (ebook)
[1. Broadway (New York, N.Y.)—Fiction. 2. New York (N.Y.)—Fiction.
3. Internship programs—Fiction. 4. Friendship—Fiction. 5. Dating (Social customs)—Fiction. 6. Gays—Fiction. 7. Jews—United States—Fiction.] I. Title.
PZ7.R85513Ri 2015 [Fic]—dc23 2013015904

Printed in the United States of America

10 9 8 7 6 5 4 3 2 1

First Edition

Dedicated to all the kids (boys and girls)
who are Justin Goldblatt,
and the adults who were

THE RISE AND FALL OF A

OF A

THEATER GEEK

All right, I have to admit it. I need a break from Spencer.

Not literally a breakup. More like a break(ish)-up.

Here's the thing—I am about to go live in *New York City*!!! I can't very well show up in the city of my dreams, a city filled with other sixteen-year-old boys who love theater like I do, and tell them, "Keep your Broadway show tickets. I can't go on a date with you because I have a boyfriend back home."

I mean, I guess I *could* say that, but I wouldn't be taking advantage of everything the city has to offer me. And that's the whole point of my time there in the first place.

See, every year in my school we have JobSkill, a two-week period where the juniors immerse themselves in what could be their future career. This has been a tradition at my high school since the sixties, when the school briefly had a hippie principal who decided homework was too "establishment," so he adopted a "go at your own pace/do whatever you want" curriculum. The parents halfheartedly went along with his ideas until spring semester. That's when they found out he had encouraged the juniors to go to a "be-in" instead of take their SATs *and* he had meticulously changed everyone's grades on their report cards to either "Cool" or "Not Cool." The school board called an emergency meeting and voted unanimously to fire him. Soon after, he was briefly institutionalized and is now leading a cult in Memphis.

Anyway, the one idea of his that's remained is JobSkill. In the spring of 1969, he petitioned and got permission from the state to allow students two weeks off to experience what life would be like after high school. Or at least, that's what he told the education board. In actuality, he called it "Jobs Kill" and told students it would be a chance for them to learn that taking any kind of a real job would destroy their souls. He claimed the only reason he had one was to "change a broken system from within," but after he left, people realized he had become principal because it gave him access to the school greenhouse, which he used to grow hundreds of pot plants. Regardless, once the state education board approved JobSkill, the school board voted to keep it. Since then, all juniors apply in September for a two-week internship that takes place in January.

Most kids wind up at Franklin General Hospital or the big law office in Woodmere or wherever their parents work. I, however, have planned ever since elementary school to spend my two weeks as near to Broadway as I could possibly get.

Of course, I couldn't wait till September to start applying, so last May I began researching my favorite Broadway directors, and by the time sophomore year ended, I had sent each of their agents a request to be an intern. Naturally, it wasn't just a letter requesting an internship. I also conveniently included a forty-five-minute professional-quality DVD that featured highlights of my performing experience going all the way back to first grade when I did my shul's Hanukkah musical and stole the show as the sassy but ultimately wise sixth menorah candle.

I was hoping that one of the directors would watch the DVD, skip the internship request, and immediately ask me to be in one of their shows. Unfortunately, I should have done more research because when I finally heard back from their agents (months later!), I found out that one director was now based in Europe, another was directing at a regional theater in Southern California, and the third was working on a television show. The most frustrating part is that all three of my DVDs were returned, and I could tell they had never been opened! Argh! How was I going to get to Broadway?

Then, out of the blue in early September, my dad mentioned that one of his patients, Irving Perlman, had a daughter named Sophia who recently started a theatrical publicity firm with her two college best friends called Big Noise Media. Mr. Perlman put in the good word for me and I called the next morning. Lou, their office manager/accountant/executive assistant, was so appreciative that I was willing to intern, because they really needed help, and he was thrilled with the idea of having an intern who loved Broadway as much as I did. He told me I'd be answering phone calls, forwarding emails, and scheduling publicity events.

I was disappointed to learn that the firm only represented a few shows *and* they were all off-Broadway, but at least I'd be in New York City working in theater! Yes, I wanted to be working *inside* an actual theater, but I'm only sixteen. I told myself I'd be getting my foot in the door and who knew where it could lead! I didn't see exactly how it could happen, but I hoped that by the end of the internship, I'd somehow be performing on a Broadway stage. Sure, it was incredibly far-fetched, but not impossible. I began to get more and more excited and kept telling myself that there were very few steps between interning off-Broadway and performing on Broadway.

Then in mid-December, everything changed.

Spencer and I went into New York City to see a matinee. I remember thinking that he looked extra adorable that day. He had put some new cruelty-free product in his orange hair that made it look tousled yet perfectly styled, and he wore one of his signature New York Civil Liberties Union shirts (with the slogan YOU HAVE THE RIGHT NOT TO REMAIN SILENT) tucked into his organic denim jeans, which showed off his always-flat stomach. I, because of our completely different body types, had my shirt *un*tucked. And, due to eight days of Hanukkah snacking, I had recently been forced to add an extra notch to my belt. Furthermore, like Spencer, I had put a new product in my hair that morning, but instead of straightening out my tight, uncontrollable curls as I intended, it simply fluffed out my entire head of hair. So, even though Spencer is much taller than me, we both blocked the people sitting behind us equally, he with his natural height and me with my extended Jewfro.

We were seeing *Phantom of the Opera* because it's my December tradition. *Phantom* (as insiders call it) was the first musical I ever saw (when I was five), and I go back every year to commemorate the anniversary of my Broadway obsession. Spencer and I went to the half-price ticket booth in Times Square and wound up getting great seats in the orchestra section. Right after the chandelier did its famous fall at the end of Act One, the lights came on for intermission, and I suddenly spotted Chase Hudson sitting two rows ahead of us! Ah! If you don't know, he was one of the stars of *Vicious Tongues,* a weekly soap about a college dorm where everyone is gorgeous and dating each other while gossiping nonstop. Chase played the student on a full athletic scholarship who's always on the verge of being kicked out because of his alcoholism. Chase dated a different girl each week on the TV show (and in real life).

I DVR'd every episode and belonged to the official fan site and at least three unofficial ones. The one positive part about the show being canceled is that my weeklong black outfit of mourning not only conveyed my devastation but also served to mask the six pounds I had packed on due to a family cruise to Bermuda and a certain all-you-can-eat dessert bar. I came out of my depression when I read an article announcing a spin-off called *Wicked Words,* but I spiraled downward again when it said that Chase wouldn't be involved.

Imagine my excitement a few weeks later when I read that Chase wasn't doing *Wicked Words* because he was coming to Broadway in a brand-new musical called *Thousand-Watt Smile!*

I could tell Chase was trying to look anonymous by wearing a baseball cap, but I'd recognize him anywhere. As soon as I saw him, I got out of my seat and started moving toward the aisle.

"Where are you going?" asked Spencer as I took a giant step over his legs.

"Chase Hudson is sitting up there," I whispered, and pointed. "I have to say hello!" I started squeezing down the aisle again but had to wait for an elderly lady to slowly move her cane out of the way.

"Do you know him?" asked Spencer, confused.

I turned around and smiled. "Not yet, but he's going to star in *Thousand-Watt Smile*! We're going to be peers!"

I was about to step over the old lady's cane when Spencer tapped me on the back and asked, "Peers? How? Aren't you just interning at a publicity firm?"

Typical. Spencer always throws the cold water of reality into my face. I turned around. "Exactly. A publicity firm that handles shows in *New York City*. He's going to be in a show in New York City!" Spencer was about to speak again, so I waved my hand in the air dismissively. "Peers, coworkers, equals, call it what you will. It'd be rude if I didn't introduce myself."

I turned back toward the aisle, but Spencer's voice forced me to turn around again. "I don't know, Justin. I've read that stars don't like to be disturbed. I know you're a fan. Why don't you wait and see if your boss can introduce you somehow?"

I paused for a moment to actually consider what Spencer said. He did have a point, but I knew the firm I was interning at was small potatoes at best. There's no way anyone there knew Chase.

And what if I spent my whole internship in the city doing busy work at the publicist's office and never got near any actor at all? This could be my only chance to meet a big star face to face. I looked toward the aisle and saw that the old lady had finally lifted her cane. I took that as my cue to quickly squeeze down the row, but in doing so, I stepped on her Playbill and ripped the cover. "Sorry," I called back over my shoulder and saw that the cane she had lifted out of the aisle was now over her head and being angrily shaken at me. I hightailed it to row C. As I approached, a very blond, very tanned man who looked vaguely familiar stood up and blocked my path. "Sorry. No autographs."

Why the H would I want his autograph?

"That's OK," I said, trying to politely elbow past him. "I'm actually interested in *his* autograph."

However, before I could enter the row, the blond stepped in front of me again. "Very funny, kid. Chase doesn't give autographs."

"How do you know?" I asked.

"Because I'm his assistant."

Aha! *That's* why I recognized him. There were always photos of him in the background whenever *People* or *Entertainment Weekly* featured a candid shot, but I had never really taken in his frighteningly overtanned face. And, I might add upon closer inspection, dark roots.

"Oh well," I said casually, and pretended to start leaving. Right when I was about to turn back around and make a mad dash past him to thrust my Playbill in Chase's face, I heard Chase!

"I'll give him an autograph. Why not?"

Ah! He sounded exactly the way he did on *Vicious Tongues.* Masculine and tough yet friendly. Whoa! He was even more gorgeous up close. Wavy brown hair poking out from underneath his cap, huge green eyes, and just a little stubble around his pouting mouth. And even though he was pretty old (he just turned thirty!), he looked like a college kid. He beckoned me forward and the blond slo-o-o-owly stepped aside. I decided to be friendly, though, and held out my hand to him.

"I'm Justin," I said.

He considered a moment and then responded. "Oo-bare," he said, while barely shaking my hand.

"Huh?" *What's Oo-bare? How are you? in some other language?*

Chase laughed. "Oo-bare. That's his name. It's spelled Hubert but pronounced the French way."

Oh, I thought. Then, *Why?* "Are you from France?" I asked.

The slight shake of the head I received from Hubert indicated he wasn't a French native. But the glare that accompanied it indicated he was well versed in their ability to convey deep disdain.

I ignored him and handed my Playbill to Chase, along with the trusty Sharpie that I always carry for emergency autographs.

"Sorry for the rigmarole," he said as he signed. "*Vicious Tongues* has some psycho fans and Hubert was just trying to protect me."

Wow! Chase thought I *wasn't* a psycho fan? Well, that's a testament to my acting.

"I'm looking forward to working with you, Mr. Hudson!" I said, exaggerating a little.

"Aw, call me Chase," he said as he handed back my Playbill. Then, "Wait. Working with me? Where?"

Specifics? Uh-oh. "Well, not exactly. But I'm sure we'll be running in the same circles." I lowered my voice in an I-don't-want-to-brag way. "I'm going to be on the staff of a big New York theatrical publicity firm."

He looked confused. "Aren't you a little young to be on a publicist's staff?"

"Well," I said, stalling, "I'm not exactly on the staff. It's complicated. . . ." I faded out and used the awkward silence to listen to Spencer's voice in my head telling me to stop trying to make it sound better than it was. I took a deep breath. "I'm in high school, and starting in January, I'll be doing an internship for Big Noise Media, which is an off-Broadway publicity firm."

"Oh!" he said. "You want to be a publicist?"

"No!" I said, a little too loudly. "I want to be an actor. On Broadway," I specified. "As a matter of fact, this is my tenth time seeing *Phantom.*"

"Wow!" he said with a smile. "This is my first. I'm trying to see as many shows as I can before my Broadway debut. This is my day off from rehearsals."

"Chase!" Hubert interrupted, willing me to go with his eyes. "Act Two is about to begin."

"Well, nice meeting you—" Chase began, but I cut him off.

"I'm sure it's a big deal to you since Broadway's been your dream ever since you played Sky Masterson in summer camp."

He looked at me with a shocked *how-can-you-read-my-thoughts?* expression.

I then explained, "I read your interview on Playbill.com." He looked visibly relieved. "Stephen Sondheim is my hero, too."

He seemed impressed. "He's the best, isn't he?"

"I have all of his shows on my iPod. Including both revivals of *Sweeney Todd!*"

"Me too!"

"Chase!" Hubert said, barging into the conversation.

I ignored him. "I'm here with my boyfriend, Spencer, and I've turned him into somewhat of a Sondheim fanatic, too."

"Boyfriend?" he asked. "Wow. No one was gay back in my high school."

"I bet they were, but you just didn't know it!"

He laughed. "How old are you, Justin?" he asked.

"Sixteen."

He nodded and spoke quietly. "Sixteen. Things sure are different from when I was your age."

I bet! "But they're also the same," he continued. "That's how old I was when I first got into theater." He looked away with a dreamy smile. "I wish I could have done an internship in New York."

Hubert barged back in. "Nice meeting you," he said while putting his arm around me and pushing me toward the aisle. I ducked under his arm and turned back to Chase because I knew this might be the last chance I actually got to speak with him. "Mr. Hudson, I may be stuck in the publicist's office the whole time I'm here, but

I hope that somehow I get a chance to watch you rehearse." Then, "I'm sure you'll be amazing in the part. Brilliant!"

That sentence was a last-ditch effort to score some points. In actuality, I had never heard him sing or seen him dance, so I had no idea how he'd do, but I thought if I laid on the compliments, it might result in him contacting Big Noise Media and inviting me to one of his rehearsals!

The lights started flashing to signal Act Two was about to begin but Chase suddenly touched my arm.

"When do you begin your internship?"

"Right after New Year's," I told him.

He looked like he was thinking. "That's the beginning of our last two weeks of rehearsal before previews, right?" he said, looking at Hubert.

"Exactly," said Hubert. "It'll be a very busy time. So—"

"So," Chase finished his sentence, "you could use the extra help!"

"What extra help?" Hubert asked.

"How about this?" Chase said to me excitedly. "Skip the publicity firm and come intern for me in January!"

"Are you serious?" I asked, too scared to hear the answer.

"Absolutely! If you want to be an actor, you should intern for an actor."

"I can't believe it!" I said, and the next thing I knew, he was handing me his iPhone.

"Type your name and number here." I did and handed it back.

Hubert was having a conniption. "Chase! I have a very specific system worked out. I certainly don't need—"

Chase cut him off. "You're a workaholic and you deserve some help." Then he looked at me. "And it's the chance I wish I'd gotten as a kid."

"But—" Hubert started, but I didn't want to wait around to have him take the internship away.

I decided to use his line against him. "Sorry to cut you off, but Act Two's about to begin. Gotta go!" I turned back to Chase. "Thank you so much and see you in January!"

Yay! This was exactly what I wanted! Hubert could do all the fetching and running an assistant does and I would do all the Broadway assisting Chase might need. You know, running lines, going over choreography, and being ready to accompany him on the piano if he wanted to sing through the entire score to *Thousand-Watt Smile* or any of the Broadway shows I can play by heart.

I ran back to my seat and quickly told Spencer the whole story. He gave me a kiss and told me that he had been wrong to tell me not to approach Chase. It felt good to have him apologize and have everything work out so well.

Now I just had to tell Big Noise Media that I was no longer available. For a brief moment I remembered the office manager telling me how much they needed an intern and I started to feel guilty for leaving them in a lurch.

But soon the lights began to dim for the start of Act Two, and I put it out of my mind.

There was no way I was going to lose my chance to work on Broadway!

Spencer and I saw *Phantom* at the start of Christmas break, and as soon as I got home, I told myself I had to call Big Noise Media and cancel my internship. But I knew the office would be closed because it was a Saturday, and since my quitting would undoubtedly upset them, I felt I should actually talk to them rather than leave a message. But when Monday came, a part of me hoped that they'd somehow forgotten I was supposed to intern and I wouldn't have to deal with canceling at the last minute. Of course, the more days I put off calling, the more last minute it became. Since it was Christmas break, I woke up late every day and spent a lot of time practicing the violin and piano because I had a recital at the end of January and knew I wouldn't want to practice once I was in New York City. I successfully avoided thinking about Big Noise Media until just a few days before I was due to begin. I checked my email and saw a message from Lou the office manager describing various projects I'd be working on and telling me he'd be calling later in the afternoon. I managed to avoid picking up my cell throughout the next two days but Mr. Perlman must have given them our home number because on the Friday before I was supposed to start, my dad told me I had a call.

I took the phone to my room, closed the door, and took a deep breath.

"Hello?" I said, hoping it wasn't Lou.

Of course it was and he asked why I hadn't responded to his calls. I hauled out the old my-cell-phone-has-been-deleting-messages routine and before I could say anything else, he told me that he was thrilled I was coming to help because "confidentially, we just lost two clients and we're struggling to stay afloat. We really, really need the help."

It seemed rude to follow that statement with the news that I wouldn't be showing up because I got a much more exciting internship, so I stalled by asking about Sophia, Mr. Perlman's daughter. I expected to hear a bland "She's fine," but instead he said she was flying to L.A. to see if the firm could branch out into movie publicity because they were "desperate, *desperate*" for new clients. Since Sophia was planning a two-week trip, the office would be understaffed starting tomorrow, so my timing was "absolutely perfect!"

Argh! Everything he said made it more awkward for me to completely back out of my commitment.

I inhaled and he took that moment to add, "Boy, do we need help!"

Stop already! Why was he making it so hard for me to leave him in a lurch?

"So . . . ," I began.

"So," he continued, "I know I said ten o'clock on Monday, but can you start at nine?"

Oy. I knew I should have just given in at that point and said yes, but that would have meant passing on the chance to work on an actual Broadway show in an actual Broadway theater.

That's the right thing to do.

Of course Spencer in my head would say that. That's one of the reasons I need a break(ish) up from him. Spencer never sees the gray between black and white. He would only see two options for me: doing an internship I don't want to do or breaking my word.

I knew there must be a third option.

Hmm . . . I took a moment to think. I know I can get out of my Big Noise Media internship *and* not look like I'm completely letting them down if I just come up with a good reason.

Do you mean you're going to lie, Justin?

I mean I'm going to tell the truth, Spencer.

In my own way.

"Hello? Justin?" Lou was waiting for an answer.

I got it!

"Lou," I said, adopting a somber tone, "I actually have bad news." I paused. Then I spoke with emotion. "My . . . my grandmother died."

Which was true.

She died when I was four.

"Oh, Justin! I'm so sorry," said Lou.

"So," I said with a little catch in my voice, "I guess you understand that I really need to be here . . . with my family."

"Of course, of course," Lou said. "Listen, I don't want you to worry about us. We'll get by without you."

"Thank you," I said with a tone that I hoped sounded brave yet devastated. "And . . ." I needed to cover all bases. "I know my parents will feel guilty that I'm choosing to stay with them instead of intern with you. . . ."

"Oh, they shouldn't. It's very sweet."

"Well, I know them. So, if you don't mind, I'm going to tell them that the internship fell through. That way they won't wonder why I'm not at Big Noise Media."

"That's very considerate of you. I understand."

I was getting a little uncomfortable from how nice he was being, so I quickly told him I had to go comfort my mother and got off the phone.

Phew. I got what I wanted without having to lie.

Well, without having to lie too much.

The good news is I paved the way to start my Broadway life on Monday! I still didn't know exactly what I'd be doing since I'd only gotten a terse phone call from Hubert last week confirming my start date. When I tried to get more information from him, he told me that being an intern meant not asking questions. It did?

I didn't care; Chase was the one I'd be working with. Hopefully. I just accepted that Hubert would always be cranky toward me.

So, imagine my surprise when he called this morning.

"Hi, Justin!" He sounded exuberantly friendly. As a matter of fact, he was so loud that I had to quickly lower the volume.

"Hi, Hubert," I said tentatively. It was enough of a struggle to remember to pronounce his name "Oo-bare," but it was even harder to know how to talk to him with his new personality.

"First of all, how are you?" he asked.

Huh? I know it was the most basic of questions, but it was so unexpected I was completely stymied and didn't know how to respond.

"Uh . . . ," I started, and paused for six seconds. Finally, I thought of a word. "Fine."

"That's great!" Hubert responded right away, sounding genuinely pleased. "We wouldn't want you getting sick before your big internship!" Really? Last time we spoke, it seemed like he would have loved it if I were bedridden.

"Justin," he said, sounding serious, "I am so pleased you're going to be able to help out."

My first impulse was to say, "You are?" followed by "Since when?" but thankfully I resisted and finally went with, "I'm going to help out!" This was based on a technique I learned from watching a PBS special on therapists. When a patient (Hubert) is acting bizarre, you can keep the situation from escalating by just echoing back what they say.

"What time do you get to New York City on Monday?" he asked.

"Anytime you need me," I said, starting to match his enthusiasm. "And I know exactly where the theater is."

"Wonderful," he said. "Why don't you come to the Dakota at ten a.m. instead."

Huh? The Dakota is an apartment building on Seventy-Second Street that's famous not only because it's sadly where John Lennon was shot, but also because it's one of the most beautiful A-list places to live. I'm planning on staying at my grandma Sally's and the Dakota is within walking distance, but I wanted to have the first moment of my internship be on Broadway, not at an apartment building.

"Is that 'cause you wanna meet at a landmark and then take the subway down together? I could easily hop on myself and—"

He cut me off with a laugh. "Justin, the Dakota is where Chase is staying."

Whoa! It's true I wanted to have the first moment of my internship be at a Broadway theater, but this was an amazing way to begin as well. I was going to see something very few people have— the inside of the Dakota! Great views of Central Park. Celebs in the elevator. Luxuriously spacious rooms. This internship was already thrilling!

"What apartment number?" I asked.

"Just introduce yourself to the doorman at the Seventy-Second Street entrance. He'll tell you what to do."

I was so excited that I almost dropped the phone as I said bye. Broadway! The Dakota! Yay! I definitely had the best internship in the history of JobSkill. Spencer's, however, is probably the most boring. Not just in the history of JobSkill, but in history . . . period. He'll be working for the local Greenpeace chapter and his main duty is making phone calls asking people to donate. Oy. I almost fell asleep writing that sentence. I mean, I admire that Spencer has such a generous nature, but why would he choose something so tedious when we're allowed to make our internships anything we want? I asked him that question last month at lunch.

"Justin," he said calmly, taking a bite of his baked-not-fried potato crisp, "JobSkill is supposed to give us a chance to see what our future careers will be like. After college, I'll be working in the not-for-profit world."

"But why can't you work in the not-for-profit world in Manhattan?" I asked, taking a handful of my fried-not-baked potato chips. "There are plenty of charities on the Upper West Side. That way we can see each other every day!"

"I committed to do JobSkill for Greenpeace when I was a freshman. Way before we were dating."

"Spencer," I said, annoyed, "not every commitment requires your extreme level of commitment." It sounds like I'm babbling, but I think Spencer knew what I meant. Not that it did any good.

Actually, now I'm glad Spencer is going to be here on Long Island and not in New York City. Maybe I won't even have to ask for an official break(ish) from him because the geographical one will be enough. I must admit, though, it'll be weird to be away from Spencer for fourteen whole days. We've seen each other pretty much every day since we started dating last spring. And no matter what, we've never missed a Sunday together. We have his whole house to ourselves because Spencer's parents spend Sundays at a yoga intensive.

Yes, a yoga intensive. In other words, take something tedious and then intensify it. Oy! Is wanting to do boring things genetic?

Regardless, every Sunday Spencer makes us a delish vegetarian meal (we both became vegetarians years ago after watching *The Simpsons* episode where Lisa stops eating meat), and then Becky comes over and we watch a movie. Becky, by the way, is Becky Phillips, not only one of the most popular girls in our grade but also *the* best actress in our entire school. FYI, I'm the best actor, and we're tied for best singer. Even though I'm pretty low on the social scale, we're great friends. It happened last year when I came up with a plan to try to become popular *and* date Chuck Jansen, the cutest guy in school. It involved me pretending to date Becky and quickly got very complicated. To this day, she thinks the only reason I pretended to date her was to help her date Chuck behind her father's back. In the end, Becky and Chuck broke up and she and I became close friends, and since then, Spencer, Becky, and I haven't missed our Sunday movie.

Tonight, though, is an even more important tradition. It's New Year's Eve Game Night. I don't know if I'll have the courage to talk to Spencer about a break(ish) but it's now or never . . . JobSkill starts in two days!

3

Well, that didn't go as I expected.

At all.

Let me start at the beginning. I got to Spencer's house at around five.

"Hi, Justin!" Becky said as I walked into the kitchen. She was wearing her reddish-gold hair in a ponytail that gave her an "I'm among friends so who cares what I look like" vibe but her casualness actually intensified her gorgeousness. If anything, having her hair back showed off her stunning cheekbones and catlike green eyes even more. Spencer was still in the middle of cooking but he turned away from the stove and bent down to give me a kiss.

P.S.: Why am I still the same height as when I was thirteen? I keep clinging to the hope that my gut will magically disappear when I reach a normal height. Hmm . . . I guess it could also "magically" disappear if I cut down on eating, but I'm holding out for a growth spurt.

"I'm psyched to spend my first New Year's Eve with you guys!" Becky said. "What's the Monopoly theme this year?"

"You'll have to wait and see," I said with a wink.

Becky was referring to a tradition Spencer and I started years ago, even before we were dating. Every New Year's Eve we play themed Monopoly. Not the kind you get in a store, like *The Simpsons* or Disney; we make the game ourselves. Our first year, it was based on gym. My playing piece was a shoe with a pebble in it since I once put rocks in my shoe so I would have a limp and be able to skip class. And Spencer's was a sock. But not a normal white gym sock. It was a black sock you'd wear with a suit. That was based on the day Spencer dressed up for a big science presentation. He remembered to bring most of his gym clothes for later in the day but forgot his socks. He was mortified that he had to do all of gym class wearing shorts, sneakers, and black nylon socks. He spent the whole period pulling them up and then pushing them down because both positions were horrific. If he bunched them around his ankles, they looked crazy because there was so much material, and if he pulled them up, they looked like my aunt's half stockings. Instead of Go to Jail cards, I made Be Picked Last for Football Team cards, and when you passed Go, you didn't get two hundred dollars. Instead, you got a Cramps card. That was because Spencer and I were incredibly jealous that girls could get out of gym just by hauling out that complaint.

Last year Spencer made a whole Broadway themed Monopoly that was amazing, and this year I themed the game on our upcoming JobSkill. The pieces all had to do with our internships.

Mine was a picture of Chase with Broadway-style lights around it, Spencer's was a whale with dollar signs for eyes (representing him asking for donations to Greenpeace), and Becky's was a gold ticket stub since she was interning at the local Starlight Theater. Since I had no idea what would happen at our internships, I based it on my hopes. Boardwalk and Park Place were actually pictures of Don Frances and Michael Monda, two cute guys who worked at the Starlight, one of whom I was hoping Becky would wind up dating. When you passed Go, you got a starring role on Broadway (my fantasy!), and the Go to Jail card was still "Go to Jail" . . . but for leading a Greenpeace protest that involved civil disobedience.

"Well, I know that this year I'm being added to the Monopoly tradition," Becky said as I pulled out the box with the game inside, "but I have to take a rain check. I've got to leave right after dinner."

"What?" It was New Year's Eve! No one leaves a party before midnight. "Why can't you stay?" I asked, shocked.

"Well," she said, briefly giving Spencer a smile for some reason, "my parents are making me come home early tonight because they want to spend time with me since I'll be gone for two whole weeks starting Monday."

Huh? That didn't make any sense. The community theater where Becky is interning is a few blocks away. She loves Broadway as much as I do but couldn't convince her parents to let her go to New York City to intern at GlitZ.

Oh, yeah . . . if you don't follow the modeling world, you might not know that GlitZ is one of the top modeling agencies in the U.S., and the only one that has solely male models. I thought it would be a great place for Becky to intern because we'd be able to see Broadway shows together and she'd get to meet tons of cute teen models and, hopefully, start going/making out with a few of them. Becky hasn't dated anyone since Chuck, and in October, I decided to make it my mission to find her a new boyfriend (and an internship). I knew she'd want someone super cute (Chuck was gorgeous!), so I started researching modeling houses in New York. A whole bunch came up, but I called GlitZ first because I remembered reading an interview with Chase where he mentioned that he started there as a teen model. I asked the woman who answered if there were any upcoming internships, and she told me they had plenty of internships available! I filled her in a little about Becky and mentioned she'd be free for two weeks starting January second. She told me Becky needed to fill out the online application but there wouldn't be a problem.

The application was super simple, so I did Becky a favor and filled it out for her. That night I called Becky with the good news. At first she was annoyed I didn't ask her before I called GlitZ and even more so when I told her I did the application without telling her, but I quickly said "sorry" and launched into details. She went from cranky to psyched when I told her what was (probably) in store for her. World-famous photographers, discounts at top designer stores, business lunches at fancy restaurants, et cetera.

After we said goodbye, I decided to research GlitZ a little more so I could tell Becky what department was most likely to snag her a future boyfriend. I was hoping there'd be a "blond male models with high IQs who love *Wicked*" department, which would be perfect for *both* of us. Unfortunately, I didn't find out much about their separate departments. Annoying. I did, however, find a few postings on various websites talking about how GlitZ "saves bundles of cash" by using "slaves" to do free grunt work all the time and warning people to stay away because it's a "living nightmare." But on the GlitZ website the internship testimonials were all glowing. Various interns wrote that it was "So much fun!" and how wonderful it was to work for a "top modeling agency that treats everyone like a superstar." That negative stuff sounded to me like sour grapes and it didn't even make sense. GlitZ doesn't need to save bundles of cash; they're one of the biggest modeling agencies in the world. And how can anyone feel like a slave when they're surrounded by gorgeous models? Living nightmare? More like a living dream! Soon, everything fell into place. Becky even got herself a great place to stay. Her older cousin Melissa is a medical resident (everyone in Becky's family is a doctor) and told Becky she could crash at her place. Melissa's apartment is right near GlitZ, so Becky wouldn't even have to pay subway fare.

Everything was fine until Becky's dad learned that Melissa has the graveyard shift at Mount Sinai Hospital and she's out of the apartment every night from 9:00 p.m. to 6:00 a.m. He didn't want Becky sleeping in a New York City apartment all by herself, so he told her she had to cancel the internship.

"Why do your parents need to spend time with you if you'll be home for JobSkill?"

"Because," she said with one of her smiles that make you feel warm all over, "I'm going to New York City!"

AH!!!

I screamed and ran over to hug her. Her father must have changed his mind. This was perfect! Her cousin's apartment was right near where I was staying.

Yes!

Becky and I would be two single(ish) teens hanging out in the big city!

"When did this all happen?" I asked.

"Last week!" she squealed. "I wanted to surprise you."

"How did you convince your dad to let you stay in the apartment alone?"

"I didn't," she said.

Huh?

Then I figured it out. "Did your cousin finally get normal hours?"

"No," she said, shaking her head. "I'm going to have a roommate."

Aha. That made sense. Becky's so popular, I'm sure she was finally able to convince one of the cool kids to change their internships and stay with her.

"Who?" I asked, thinking it was a toss-up between Savannah Lichtenstein and Julianne Taylor.

I was wrong.

"Hey, roomie!" Becky said as she ran over to Spencer and hugged him.

What the—?

Spencer was going to be in New York!

Oh no! I had hoped that his being on Long Island and my being in Manhattan would save me from having to officially ask for a break(ish)-up. Now I will have to go through the conversation of asking for an official separation. Thanks, Becky!

But wait. Something else was bothering me.

"I don't get it," I said to Spencer as we all sat at the table. "What happened to the whole 'I committed to Greenpeace'?"

Becky answered. "I told him that he didn't need to treat everything as set in stone."

Spencer shrugged. "She was right."

"I always believe there's room for flexibility," Becky added firmly.

Argh! That's exactly what I said to Spencer at lunch a few weeks ago, but his only reaction was to take a sip of soymilk.

That always seems to happen lately. For instance, I told Spencer a month ago that he had to watch this new reality show (*Double Divorcées* about women who divorced the same husband *twice*) because it's so incredibly stupid. I even told him that I programmed his DVR to tape it for him when I was at his house. He shook his head and said he wouldn't have time to watch it. Fine. But then at lunch a few days later, Becky started telling him how stupid the show was. I got up to get some more veggie hot dogs and when I came back, he was hunched over an iPad, sharing headphones with Becky and watching that stupid show!

What nerve! *I* said it was stupid first!

Becky snapped me out of my irritating memory. "I knew my dad would let me come to New York if Spencer stayed with me."

I wasn't surprised. Spencer is the most reliable kid in school. He's at every school event doing the things no other kid wants to do. He's been the head of the cleanup committee for the bake sale *and* the car wash, the curtain puller for the school musical, and the so-called explosion preventer at the school science fair, which involved hauling around an industrial-strength fire extinguisher and wearing a hazmat suit.

Spencer scooped out a sensible-sized portion of tofu curry stew for himself. "After Becky convinced me, I called Greenpeace and asked them if I could do volunteer work this summer instead."

Hmph. If I had suggested that, he would have done his typical soymilk sip/ignore me routine. I scooped out a sensible-sized portion of the stew for myself. And then another. "So where are you going to intern in New York?" I asked Spencer, annoyed. "The Human Rights Campaign Fund? Save the Whales? More Math in Our Schools?"

"I'll answer that," Becky said proudly. "I got him an internship!"

"You did?" I asked, confused.

"That's right," she said while squeezing lemon into her water. "He'll be with me at GlitZ."

WHAT!

I was speechless.

I didn't know what I was feeling. It felt like jealousy. But why would I feel jealous? Because I introduced Becky to Spencer and now it seems they have a friendship completely separate from me? Because the two of them were going to spend every day of their internship together? Because Spencer was going to spend two whole weeks immersed in the glamorous world of male models?

No, I decided, there was no need for jealousy. This whole situation was actually a positive thing. I'm glad they've become so close. It shows what good taste I have in friends. And I'm glad Spencer will have tons of cute boys around him. Maybe this will get his mind off the heartbreak he'll feel when I tell him we need to break(ish) up.

But it still didn't make sense. Where's the nonprofit part of GlitZ?

"GlitZ has a 'save the environment' category of modeling?" I asked.

"No, silly," Becky said. "Spencer isn't just an activist. He likes other things as well."

GlitZ has a yoga department?

"I got him an internship in the accounting department."

Accounting? Only Spencer could find a way to make a modeling agency boring.

Spencer high-fived Becky. "Numbers all day long!" he said as my eyelids drooped. Wow. I'm glad I drank some coffee before I came over.

Hmm . . . I had always fantasized about spending JobSkill in the city with my friends and it would be like a preview to our lives after college. Then I was forced to come to grips with the fact that I'd spend those days without the two people closest to me. Now they're *both* going to be living right near me . . . and I'm not sure how excited I am. It's weird how things change. In September, since there's no fall play and therefore no afternoon rehearsal, I had been able to go with Spencer to all of his after-school activities. I would sit on the side and do my homework during math team or yoga and then I'd walk Spencer home. After I dropped him off, we'd chat on the phone till I got to my house. *And* we'd always have a nice long conversation before we went to sleep. But recently I've been thinking about all the possible boyfriends out there I could have if I weren't dating Spencer. I mean, even if you love vanilla ice cream, don't you get sick of it after a while if it's all you ever eat? And Spencer's not even so much fun to be around these days. Lately I feel like he's always vaguely complaining about things I do. Furthermore, even though he and Becky think I don't notice, they sometimes roll their eyes to each other after I say something. And last week, during our nightly chat, he cut me off in the middle of a story—before I even got to the good part—claiming he had to go to bed. All these things are getting on my nerves, and I know it's time to take a small break from him. During our time apart, he'll realize how amazing I am and get his act together. And I'll be refreshed after a quick winter fling with a city boy or two (three, maximum) and come back to school ready to reenter the relationship.

As I was briefly fantasizing about what kind of boy I'd date in the big city, Becky got up from the table and put on her coat. "Spencer," she said, "my dad'll come at eight a.m. Monday, but if we're running late, I'll call your cell." And with that, she gave us both a quick kiss and left.

Hmph. Her dad's driving them? I'm stuck taking the Long Island Rail Road to New York.

"Justin," Spencer said as he washed dishes and I dried, "let's talk before Monopoly."

Good ol' Spencer. He can always read my mind. He somehow knows I need a break and wants to save me the awkwardness of telling him.

"I agree," I said.

I took a deep breath but he held up his hand. "I know you probably want to start, but I'd like to say what I have to say first."

Sweet! He wants to make sure we can still hang out in New York even if we aren't "officially" dating.

"OK, Spencer," I said, deciding on three nights, max.

"Justin, I think we should break up."

What?!?!?!?

4

Hello From Fabulous New York City!

I know I seem too happy for someone who was just dumped, but the shock of Spencer's nerve is much easier for me to take while I'm surrounded by the greatest city in the world. On Saturday I went home and thought through what Spencer said. The first mind-boggling thing he claimed was that I was trying to change him.

"I never try to change you!" I yelled after that moronic statement. "That's why I'm slowly going crazy. I don't say anything about your weird fascination with math boringness and yoga snoozery!"

"See!" Spencer said in an I-just-proved-my-point manner. "That's what I mean. You don't want me to be who I am."

"Yes, I . . . I do," I sputtered. "But I'd also like to help you grow!"

"Grow?" he asked, with an I-completely-don't-believe-you look.

"Yes, grow!" I responded. Then, using his own Eastern religion double-talk, I added, "Into your better self!"

"Ha!" he laughed, a little meanly.

"What's so funny?"

"I think you mean you want me to grow into *your* better self."

What was that supposed to mean? I decided to leave before it got worse. After all, I got what I wanted. Maybe a little more than I wanted, an entire breakup instead of a short break(ish)-up, but it's probably for the best. It's clear that Spencer and I are just too different to be together.

We gave each other a light hug goodbye.

Silence.

Spencer said, "I hope we can stay friends."

"Me too."

No, I didn't. I was actually hoping to avoid him completely and immediately get a new boyfriend who likes the things *I* like and is interested in what *I* have to say.

The good news is, I left his house a day and a half ago and already I feel rejuvenated.

I took the Long Island Rail Road to Penn Station this morning and then the subway up to Seventy-Ninth Street. My grandma Sally lives on Eightieth Street in a beautiful brownstone. She has a floor-through, which means her apartment has a window in the front living room that overlooks the street, and then you can walk all the way through her apartment and there's a window in her bedroom that overlooks the backyard. Her guest bedroom has no window, which some people would find too dark and depressing, but I love it because it makes me feel like a real New Yorker.

I buzzed when I got to my grandma's place and she opened the door in her usual mood. Crankiness.

"You're wearing *that?*"

I didn't even know what the "that" referred to—my coat? Hat? Pants? Shoes?

Turns out, none of the above. "Take it off!" she barked while moving the straps of my knapsack off my shoulders. "It's bad for your back."

Ironic advice to be getting from a woman who has what is affectionately known as a "dowager's hump" among polite society or simply a "hunchback" among fans of the Disney film.

"Hi, Grandma Sally," I said, and gave her a kiss.

"Did you eat breakfast yet?" she asked as I carried my suitcase to my room.

"I'm starving!" I responded, not actually answering the question. I was too embarrassed to admit that less than ninety minutes after eating two bowls of hot cereal at home and twenty minutes after a glazed donut at Penn Station, I was raring for more.

"I thought so, so I made you a little something."

Yay! A "little something" is Jewish for five courses. I went into the kitchen and saw eggs, bagels, cream cheese, muffins, blintzes, and both buttermilk *and* potato pancakes (with the requisite apple sauce).

I dug right in. I poured on the maple syrup knowing I'd burn it all off at rehearsal. I didn't know exactly what I'd be doing for Chase, but I assumed I'd be going over dance steps with him, running scenes, and possibly stepping in for him during some of the run-through if he needed a rest.

Grandma Sally stood over me. "Are you done?" she asked unpleasantly.

I couldn't tell if she meant, "You're done so soon? You barely ate!" or "Are you finally done? You've eaten way more than your share." The one thing I did know was that her question was overflowing with disapproval.

I was in the mood for another bagel, but I didn't want to be late to meet Chase, so I told her I was finished. Naturally, she sighed. I didn't have time to figure out what new dissatisfaction she came up with, because I had to flatten my hair and floss. Chase was used to hanging out with male models. I couldn't greet him in his amazing Dakota apartment with a high-rise of hair and veggie cream cheese between my two front teeth.

I fixed myself up, did a quick Listerine, said bye to Grandma Sally, secretly got my knapsack so she wouldn't see, and left at 9:40. The Dakota is only eight blocks away from Grandma Sally's brownstone, so I was able to walk casually and take in my new neighborhood. I loved it! I've visited the Upper West Side many times before and had had a few overnights, but because I'm staying for two whole weeks I feel like I really live here. I started nodding to people on the street with the subtext of "Hi, fellow Upper West Sider. I, too, am a resident." When I got to the corner of Seventy-Seventh Street, the light turned red and I decided to try complaining like a real New Yorker.

"Ugh!" I said to the well-dressed woman standing next to me. "This light always takes so long!" I looked at her with an *Aren't you sick of it, too?* expression, hoping we could commiserate as two long-term Manhattanites.

She looked confused.

"The light?" She glanced at the traffic light and then back at me. "It's been broken and finally got fixed last night."

I looked away. She continued. "I guess you just got here this morning."

I immediately started crossing the street even though the light was still red.

"Watch out!" she yelled, but I successfully dodged an oncoming taxi *and* any more of her incisive yet sadly revealing comments.

The morning wasn't going quite as I expected. I'm fairly numb to Grandma Sally's crankery, but I didn't like being spotted as a non-native within minutes. It didn't really matter, though. I was about to see one of the most exclusive places in New York: the inside of the Dakota! Last week I did a little research and saw that an apartment there was recently on the market for twenty-eight million dollars! I was hoping I could get a few photos of myself by Chase's living room window with a snowy Central Park behind me. It would make a great Hanukkah card for next year. As I approached the Dakota, I looked up at the beautiful gas lamps that lined the path to the inner courtyard. Instead of having the doorman located inside the building like most apartments, he's located outside in a kiosk. I approached the uniformed man and smiled.

"I'm Justin Goldblatt," I began.

"Oh yes, Mr. Goldblatt," he said right away.

Mr. Goldblatt? I definitely was expected! I waited for him to call up to Chase and tell him I was here. I was hoping the apartment was on a high floor with a great view all the way to the East Side.

As I was fantasizing about whether it was on the tenth or eleventh floor, the doorman handed me a package that I assumed he wanted me to take up to Chase.

"Oh, thanks," I said. "What apartment?"

"What apartment what?" he responded.

"What apartment am I going to?" I clarified. *Needlessly,* I thought.

"Uh, I don't know, sir."

How could he not know? It was his job to know where everyone lived. Nevertheless, I spelled it out. "What apartment is Chase in?"

He shook his head. "I can't tell you that. We're not allowed to give out residents' information."

What? He obviously knew I was expected but was now acting like I was a crazed fan trying to break in.

This was a continuation of my annoying morning (which, quite frankly, began Saturday night), and I decided to put the kibosh on it before it got worse. I took out my cell phone and called Hubert.

"Hello?" he said after it rang twice.

"Hubert, it's Justin Goldblatt."

"OK." I guess that meant "hi." "Did you get the package?"

Package? Oh, right. The one in my hand.

"Yes, I did." Then I lowered my voice. "I just can't find out from the doorman where to go." I kept scanning the apartments, hoping I'd see Chase in one of the windows. No luck.

"Where to go? How would the doorman know?"

Huh? This was getting more and more bizarre.

"Just read the letter in the package," he said, sounding irritated. "I need to go." And with that he hung up.

I ripped open the package. Inside was a small glass jar of something that looked like lemonade. Maybe it was a lemony throat remedy for Chase?

I looked back in the package and saw a letter. Finally, some info.

Turns out, while I was staring up at various windows like an idiot, Hubert and Chase were nowhere near the Dakota ... They were already at the theater! Hubert wrote that Chase wanted to get there early to warm up. Then why didn't he take his throat remedy with him? And if they already left for the theater, why wasn't I with them right now helping out?

Well, the rest of the letter gave me the answer.

Hubert wrote directions that told me where to go today and it was not to the theater. Not at all. I had to take a subway *and* a ferry to Staten Island! And then I had to take a bus to a doctor's office. Specifically, a veterinarian where I would drop off the jar. Apparently, the jar I was holding was not a lemon-based throat soother. It was an ammonia-scented urine sample! According to the letter, Mookie possibly had a bladder infection and Staten Island had the best dog bladder/spleen vet specialist in New York. I hoped I'd be able to drop it off and rush to the theater to watch the rest of rehearsal.

Apparently not, since the end of the letter told me to wait at the vet until it was analyzed. Just in case I thought there was a chance I'd be able to stop by the theater, the letter ended by saying it would "probably take most of the day."

Well, at least I could tell people I spent my first day of interning in New York on Broadway.

That's right ... Dr. Geraci's address is 127 Broadway, Staten Island.

5

What a day. While the Staten Island Ferry is fun to ride with your grandparents when you're a little kid, it's not fun to ride in the deep freeze of winter. The river was so choppy from the waves that I began to feel seasick. Unfortunately, someone actually got seasick but wasn't able to aim it overboard. He wasn't even able to make it to the outside deck. So ten minutes into the thirty-minute crossing, the entire inside smelled like a vomitorium and I had no choice but to spend the rest of the ride outside in the freezing cold. I stayed at the vet for the bulk of the afternoon, and when I finally got the result of Mookie's test (negative!), I had to take the whole ride back.

I figured that today was a pet emergency and tomorrow would really begin my stint working on a Broadway musical.

By the time I walked into Grandma Sally's apartment, I was feeling better. That feeling was immediately cut short by her yelling, "Don't get mud everywhere!" I don't know what she could have been referring to considering I took off my boots *outside her apartment*!

"Grandma Sally, I'm wearing socks. How can I track in mud?"

"Socks!" she shrieked as she impressively changed what she was mad about within one second. "You're going to slip on the wood floor, and I don't have time to take you to the hospital. My friend Devon is coming over to play cards."

Devon? Who was that? Some widower looking for a wife? Before I could ask, she said the thing I expected. "Put on the guest slippers."

Oh no. She was holding one of the pairs of slippers she'd been giving guests since before I was born. She has four pairs that she keeps in her closet for whenever it rains/snows/sleets/is icy outside and they've been the same pairs for as long as I can remember. And they've never been washed. Ever. A part of me needed to prove it, so one year I decided to do an experiment. We had come over for Rosh Hashanah dinner during the year I was Bar Mitzvahed. There was a big rainstorm that day and we were all forced into the slippers. My father dangled my pair in front of his face and said the same thing he always does. "Ma . . . these look like the same ones I wore when I was a kid."

Grandma Sally then gave the same response she always does.

Silence.

Neither confirmation nor denial.

Right before we left that night, we pried them off and put them back in her closet. I took out the rattiest pair (they were red, white, and blue and said '76 across the top) and put one of my remote control cars inside the right slipper. When we came back for Pass-over, I brought my remote control console, opened the closet, turned it on, and guess what came riding out of the closet? Of course, I had to throw the car out because it had spent six months inside a stench factory and reeked worse than the inside of today's Staten Island Ferry.

This time, however, I came prepared.

"Thanks for the offer, but I actually have my own slippers," I said while heading to my suitcase.

"Not anymore!" she yelled. "While I was unpacking your stuff, I threw them out."

"Why would you—"

"Covered with dog hair!" she said, and thrust out a guest pair.

Argh! She somehow figured out a way to thwart me thwarting her. I gave up. I knew I had to put on the slippers Grandma was threateningly holding toward me but I also knew it meant I'd have to throw out the socks I was wearing. I attempted to shut myself down emotionally as well as olfactorily and slipped them on.

"That's better . . . ," Grandma Sally said, and then one second later she started screaming again. "You're dripping!" She pointed to my winter coat, which was wet because it was still sleeting out-side. I hightailed it to the bathroom and hung it in the shower so it could dry but immediately wanted to put it back on because it was freezing in the apartment. I went over to see if the radiator in the living room was working and as I got near it, I saw that the window was open!

"Grandma Sally!" I yelled to the kitchen. "You left the window open."

"Don't touch it!" she yelled back. She walked in, drying her hands and wearing an enormous down coat. "Every time I open the closet, the whole apartment smells like sour milk for some reason. I've got to get that stench out of the apartment."

"For some reason?" Surely she must know the reason the closet lets loose a smell from hell is because of those stank bombs from 1976.

"You know what it is, don't you?" she asked. Before I could answer, she did it for me. "It's that old Russian couple in the next apartment cooking cabbage soup. That closet wall must be paper thin."

Huh? The closet wall was made of brick. How could it be thin?

I told myself that I was getting a rent-free apartment on the Upper West Side and decided not to question her. But I did need something to warm myself up.

"I'm freezing," I said as I headed toward my room for a sweater.

"Wait a minute." She went back to the closet that held the slippers. "This'll keep you nice and toasty." She walked over and placed a knitted shawl around my shoulders.

Not only did it smell like the closet, but it was an ugly mustard color. And it was also stained in three places with actual mustard.

She must have seen me looking. "Don't mind the stains. They're permanent because you can't wash wool."

Huh? "Well, you can dry-clean wool—"

"And you can pay for it, Moneybags!"

I couldn't wear something so ugly and that was stained and had the permanent slipper smell embedded in it.

"I think I'll get one of my really warm sweaters," I said as I walked toward the suitcase in my room.

"Don't go in there!" she yelled. "I washed your floor and it needs a half hour to dry."

Washed my floor? I just arrived that morning. How dirty could it be? She drives me crazy. A complete neat freak over things that need no cleaning yet zero concern over things that are actually disgusting.

"It's so cold," I muttered, half to myself.

Unfortunately, she heard the other half. "You lose eighty percent of your body heat through your head."

She plopped one of her fur hats onto my hair.

She stepped back to admire it. "My mother used to wear that back in the day when New York really got cold. Not this global warming crap."

The doorbell rang.

"That's Devon!" she said as she scurried back to the kitchen. "You get it while I finish making dinner."

I looked crazy but I assumed I was safe; anybody who was friends with Grandma Sally had to have some sort of a screw loose. If he was anything like the eligible widowers she'd dated before, I knew my outfit would be more attractive than his polyester suit.

I opened the door.

A teenager stood there.

He was taller than me and had blond hair and dark blue eyes. I couldn't help but notice his leather jacket clung to what was undoubtedly a muscular chest and then tapered to a thirty-inch waist.

I stared.

He took off his Banana Republic glove and stuck out his hand.

"Hi, I'm Devon." He flashed a smile.

No two ways about it, he was C-U-T-E!

I snapped out of my state of shock and put my hand out but it got caught in . . . Argh! My stupid shawl! I struggled to untangle it and it finally fell to the floor. I kicked it away but in doing so, one of my slippers flew off and bounced down the hallway.

"I'll get it," Devon said, and jogged off. He came back with the slipper but I noticed he was holding it farther away from himself than I had held Mookie's pee jar.

"Thanks," I said, slipping it back on. I instinctively went to pat my hair to make sure it wasn't in its highest Afro. Instead of feeling my Jewish curls, however, I felt soft fur and faced the horrifying fact that I had opened the door wearing never-been-washed slippers, an old lady shawl, and a squirrel hat from the 1940s.

"Come right in," I said, and as soon as he did, I muttered, "Excuse me" and ran into my bedroom. I didn't care that the floor was just washed; I needed to counteract the first impression I had just given Devon. I peeled away the slippers and put on my sneakers. Off came the shawl and on came a baby blue sweater from Macy's. I also squeezed two handfuls of product into my hair to shape it into something that would erase his memory of the dead animal on my head.

I came out and Devon and Grandma Sally were already sitting at the table.

I looked at Devon's feet to see which pair of disgusting slippers he was forced into.

What?

He was still wearing his Nikes!

"Devon said it stopped sleeting out," Grandma Sally said, following my gaze.

Unfair!

"Justin," Devon said while pouring himself some water. "Your grandma's told me all about you."

Wow, I thought, looking at him. Who cares about the slippers? He's cute. I better work it.

"Well," I said, flashing a grin, "I'm here for a school project—"

"Didn't you just hear him? He knows! I already told him you're working with some model who's starring in *Phantom of the Opera.*"

"What? No . . . I mean, yes . . . He *used* to model in the old days and I ran into him at *Phantom,* but I'm actually—"

"—interning for Chase Hudson while he's rehearsing *Thousand-Watt Smile,*" Devon said, then added, "And today you got to go to the Dakota."

"How did you—" I began.

He looked embarrassed. "Justin, please don't think I'm a stalker, but I go to your website once in a while."

Huh?

"Your grandma told me you'd be visiting and joining us for

our weekly dinner, so . . ." He smiled sheepishly. "I couldn't resist doing a quick Google search to see who you were."

"Isn't it pronounced 'goggle'?" asked Grandma Sally.

We ignored her and he started rattling off information.

"When I put in 'Justin Goldblatt' and 'Long Island' there were too many results, so I added words like 'Broadway' and 'high school.'"

Smart!

"There were three Justins that seemed likely, but I wound up not having to check them all because I could tell that the first website I went to was yours."

Oh! Now it was making sense. "You saw one of my daily blog postings?"

"What's a blog?" asked Grandma Sally.

We ignored her.

"Your grandma didn't have any photos of you—"

"I have 'em, but they're in a good place," Grandma interrupted as she passed me a platter of veggie lasagna. She keeps all photos in a shoebox on the top shelf of her closet. "Once you take 'em out, they start to get yellow."

"But," clarified Devon, "your grandma described you, so as soon as I saw your profile pic, I knew it was you."

"Yep," Grandma Sally piped up again. "I told him how you're always complaining about your weird, curly hair." I dropped a fork, hoping it would distract her. She continued. "What do you call it? A Hebrew do? The Jewish curse? A curly Jewfest?"

"A *Jewfro*," I finally said to shut her up. I glared at her, but she didn't see because she was busy diving into her lasagna.

"*That's* it!" she said with cheese hanging out of her mouth.

I tried to start another sentence but she kept talking. "And I told him how I gave that pep talk to you about your dad also having a large belly and big backside like yours. What did I tell ya, kid?"

I didn't respond.

"Justin! What did I tell you about your large, large—"

I cut her off before she could reiterate. "You told me to wait it out like Dad did," I said through gritted teeth.

"Yep! Most of the lard melted away once he turned eighteen," she said, nodding.

I smiled and mentally tried to signal the end of the conversation.

She squinted her eyes and looked closer. "I got no advice about the pimples, though. They seem to be relentless."

"Of course," Devon thankfully broke in as I passed him the lasagna, "the picture made me pretty certain it was you, but when I saw your blog update called 'Moving to the City of My Dreams,' I knew for sure."

Why couldn't he have said that before my physical faults were spelled out by the Wicked Witch of the West (Side)?

I started to eat and tried to counteract my devastation by bragging a little. "My favorite blog so far has been 'Chase and I.' It's the one where I wrote about how excited I am to be working with him."

"Aren't you working *for* him?" Grandma Sally demanded.

I kept my eyes on Devon and spoke confidentially. "Well, it's officially an internship, but he kind of handpicked me so . . ." I shrugged to imply *He not only wanted an intern, but he also wanted someone who could inspire him. Yes, the innocence of the student might indeed rekindle the flame within the master.* That was a lot of information to get into one shrug, but I think I was clear.

Then I remembered something Devon first said. "Go back a bit," I requested. "Weekly dinner?"

"Well, I'm also doing a school project, just like you," he said while wiping tomato sauce from his mouth. "My school's guidance counselor said that colleges like to see some sort of volunteer work, so—"

"He was coming to the senior center where I go on Sundays," Grandma Sally explained. "We wound up playing Scrabble."

Devon laughed. "Your grandmother loves Scrabble."

Hmph. More like she loves competing. She refuses to play unless she has stiff opposition. She flat-out forbid me from even asking to play Scrabble with her until I turned thirteen.

She'd always repeat the same sentence: "No way can you have any kind of Scrabble knowledge until you're *well* into puberty."

I was too scared to ask what her version of "well into puberty" meant. When I turned thirteen, I kept my mouth shut because I was afraid that if I asked to play, she'd put on rubber gloves and begin a Scrabble physical.

Finally, last year I brought out the Scrabble box but she immediately slapped my hand away.

"Don't open it!"

She grabbed the box and clutched it to her chest.

"First, give me four three-letter words that have the letter *Q*."

"Um . . ."

She held out her hand to silence me. "All right, that's it." She passed the box back. "Put it away," she said, shaking her head, and I haven't had the nerve to ask to play since.

I looked at Devon. "You won?"

"What?" Grandma Sally said with a cackle. "I kicked his behind!"

"But it was close," he reminded her.

"That's the point," she said, slamming her hand on the table. "All those other codgers can't play Scrabble worth a wooden nickel. When they saw me with the board, they started whining and asking if they could play. I was hoarse from saying no so much." She pointed at Devon. "I told this one I'd make him dinner once a week if he'd come over and play here in peace."

"So, we started a tradition. Every Monday I join your grandmother for a little Scrabble and some dinner."

I passed him the salad bowl and he started to take some.

"Devon!" Grandma Sally yelled in his direction. "Don't take all the tomatoes!"

I guess he'd been coming for a while if she felt comfortable enough to scream at him. Then I rethought my conclusion because she screams at everybody.

"So," I said as Devon passed me the salad dressing, "I guess you went to my website today?"

"Yeah," he said, looking embarrassed. "I got hooked on your daily updates and I wanted to know what happened on your first day in New York."

I smiled.

"I didn't see anything about Chase, though," he continued. "Was he glad to see you?"

I stopped smiling.

"Uh . . . ," I began, "today was not my official start day." He looked confused. "You know, the theater is usually 'dark' on Mondays," I added.

That is technically true. Most Broadway shows start their performance week on Tuesday and end with the Sunday matinee. If there is no show, the theater is "dark" for that day. Of course, Chase's show is in rehearsal today, so the theater is anything but dark, but Devon didn't need to know that.

"I know it's usually dark, but I looked on Playbill.com and it said that there are Monday night shows for the first month of *Thousand-Watt Smile* performances, so that usually means there are also rehearsals on Mondays."

I was a combo of mortified and impressed. He definitely had my investigative skills, or what Spencer calls my relentless obsession with snooping.

"Are you into theater?" I asked, sidestepping the conversation.

"He's just like you," Grandma Sally said, with her mouth full of cucumbers. "What do you call it? A Broadway loser? A theater freak?"

"Theater *geek*," I clarified.

"Yeah, that's me!" he said. "I pretty much spend all my free time trolling the Internet for message boards and videos about Broadway."

Wow! Was this my (much better-looking) twin talking? I had hoped I'd meet someone like this at some point during my internship. And I'm meeting him the first day! I thought maybe we could hang out after dinner watching fun YouTube videos and then go out for a little dessert.

"I'd love to show you this obscure Tony Awards clip that—" I started to say.

"Do it on your own dime!" Grandma Sally said. "We're playing Scrabble." She then stared me down. "Privately."

"Of course," I said, forcing myself to smile at her. Then I looked at Devon with a real smile. "But maybe after—"

"*Af-ter,*" she said, "Devon's heading straight home. Scrabble wears me out and I can't have any chattering between you two that'll keep me up."

"Oh, but—"

"Justin, bring the plates to the kitchen. Devon, pick your tiles."

I wanted to argue but couldn't bear to be cut off again in front of him.

"Have a great night," I said instead, as I carried the plates away.

"Nice meeting you!" Devon yelled as I heard Grandma Sally spill out the Scrabble tiles.

Now what? What the hell was I supposed to do while they played? I figured I'd call Becky from my room for some privacy. Then I remembered that Becky was two blocks away, and the good news was for two whole weeks I wasn't living with my parents, who wouldn't let me go out on a school night! I already told Grandma Sally I needed my own set of keys because I'd have to do some interning at night. How would she know that my interning was actually a vanilla latte with extra whipped cream? I quickly texted Becky after I put the plates in the sink.

ME: *Had an interesting first day. You?*

BECKY: *Don't even!!!!*

ME: *Wanna meet?*

BECKY: *Starbucks near your grandma's?*

ME: *If you say so. Ten minutes.*

BECKY: *Order me a latte. Double shot.*

Starbucks? Double shot? Becky had proudly given up coffee over the summer because she felt she was getting addicted to it and was sick of spending ten dollars a day on various caffeinated drinks. What had happened today that made her go back to what she called "the devil's beverage"?

I was about to find out!

6

I went to the really nice Starbucks on Eighty-Sixth and Columbus Avenue. Some of New York's Starbucks are so small you can't ever get a seat, or if you do, it's at one of the long bars by the window where you never know who's going to be sitting next to you. It's one thing to be in an elevator next to someone I've never met and be forced to stare straight ahead for several floors, but I don't want to be one inch away from a stranger when I'm slowly licking whipped cream off the sides of my mug. Anyhoo, I got a great table and waited for Becky. I looked down Columbus Avenue and saw her red-gold hair flying in the cold breeze. I waved her over as soon as she walked in and I pulled the cover off her latte.

"Thanks, Justin," she said, and took a lo-o-o-ong sip.

She put it down and I noticed there was barely any latte left in her cup. "Whoa," I said. "You are off the wagon!"

"Justin, GlitZ is a nightmare!" she said right away.

Uh-oh.

"What do you mean?" I asked, nervously trying to figure out a way to deny I ever saw any postings online forewarning me.

"It's not an internship. It's . . . it's . . ."

I said the first thing that came to mind. "Slave labor?"

She cocked her head. "How did you know?"

Uh-oh.

"Just a wild guess," I said with a laugh. "Just an out-of-the-blue thought." I couldn't stop babbling. "It could have been way off base because it was totally based on conjecture"—I was losing track of what I was saying—"and not, you know . . . based on previous knowledge. Because I didn't have any"—what did I call it?—"previous knowledge." Phew. I finally faded out. Luckily she looked like she had also faded out on what I was saying because she was too involved drinking the last third of her latte.

She wiped her mouth. "I thought I'd be hanging out with models, or at least that's what you told me. . . ." She then reached across the table and took my coffee. Did she want to smell it? Surely she didn't want a sip. She just drank an entire venti ten seconds ago. And I only ordered a grande. And every drop is delicious!

Gasp! She gulped the whole thing down!

"I don't get it," I said, trying to avoid focusing on the fact that she not only finished my delicious drink, but she also got all the sugar that accumulates on the bottom of my coffee. Argh! My favorite part!

How could she not have spent the day hanging out with models? This totally threw off the timeline I had planned for her. I was hoping by now she'd have three prospective boyfriends.

Hmm . . . I suspected it might have been good old-fashioned shyness. "Becky! All you have to do is say hello. Then the invitations will start pouring in."

"Say hello to who, Justin?"

Huh? "You know," I said, "to all those cute models!"

"Justin," she said, sounding exasperated, "there's no one to say hello to!"

What?

"I don't see anybody! I'm on a special floor where none of the models go."

"Why?"

"It's where they keep all their records," she said, putting her finger in the empty cup, scooping out what was left of the granules of sugar and licking them off each individual finger.

"The penthouse?" I asked, hoping for the best.

"The basement!" she yelled.

I kind of predicted she'd say that.

I needed clarification. "What exactly do you do?"

She rubbed her eyes. "It's so tedious. GlitZ started so long ago that they have tons of photos from before anything was digital."

"So?" I asked.

"So . . . my amazing internship is to take all the old photos and scan them one by one so they can be put into their database." She leaned forward. "And, Justin, there are thousands!" She was getting loud. "*Thousands!*"

Well, that's all it took for a barista to send a severe glare in our direction. I looked back at him with a face that was half apology and half asking for waiter service. Becky drank my latte and I desperately wanted another one. The face I got back told me I should get my own drink. And that my apology wasn't accepted.

I focused back on Becky. "That part sounds awful. What else do you have to do?"

"That's all I'm *allowed* to do! From now on, I don't even enter the main GlitZ office. I'm supposed to go directly to the basement and stay there all day."

"Well, are you at least working with fun people?"

"No. It's just me in a creepy basement with tons of file cabinets." She looked at her iPhone, which was sitting on the table. "I don't even get cell service."

It sounded much worse than my day on Staten Island.

"Becky, I can't believe I'm saying this, but why don't you quit?"

She looked at me like I was crazy. "How? Where would I go? Pamela Austin took my internship at the theater. There's no way I'd be able to find another one this late. And don't say I should just not intern at all because then I wouldn't get any credit for all of JobSkill, my parents would ground me, and I wouldn't be able to do the spring musical!" She put her face in her hands, but I could still hear her. "I'm stuck. Stuck! Stuck!!"

I looked up at that moment and then *I* wanted to put my face in my hands. Spencer was in line and waving at me! I couldn't believe Becky invited him. Ugh! Why did I say I wanted to remain friends with him? Couldn't he see through my lie? Was I that believable? Sometimes being an amazingly talented actor backfires.

"Spencer's here," I said, and Becky lifted her head.

"Good, I'm glad he came," Becky said. She looked at him with pity. "He had it just as bad as I did."

I hoped my smile wasn't obvious.

Spencer walked over holding a cup with a tea bag string coming out of it. Decaf, no doubt. And organic. Hmph. Even holding a drink, he can make you feel shallow.

"Hi, Spencer! How are you?" I said with a broad smile. I decided to start big. Why be awkward? Especially when I'm already planning on getting Devon's number from my grandmother's easily accessible address book.

"Good, Justin, how are you?"

"Fine."

Silence.

I was able to start big but I wasn't able to continue it. It was too weird. I mean, I was just at his house two nights ago eating dinner as part of a couple and now we're broken up. I didn't expect it to hurt, but it did. Yes, I wanted to break(ish) up but I didn't expect it all to end completely.

OK. I decided to focus on Devon. His cute face, his tiny waist, his . . . Wait, what color were his eyes again? Argh! I don't know him well enough to distract me from my feelings of rejection.

Becky was too into her own devastation to pick up on the awkwardness. "Spencer, what did we get ourselves into?" She reached across the table and took a sip of his tea. Wow. She was now a liquid kleptomaniac.

"Did Becky tell you about our day?" Spencer asked me.

No! And I don't care!

I didn't say that. I took a breath and decided not to hold on to my anger. For now. Spencer and I were friends for years before we became a couple, so I at least owed him the courtesy of listening to his problems. Even if I was secretly overjoyed he was having them.

I gave him a caring look. "Becky told me about hers, but she didn't tell me about yours."

He shook his head. "Just as bad."

"Why?" I asked. "I thought you liked accounting."

I decided to leave out "for some reason."

"I do like accounting," he said, and put his usual one pack of sweetener into his tea. Yes, I mean sweetener, not sugar. He would never use actual sugar or what he calls "poison in a pink packet" (Sweet'N Low). His choice, as usual, was all-natural Stevia. Of course, he never worries about whether the restaurant he's in will have it. Why? Because he *carries it around with him.* Does that show you the kind of person he is? He's a Goody Two-shoes who goes two steps further. His goody two shoes are also vegan *and* made of all-natural recycled rubber.

"The problem is," he continued, "I'm not accounting."

"I thought you're in the accounting department."

"Justin," he said with a sigh, "I thought so, too."

What did that mean? "Thought?" I asked.

He explained with some anger. "I'm on the same floor as the accounting department, but I'm not doing anything and I mean *anything*"—he brandished his tea for effect—"with numbers." He started listing off his expectations while tearing open the Stevia packets and putting them in his tea. "I thought I'd be dealing with numbers all day." Two packets. "I thought I'd be double-checking computer equations nonstop." Three packets. "Multiplying, subtracting, dividing." Four packets. "Formulating equations, solving problems . . ." Five packets. "I'm doing none of that!" Wow! Three more packets at the same time!

I know it doesn't seem like a big deal, but this was Spencer completely out of control. Essentially, his version of binge drinking is an overdose of all-natural sweetener.

"What are you doing instead of all that?" I dared to ask while hoping it wouldn't trigger him to add seven more packets and put him in a non-GMO diabetic coma.

"I'm a . . . receptionist!" he said with disgust.

"What does that mean?"

"What do you think it means, Justin? I answer the phone!"

"And?" I asked.

"That's all! Period!"

It didn't sound that bad.

He must have read my facial expression.

"Do you know what kind of torture that is?" he asked. "I can hear them doing math right in the next room. Calling out numbers, yelling sequential integers, asking each other for help with complex numerical systems and"—his face registered pain—"I can't join in!"

He put his head down. It was the same head-in-hands position Becky had just been in. "I thought I'd be doing math," he said with his face to the table.

Even though I didn't understand, I realize that he loves math like I love theater. He kept talking to the table. "I even thought I could somehow use my math to help the world."

At a modeling agency? That's just like Spencer. He can't simply enjoy something. It always has to be for the greater good. I knew I should say something to cheer them up, but what? I wasn't loving my internship so far either, but I had hopes it was going to improve. The two of them seemed set that theirs was a dead end.

I decided to put the ball in their court. "What can you do to make it more fun?"

Becky turned so fast that her hair whipped like a tornado. "What can *we* do?" she asked, dripping with anger. "*We* can't do anything."

"Yes, Justin, we're stuck," Spencer said, and gave a quick look to Becky.

Huh?

"What's that look about?" I asked him, a little too loudly. I lowered my voice. "Why are you both acting like it's my fault? I don't run GlitZ."

They looked at each other.

"Well?" I raised my voice again.

"It pretty much is your fault, Justin," said Becky. Spencer nodded as he drank his tea.

"What is 'pretty much my fault'?" I said, imitating Becky's slight Long Island accent.

"The horrible time we have in store for us," Becky shot back at me.

That was so unfair. "What did I do? I've never even been to the GlitZ offices."

"So? It didn't stop you from getting me an internship there without even asking me if I wanted it!"

"Exactly," Spencer added. "And now I'm stuck there, too."

Wow. Within one minute they had completely ganged up on me. Becky is always emotional, but I didn't expect this from Spencer. I looked him straight in the eye. "Spencer, I didn't make you go to GlitZ."

He looked right back at me. "I took the internship, Justin," he said in a measured tone, "because I wanted to be in New York with you." He did? "After I accepted the Greenpeace internship, I thought about what you said and decided it *would* be nice if we were together for JobSkill."

That was sweet.

He threw his head back. "Ha!"

That wasn't! "Why the laugh?"

"I thought it would help our relationship." He shook his head. "That was before I realized I needed to end it."

How dare he say that he broke up with me? Even though it's true!

I refused to let him see I was hurt. "Well"—I shrugged—"I see you've bounced back pretty quickly and I'm sure you'll make an excellent assistant." Spencer's eyes widened. "Sorry, *secretary*." He looked stricken. "Oops," I said, then slowly stated, "receptionist."

Becky gasped. "Justin!"

"What?" I asked. "I'm trying to be supportive," I lied. "Which is pretty amazing of me since you're both acting as if I ruined Job-Skill for you."

"You pretty much did!" Becky said with her eyes ablaze.

"How? All I did was get the offer from GlitZ. There was no commitment. You didn't have to say yes!"

Becky laughed. "Please. You would have found some way to trick me into going."

"That's not true! I accepted that you had to turn down GlitZ and were going to do JobSkill on Long Island. You completely surprised me on New Year's Eve, if you can remember all the way back to Saturday night."

She snorted. "Oh, really, Justin? We all know you'll pretty much do anything to get what you want." *What did that mean?* "I'm sure you had some plan up your sleeve to call my parents and ask them to drive me back and forth to the GlitZ offices. Or ask the theater to let me do mornings at GlitZ and afternoons on Long Island? Or—"

I let her prattle on. Of course she was right. I *was* planning on getting in good with Chase right away and then, after a few hours, asking him to let Becky stay in one of his extra rooms at the Dakota so she could quit the Starlight Theater on her first day and start interning at GlitZ by tomorrow.

I waited until she took a breath and then defended myself. "Even if I was planning on helping you figure out a way to do GlitZ, it's because you wanted to intern there."

"Justin, *you* wanted me to intern there. Why? Because you always think you know what's right for everyone."

Well, I do! I thought.

Then I clarified my thought. I mean, I don't always *think* I know what's right for everyone. I always *know* what's right for everyone! Wait. Is that the same thing? Isn't one better than the other?

Spencer spoke. "I think what Becky means is sometimes you're . . ." He trailed off.

"I'm what?" I asked.

"Well," he slowly said, "you can be a little . . . selfish." *What?* "I mean, you sometimes bulldoze your way into getting what you want without thinking how it will affect anyone else."

Selfish? Me?

Becky joined back in. "Justin, I never asked you to get me the GlitZ internship."

That's like someone saying, "I never asked for this pot of gold." Where was the gratitude? I mean, maybe the internship wasn't turning out the way she wanted, but it was high profile and in New York City! I shook away any doubt about my actions and went on the attack. "Yeah," I said, feeling mind-boggled that she wasn't more appreciative, "you're right. I'm completely to blame. I made the call, I gave them your name, and I got you an internship at a world-famous place. You didn't have to do anything." I should have stopped there. Unfortunately, I added another sentence. "As usual."

It was like all the noise in Starbucks was sucked into a vacuum. It seemed totally silent.

Becky finally spoke. Slowly. "What does that mean?"

Well, I started it, I thought. *I might as well finish it.*

I spoke calmly. "You don't usually do things for yourself, Becky, if you haven't noticed."

"No, Justin, I haven't noticed."

Really? How could she not realize all I've done for her? "Then let me spell it out for you. When your dad was about to transfer you out of school, *I* figured out a way to stop him. Remember? And I was the one who pushed you to audition for the chorus solo, which you then got. Then I was the one who gave you the opportunity to sing at last year's Spring Fling, which finally convinced your father you didn't want to be a doctor. I was also the one who told you about Usdan summer camp and talked the camp director into letting you come to the callbacks even though you missed the auditions. And those are just the highlights."

"You've been keeping score? How could you—"

"So, yes," I interrupted. "I knew I'd have to find an internship for you because you always need someone to hold your hand!"

That was it. Becky and Spencer both looked at each other and then, as if choreographed, they got up and walked out of Starbucks.

I sat there by myself and watched them walk down Columbus Avenue.

It was my first night in New York City and I was now friendless.

7

I sat in that Starbucks for around an hour.

At first I stared out the window till I could no longer see Spencer and Becky. It was getting crowded but I felt very alone.

Over the past year, whenever Spencer and I had a disagreement, I would go to Becky to talk it through. And the few times I'd had it with Becky's wishy-washiness, Spencer helped me get past my annoyance. I had no backup plan to deal with both of them teaming up and dropping me.

Spencer called me selfish! And Becky said I would do anything to get what I wanted!

Was that true?

I knew I could call my parents, but whenever I have a problem, they're not interested in just listening. Instead, they immediately spring into action and try to solve it. It always involves some wacky scheme that backfires on all of us or some New Age/love-yourself technique they learned from watching *Oprah* reruns that doesn't work but involves things like being barefoot and chanting. If I told them what happened, they'd probably drive into the city, pick me up, take me to Spencer and Becky's apartment, and then make us act out our feelings in a game of charades. I considered turning to my grandmother for comfort but then realized I could simply walk in front of a cab and get the same result. I had a quick inclination to track down Devon just to have someone to chat with about it, but I just met him and I want to maintain the image that I'm totally together. Why would he ask out someone who was just dumped by his ex-boyfriend and his best girlfriend? Yes, he'd probably give me comfort but a part of him would wonder if I deserved it.

Frankly, *I* wondered if I deserved it. After all, I did see those posts online about GlitZ and didn't tell Becky. And I guess part of me knew that the praiseworthy posts were probably planted by someone at GlitZ. And even though I was trying to be helpful, I did harass Spencer for weeks, telling him to intern in Manhattan.

Was it all my fault?

Argh! I needed to talk to someone but who? I reached for my iPhone twice before I realized I couldn't call Becky or Spencer.

I stared at my empty cup and felt very immobilized.

Finally, I realized I had to move. Whenever I feel upset, I know that I can only feel better if I do something. First, I made a decision that none of what happened was my fault.

At all.

I mean, yes, I set their internships in motion, but Becky could have said no and Spencer never should have said yes.

They were both free agents and I bore no responsibility for their current situation. Case closed.

I took a deep, cleansing breath and the guilt washed off of me. Ahhhh.

Then I got myself up and ordered another latte. It was essentially my first latte of the night since the one I ordered before was polished off by ol' Sticky Fingers. Right before I took the first sip, I snapped a picture of myself with the latte next to my mouth (I love that reverse photo thing on iPhones) and posted it on my blog. Excellent! I looked 100 percent happy. I captioned the photo with "Yay NYC. Finally *freedom*! No teachers, parents, or ANYONE ELSE telling me what to do!" I hoped Spencer would go to the site tonight and see how unaffected I was by his and Becky's betrayal. I also hoped Devon would read it and consider asking me out. I looked like an independent guy who was totally at peace sitting by himself for hours. After I posted that picture, I immediately became anxious from sitting by myself, so I gulped the rest of the latte down and hightailed it outta there.

Even though I decided the night's events weren't my fault, I still felt bad about some of the stuff I said. And I really felt bad about some of the stuff they said to me. I wanted to shut the dialogue out of my head. I thought I would go lie in bed blasting *A Chorus Line* through my headphones, but when I got to the corner of Eightieth Street, I didn't turn to go to the apartment. I took a quick look at my watch and saw that only an hour had passed, so Devon could still be there playing one of Grandma Sally's endless games. I was scared that as soon as I walked in he'd be able to tell I was depressed and that would ruin the chances of him asking me out. I hoped instead that he'd go home tonight, look at my website, and want to be part of my amazing happy-go-lucky life. I know I have a much better chance getting a date from him if he envies, not pities, me.

I continued down Amsterdam Avenue and passed by Josie's. There was a couple sitting next to the window, both eating from one big bowl of roasted vegetables. Seeing all those veggies made me immediately think of Spencer and his fondness for unpronounceable food like quinoa. I'm a vegetarian but at least I have the courtesy to eat things like tofu and beans, words that sound like they're spelled. Still, quinoa is one of Spencer's favorites, so I walked over to the menu in the window to see if they carried it. Yes! I opened my phone to text him but when I did, I saw the picture of me sitting alone at Starbucks and I suddenly remembered everything that happened. I immediately put my phone back in my pocket and crossed the street. Unfortunately, the next thing I passed was Levain Bakery, which has the best chocolate chip cookies in New York. Even if you don't want to go in and buy one, it's difficult to resist because the smell of the cookies wafts out and permanently settles in the air, forcing you to enter and purchase a dozen. Mmm. I stood right outside the door, and though the bakery was closed, I still had the delicious sensation of living inside a cookie. I breathed in the chocolaty sweetness, which made me think of the brownies I baked and used to manipulate Becky into trying out for the chorus solo last year. Ah! Why did my mind keep going to Spencer and Becky? If they were able to walk out on me at Starbucks, why couldn't they also walk out of my memory?

Why don't you try to work it out? Tell them you're sorry for whatever you did wrong. They're both upset and need your support.

N-O!

I refuse to have Spencer in my head telling me to apologize to Spencer in real life! I put my fingers in my ears and started walking briskly down Columbus Avenue.

Excellent. I didn't hear Spencer anymore.

I kept walking down Columbus Avenue till I got to the famous Magnolia Bakery, which made me think about Chase. I don't know why it made me think of him, but his face suddenly popped into my head. Hmm . . . maybe because I had passed by Seventy-Second Street and the Dakota. Or . . . wait a minute! Maybe his face popped into my head because I just passed his face drinking a cappuccino! I walked back up Columbus and looked in the window again. He was wearing a baseball cap like he did at *Phantom,* and this time he sported sunglasses, giving the full celebrity "Don't recognize me" look. I suppressed my need to walk in and tell him that wearing sunglasses after nine o'clock at night actually draws more attention. I stopped myself because I knew he probably didn't want to be disturbed, but I couldn't resist taking a closer look. If the rest of my internship is anything like today, I may never get to spend any time with him and I didn't want to go back to Long Island having never been near him at all. Also, he had a laptop open in front of him, and I was excited to use the snooping skills I've perfected over the years on an actual famous person. I decided I'd look at the menu in the window as my ruse to get close to him.

I walked right up to the glass, but annoyingly, the lights from passing cars kept reflecting through the window and onto the screen of his laptop, so I was having trouble reading it. I knew I'd be able to see the screen clearly once there was a red light and the traffic died down, but then I noticed that what I thought was a menu in the window was actually the grade that the board of health gave the restaurant. I realized I couldn't stand there much longer without arousing suspicion, because how long could I pretend I was reading the letter "A"? Suddenly, Chase looked up from his computer and right at me. I quickly turned my head to leave but dropped my bag, and various pens and pencils fell out. Ah! As I was fumbling on the ground to pick them up, I heard my name.

"Justin! Come out of the cold!"

Chase was holding open the door. Wow! He knew who I was.

"Hi, Chase!" I said, standing up. A big star inviting me into a restaurant. Yes! What a nice way to end a crappy night. Take *that*, former best friends!

Then I thought about what he said. It wasn't an actual invitation to join him. All he did was tell me to come out of the cold. Maybe he was just concerned I'd get sick and not be able to intern for him anymore. Selfish. And yet . . . while I was hanging up my coat, he sat back down at his table and I noticed there was another chair that I could easily sit in.

Dare I?

Hmm. Better be certain.

"Is Hubert sitting here?" I asked, forcing myself to pronounce it the moronic French way. I eyed the door to the bathroom where he probably was.

"No," said Chase. "Sit down."

Wow! No way to misinterpret that! I was so excited to have a one-on-one conversation with him! I sat down and decided to start off with a bang. I knew the sick passenger on the ferry story would get a laugh and if he thought I was funny, he would tell Hubert I had to spend all day by his side at rehearsal. But before I launched into it, he got a text.

He read it, then looked back up. "Sorry, that was my publicist. What was I saying?" he asked. "Oh, Hubert," he answered himself. "I gave him the night off. He had a rough day."

He did? I thought. I'm the one who went all the way to Staten Island today.

"Yeah," he continued. "He went all the way to Staten Island today."

Wait. Didn't I just think that sentence but with a different pronoun?

"What?" I asked.

"I said I gave Hubert some time to decompress because he spent the day on Staten Island."

"No, he didn't—" I started, but then realized I should probably be careful, so I repeated myself but this time changed my outrage to empathetic shock. *Gasp!* "No! He didn't!"

"Yes! Poor guy," Chase said, and shook his head. "He was stuck there all day."

What a crock! But I knew I shouldn't reveal the lie.

"He was checking to see if my dog had a bladder infection."

I was outraged about the lying but Chase misinterpreted my facial expression.

"You look so concerned! Don't worry, he's fine." He smiled broadly.

I was about to tell Chase that Hubert was lying but then thought twice. I'd be seeing Hubert tomorrow and didn't want to make him an enemy. Right?

But shouldn't Chase know the truth about someone who worked for him?

Ugh! Where were Spencer and Becky when I needed advice?

"Thanks for sitting with me," Chase said, indicating his laptop, which was still open in front of him. "I needed a break."

I knew I shouldn't be nosy but couldn't resist. "What are you doing?" I asked, trying to use X-ray vision to see through the back of his laptop.

"I'm going over new lines and trying to memorize them."

"Do you need help?" I asked anxiously. *This* is the kind of thing I wanted to do for my internship! "I can read the other lines with you."

He suddenly lit up. "That would be great!" He started turning the laptop toward me. "I could have used help this afternoon but Hubert was on Staten Island and I knew you didn't get into New York till the evening."

"What do you mean?" I asked.

He looked confused. "Hubert said you were taking a late train to the city and had to get settled. Right?"

Boy, Hubert was pushing it with the lies. I decided I shouldn't contradict him. Yet.

"Right! What I meant was that my train got in late afternoon but it took through the evening to get settled."

He nodded and told me to begin at the top of the computer screen. The lines were in two different colors.

"Are we only reading the red lines?"

"We're reading everything. The red lines are the new ones that were just added."

It was exciting to actually see the script. I had read on Playbill.com that the show was about two small-time 1940s Southern jewel thieves, a guy and a girl, who wind up in the same town. At first they try to sabotage each other, but at the end of the first act, they decide to team up and pull a big heist. By the finale, they wind up falling in love and leave behind their life of crime; he becomes the sheriff of the town and she becomes the mayor. It's a light story, but the rumor on all the Broadway message boards is that the score is great and the dialogue is fast and funny.

"OK," I said, scrolling to the top of the screen, "here I go."

"Oh, Jake!" I said with a Southern accent. "You're always jokin'! You pulled my leg twice. What are you gonna pull next?"

"Well, you know what they say," Chase replied. "The third time's the arm."

Huh?

That was a joke?

I then realized that it was a play on the expression "third time's the charm." Oy! If the audience took as long as I did to get the joke, then Chase's line would be followed by dead silence for ten seconds and then slight, barely discernible smiles.

"Is something wrong?" Chase asked. "Did you lose your place in the script?"

Uh-oh. I was concentrating so hard on understanding the joke that I forgot to come in with my next line. But since we were stopped, I decided to ask a question.

"That last joke was in red. That means it's new, right?"

"Exactly." Chase grinned. "The joke that was there before was too funny."

Huh? "What does that mean?"

"During rehearsals, it always got a big laugh from the rest of the cast, so . . ." He looked like he was waiting for me to say his next sentence. I didn't know where he was going with it so I slightly shook my head. Finally, he spoke again like he was reciting an age-old theory. "Big laughs on Broadway are for the comic sidekicks." He sat up straighter. "I'm the leading man. It's bad to confuse the audience." He winked. "I'm glad my intern is learning something!"

What the—

I wanted to say, "*You're* the one who needs to learn something! It's fantastic if a leading man gets laughs. It makes the audience like him more."

I was about to pipe up when he got another text.

"It's from Hubert."

Another lie about me?

"Oh no!" he said. "I totally promised to get milk." Then he flashed his famous Chase smile. "Hubert's having a late-night cereal attack." He grabbed his coat. "I better go."

Promised to get milk? That means Hubert stays with him. Were they a couple? No way. I read in *Us Weekly* that Chase has been dating the girl he played opposite in *Vicious Tongues* off and on for years. Of course, whenever they break up, he has some beautiful supermodel on his arm.

But still, Hubert lives in his apartment? I mean, I'm sure those Dakota condos have a multitude of guest rooms, but wouldn't Chase rather have his own place?

And why is Chase buying the milk? Isn't it more important that he learn his lines? Quite frankly, does Hubert do any actual assisting?

"Thanks for your help, Justin." He put down a twenty-dollar bill and smiled. "Get yourself a cupcake on the way out."

Nice! "Thanks, Chase." Definitely yellow cake with chocolate frosting.

"I hope I see you tomorrow," he said as he pulled on his North Face winter coat.

"I'll be there bright and—"

"But Hubert already told me you have an intern orientation meeting tomorrow"—*I do not!*—"so you can't come by the theater tomorrow." *I can too!* "See ya soon!" And he was gone.

Ding.

Now I was the one getting a text from Hubert. Hmm, maybe Chase got it mixed up. Maybe Hubert was texting me to meet him at *Thousand-Watt Smile* rehearsal tomorrow morning.

Hi, Justin. I need you to do a few errands tomorrow. List with the doorman again.

OK, I sent back, deciding not to challenge him till I could figure out what was up. Hubert was so friendly to me when we spoke on the phone before my internship, but now it's like he's purposefully keeping me away from rehearsal. Why?

I desperately needed to hash this out with someone, but the only people I want to call are no longer my friends. I decided that I alone would figure out a way to bypass Hubert's Broadway blockade. I had to find a way to get into that rehearsal! But first I had to eat that cupcake.

Delish.

When I arrived at my grandmother's brownstone, I put my phone on reverse photo again so I could take a quick picture to put on my website. I had posted one of myself arriving this morning and I thought it would be cool to bookend it with one of me arriving in the same place at the end of the day. I took a pic with the flash (angling the camera from the top to make my double chin look more like an extended single chin) and uploaded it right from my phone to the website. Then I captioned it "After a long day of nonstop Broadway (and coffee with Chase!) I need some sleep!" I posted it while standing on the street and then compared the morning photo of me arriving with the nighttime one. Wow. A lot had happened in the time between those two shots. I traveled to Staten Island, lost two friends, met a new friend/possible boyfriend, and hung out with a Broadway star. The perfect description of ups and downs.

As I walked up the stairs to enter the building, I saw an envelope taped to the door with my name on it. Exciting! Was it a handwritten apology from Spencer? A business card with Devon's contact info?

Before I opened it, I glanced at my watch and was relieved to see it wasn't that late yet. Only eleven o'clock. Excellent! I could still call Spencer and accept his apology or call Devon and say yes to his request for a date. Either way I win!

The envelope had one sheet of paper in it. I unfolded it and read it. It was in all capital letters and black Sharpie.

HE'S A FAKE!

I stood there, staring at the note and thought three things.

What did that mean?

Who was it about?

And, more important, who sent it?

8

My alarm went off the next morning and the anonymous letter was sitting on my chest. I lay down in bed with the express purpose of staying up for hours analyzing the letter's handwriting, but I only got in a solid four minutes before the deliciousness of the down quilt lulled me to sleep. I got myself out of bed, had a quick shower and breakfast, and put the letter in my bag. I saw my grandmother emerge from her bedroom as I was getting my coat.

"What's going on out there?" she asked, holding her ears. "The Watts Riots?"

Typical. Grandma Sally was always referencing something that was incredibly timely during her heyday but sounded like made-up words to anyone born after 1980.

"Sorry I woke you," I said.

"I don't care about that. It's the people upstairs who always complain if there's the slightest noise." She went into the kitchen.

I knew what she was talking about, but they don't complain

when there's "the slightest noise." They complain when there's a crazy amount of noise. Grandma Sally only owns one radio and she insists on keeping it in her kitchen. When she cleans the apartment, she puts the radio on the highest volume possible so she can hear it from anyplace in the apartment. Or, more honestly, anyplace in the apartment building.

I followed her into the kitchen and saw her open the refrigerator.

"I was gonna make you a little something," she said, taking a dish out of the refrigerator.

A little something? She was holding up an entire brisket. Grandma Sally often forgot I was a vegetarian.

"Aw, thanks," I said, and gave her a little kiss. "But I'm going to eat at the theater. See you later!"

I walked out of the building and took the same path to the Dakota. This time I knew what to do when I got there. I approached the kiosk, and instead of asking to be let in like I foolishly did yesterday, I asked for the envelope from Hubert. I opened it and noticed that this time, instead of one major errand, it was a list of many, many errands. In all different parts of town. So, now instead of one incredibly long trip to an outer borough, I was supposed to go all the way up to Harlem (drop off a bouquet of flowers to the owner of Sylvia's Restaurant), down to a handmade furniture store on the Lower East Side (take photos of available coffee tables with mosaic tops because Chase is redecorating), across town to Chelsea (get a dozen cupcakes from Billy's Bakery), and back up to Chase's chiropractor on East Eighty-Eighth Street (drop off the cupcakes). And that was just the first page. I decided to start with the ones farthest away from the Upper West Side to get them over with and then "reward" myself with the ones that were closer to home.

Ding.

On my way to the subway, I got a text from Devon. Yes!

Your grandma gave me your number. Hope you don't mind.

Hi, Devon! I'm on my way to the subway. Are you in school?

He wrote back right away.

Yes. But I have a free period.

What's up?

I was watching Kristin Chenoweth clips on YouTube and was wondering if you like her best when she sings soprano or when she belts.

I was about to answer when he texted again.

Or sings country?

Well, that does change it, I thought. I started to respond but my phone dinged again.

Or do you prefer her acting over her singing?

Hmm. Now it was a lot of choices. As I was thinking, I heard *ding.*

Sure enough, on my screen there were more choices.

And if acting is your preference, Broadway or TV?

The light was turning red, so I ran across the street toward the subway entrance and took out my phone to respond. There was another text on my screen.

Or films! Don't forget, she was great in "Bewitched" ☺. I decided to go down the stairs to the subway and wait three minutes to see if there were any other addendums. Nothing. Finally, I took my phone out again to text him but it said I was out of range.

The number 1 train pulled into the Seventy-Second Street station and I got on easily. In the morning hours, everyone is rushing to go downtown to work, but the uptown trains are deliciously empty. I sat down and was mulling over all of the choices Devon presented to me and then decided on a way I could turn this exchange into something more. I would tell him I was undecided and that perhaps we could discuss it later. Over dinner. It wouldn't officially sound like I was asking him out, but he could think of it that way if he was interested. The train pulled into 125th Street and I had service again. I wrote Devon the text I planned out and waited for the immediate *ding*.

No response.

I opted to not be devastated by the outright rejection and instead decided that he had to go back to class and therefore couldn't text me. I focused on getting all of my Hubert work done so I could then go to the theater and somehow get in to watch some actual rehearsal.

The whole morning was a nightmare. Besides having to run to all corners of Manhattan on increasingly crowded subways, the other bad part was that my thoughts kept going to Spencer and Becky. I wondered what they were doing. Did they have breakfast together? Were they talking about me? Were they still mad at me? Argh! My brain was relentless. I continuously checked for a text from Devon to cheer me up but my phone remained silent.

By 12:30, I finished the errands that were in the most difficult-to-reach places and now only had to do the ones that were closer to where I lived. They were actually easy and went much faster than I expected: pick up some organic shampoo at the Lush that was being held for him, get some fresh parsley at Citarella and drop it back at the Dakota, and buy and gift wrap some vegetarian dog biscuits at Spot, an upscale doggie store. I was racing through them! I'm sure Hubert thought these errands would take me all day, but I know my way around town. I only had one left (dropping off a big envelope to an address midtown) and would soon be able to spend some quality Chase time at the theater.

I took a downtown bus to Columbus Circle and when I got off, I took a look at the entrance to Central Park. There was still snow on the ground and trees from the New Year's Eve storm and everything looked so pretty. Spencer and I always talked about one day walking through Central Park from where it began on Fifty-Ninth Street all the way up to the north side on 110th Street. I knew that I'd probably only last ten minutes and then beg him to let us take a cab the rest of the way, but it didn't even matter now because I'd never get the chance. We were officially broken up.

All right. I admit it. I miss Spencer. Not the annoying stuff. The good stuff. What little of it there was. Well, I guess there was more than a little. Regardless, I missed however much or little there was.

Then why don't you reach out?

No way!!!

If Spencer and I were going to date or even be friends again, it was not going to be from me begging. I needed to accept the reality that it was over. It would, however, be easier to accept if I got a text from Devon confirming dinner. I decided to focus on finishing this last errand so I could crash today's rehearsal. I got to the address on Sixth Avenue that Hubert had written down and walked into the very modern and expensive lobby. It had a whole wall that was a waterfall. Nice! I looked again at the Hubert memo, which simply told me to drop off the enclosed 8 x 10 envelope on the thirty-eighth floor. I took the elevator up and when the doors opened, I immediately wanted to turn around. I was right at the welcome desk of GlitZ!

Ah! I didn't want to run into Spencer!

Yet, if I didn't finish these errands, I'd never be able to visit Chase at rehearsal.

The elevator doors closed behind me but I didn't move. I was standing there debating what to do for so long that the very skinny, very blond, and very long-haired (obviously extensions) receptionist asked if she could help me. Well, the longer I was there, the more chance I had of running into Spencer, so I realized I should just drop off the envelope and get out.

I did just that. I went to the desk, placed the envelope down, and quickly said, "These are for you. Take care!" I turned around, speed-walked to the elevator, and pressed the DOWN button. *Come on, come on!*

"Um," I heard her say. I turned around and saw that she was brandishing the package away from her like it was the urine sample I carried yesterday. "What is this?" She put it on the desk and pushed it away from her to the edge.

I was forced to go back.

"They're from Chase Hudson," I said, standing at the desk as I gently pushed the envelope back toward her.

"Like I said, what is it?" she asked again, pushing it toward me.

I looked over my shoulder at the elevator. It was on the eighteenth floor and slowly rising. I knew she must have had some policy about not accepting anything unless she knew the contents. Annoying! I quickly opened the envelope and showed her the inside. It was filled with photos and negatives of Chase modeling as a teenager.

Wow. Did he never have an awkward phase?

She pointed a lacquered nail at the elevator.

"Those are for the archives. Take the elevator to B and drop them there." And with that, she picked up her cell phone and turned away from me.

Well, at least it looked like I could escape before Spencer saw me. I walked to the elevator and waited while she whispered on her phone. I couldn't hear her whole conversation, but I managed to hear the words "works for Chase," "stupid Broadway T-shirt," and "something between an Afro and a home perm." I held my chin high and preferred to think she was talking about someone else with my exact same wardrobe and hairstyle.

The elevator thankfully came and I got in and pushed B. It went straight down and when the doors opened, I was suddenly looking into an area that had none of the glamour of the upstairs GlitZ offices. It was basically a dimly lit hallway with a bare lightbulb hanging in it. What a downer. I got out and the elevator door closed behind me. Where do I go? Then I saw a handwritten sign taped up on the wall that said ARCHIVES with an arrow pointing to the left. When I walked, every footstep echoed. Creepy. I got to the only door and knocked. It opened and there stood . . . Becky!

Ah!

I totally forgot she was stuck in this dungeon. We stared at each other. I looked past her and saw that her "office" was a mess. There were enormous file cabinets everywhere and every open surface was covered with photos. Because it was the basement, there were no windows and whatever lightbulbs GlitZ was using made Becky's skin look white *and* green at the same time. I felt a little sorry for her, but not enough to be friendly. I hadn't forgotten how she and Spencer teamed up against me last night.

"I'm not here to accept your apology," I said. I knew she would think "what apology?" but before she could respond, I walked in, brandishing my envelope. "I'm here because of my exciting internship."

I held the envelope out to her.

Becky stared at me as she absentmindedly flipped her hair away from her face. Yes, the light made her look sickly, but of course, she still was gorgeous. She took the envelope.

I started walking back toward the door.

"Is that all, sir?" she asked.

"Yes, it is, *ma'am*," I said, and then made sure she saw me look at my watch. "As you know, I'm working with a big Broadway star, so I have no time to take you up on your invitation to linger."

I turned to leave. But when I opened the door, I stopped dead in my tracks. There in the doorway stood . . . Scotty Preston.

Gasp! And *sigh!*

He's not only the hottest teen model right now, but he's also starring in his own Disney TV show (*Scotty . . . with an S*) and has a hit song on the Disney label ("Singing . . . with an S"). And the big news is, all the cast members on his show are part of a new campaign against bullying. Each kid has a topic; the lead girl's focus is about body image, Scotty's sidekick (who has cerebral palsy) focuses on bullying kids in wheelchairs, and Scotty's campaign is about gay kids! The most recent one is a picture of him looking right at the camera, and underneath it says, "Bullying gay kids isn't just mean, it's *stupid*. With an *S*." The extra sentence doesn't really make a lot of sense, but I have no problem with the campaign since it features him wearing a tight blue T-shirt that shows off his triceps. Or biceps. Hmm . . . traps? I don't really know the difference. Let's just say his arms look amazing in the photo.

Even though I said I had no time to linger, now all I wanted to do *was* linger. And stare.

"Hi, Becky." What the— Scotty knows Becky!

Wait a minute! This could be more than a staring session for me. If Scotty knew Becky, then she could be the middleman (girl?) who sets us up on a date.

"Hi, Scotty, come on in," she said with a smile.

He walked past me and I let the door shut. Unfortunately, I left my mouth open. I knew I looked crazy and forced myself to close it.

There. I then put a relaxed expression on my face.

"I have everything right here," he said, and put down an envelope.

Uh-oh. That was it? What if he was about to turn around and leave? I had to have Becky introduce us before he was out the door. Yes, we were in a fight, but I hope she knew that this kind of thing trumped any kind of disagreement we had. We could always go back to not speaking.

I looked toward Becky and made my eyes super big, then quickly looked back and forth from Scotty to Becky (without him seeing me).

She smiled at me and nodded. "If you'll excuse me a minute, Scotty."

"No problem," he said, and Becky walked over to me.

As soon as she was within earshot, I whispered, "I've always had the biggest crush on him. Can you please, please, please introduce me?"

She responded in a normal volume. "Thank you for dropping off those pictures."

Huh?

She then opened the door and gave her dazzling smile.

"But—"

"I'm sure you remember the elevator is just down the hall."

What was happening?

"I—"

She put her arm around me in a friendly way, but she was actually pushing me out.

"I remember you just told me that you have 'no time to linger,' so I don't want to keep you."

I was almost out the door at this point.

"Becky—" I started. Then stopped. Scotty was looking at us. I didn't want his first impression of me to be me standing in the door, yelling, "I demand you set me up on a date with him!"

I pasted on a big smile. "Thank you for all your help today." Then I grabbed her hand and shook it. "Believe me when I say"— I looked into her eyes—"I'll *never* forget it."

Becky removed her hand. "Take care," she said as she let the door shut in my face.

How dare she!

I walked back to the elevator and took it up one flight.

I stood in the lobby. Argh! I had lost my chance to meet him. And I can't date him if I never meet him. The nerve of Becky. After all I've done for her!

Then I realized I actually could still meet Scotty! I just had to wait for him here. She can't control the lobby. When he gets off the elevator, I'll introduce myself and bring the conversation around to the bullying campaign he's doing. I'll tell him I have a few ideas on how to help even more gay kids and that I'd love to discuss them over lunch.

In truth, I don't have a few ideas. I actually only have one: start dating someone like me so that average-looking gay kids across the country can have some hope they'll one day date a TV star. We'd both be doing a big public service.

My phone vibrated. Oh, right! Cell reception doesn't work in the basement, and I probably had a buildup of texts from Devon.

Wow! Two prospective boyfriends to choose from! I looked at my phone but instead of a slew of texts from Devon, I only had one. And it was from Hubert. In all caps.

CHASE NEEDS HIS WOOL SCARF PICKED UP FROM THE DRY CLEANERS ON 72ND STREET AND BROUGHT TO RE-HEARSAL BY 2!

I checked my watch. It was 1:20. I had ju-u-u-st enough time if I left now.

But . . . Scotty was still downstairs! I can't leave. This may be my last chance to meet/date a TV star.

Hmm . . . I considered pretending I never got the text . . . but what if Hubert fired me?

But Scotty! How could I leave him before he even got a chance to fall in love with me? Or ask me to lunch? Or at least nod politely when I told him I "liked" his Facebook page?

But if I didn't have an internship, my parents wouldn't let me stay in New York. And date Devon. Possibly. And be able to see a Broadway rehearsal. Possibly.

I forced myself to walk away from the elevators.

I rechecked the text to make sure I had read it correctly.

I had.

Then I rechecked to make sure there was no text from Devon. There wasn't.

I started to walk out of the building.

I hoped it wasn't sleeting.

It was.

Once I was on the street, the cold air and wet sleet on my face helped me clear my head. I don't need to date a Disney star; I have Devon!

Sort of.

Yes, I still hadn't gotten a text back from him, but I began to think that maybe he had his phone confiscated at school and therefore had no way of reaching me. He's probably been frantic! I briefly considered making a detour to his high school and dropping off a note at the front office asking him to meet me tonight for dinner but then decided it might be perceived as desperate. And I knew that if *I* thought something was possibly desperate, it undoubtedly was.

I waited an extra few minutes in front of the GlitZ building, hoping to catch Scotty on his way out, but Becky must have been chatting his ear off.

I checked my phone again to see if I had somehow deleted a text from Devon.

I then went to text Spencer to tell him I had a great story about how Becky pretty much threw me out of her office, but I stopped as soon as I typed in his name.

I looked at my phone and got an idea; I would delete all of Spencer's texts from my phone. After all, he had deleted me from his life, hadn't he?

I waited at the bus stop and scrolled to the oldest text I had from him, but it was so nice I decided to save it. I mean, how often will I have a text from someone saying my hair looked amazing? I waited for the light to change and went to the next text, but it was really funny, so I decided to save it for when I wanted an easy laugh. The next one was super sweet (he signed it "Your best friend and boyfriend, Spencer"), and at that point I decided it wasn't productive to focus on this task anymore.

OK. It was time to focus on *me*. First, I took a picture of myself in the sleet and posted it immediately on my website. The caption was "It's cold outside but *Thousand-Watt Smile*'s lookin' hot." Of course, I had no idea how *Thousand-Watt Smile* was looking since I haven't been allowed anywhere near it, but it was sort of truthful because I was on my way to rehearsal. I got on the uptown bus and before I went back to thinking about any of my two possible boyfriends and one annoying ex, I redirected my brain into figuring out who left me that note last night.

Nothing.

It was difficult to even begin because I had no idea what the note meant. *Who* was a fake? I wish I could appeal to the anonymous note writer to be more specific next time.

Wait a minute! I suddenly thought. I actually could. Whoever left that note knows who I am, and anyone who knows me has to know I have a website. I took a quick photo of myself looking quizzical and captioned it, "On New York City bus wondering who's a fake?" I hoped the note writer would see it and respond somehow. Of course, it's a completely bizarre sentence to see underneath a photo, but I figured anyone reading it who didn't write the note would think I was being philosophical about New Yorkers. I've discovered that when you write something that doesn't make sense, you can pawn it off by saying you were being poetic and then make people feel stupid for not understanding. I once uploaded a picture of me in tap class and captioned it "Dancing to a great song . . ." Unfortunately, I didn't proofread the auto correct, so it wound up being posted as a picture of me doing a time step with a caption that read "Dancing to a grid soul . . ." Before I could delete it, the head of the school poetry magazine (Anna Kinstler) came up to my lunch table and asked if she could publish it in the spring issue. I immediately said yes but had no answer when she then asked me, with deep concern in her eyes, "Isn't every soul simply part of a grid?"

Huh? Thankfully, I was taking a sip of Crystal Light when she laid that question on me, so I just held up my cup like I was toasting her and that was enough for her to smile and walk away. Of course, Spencer was sitting with me and heard the whole thing. We both laughed up a storm and ever since then, we've called Anna

"Grid Soul" or "GS" for short. Ah! Why did every memory end with me missing Spencer?

I snapped out of my remembrance and noticed we were stopped at Seventy-Second Street so I ran off the bus, picked up the scarf from the dry cleaner, and hopped on the subway to Times Square. I took the escalator out of the station and started walking.

Within two minutes, I heard my phone *ding.*

Hubert, of course.

WHERE ARE YOU?

It wasn't two o'clock yet. Why the anxiety?

On corner of 44th Street. Walking to theater.

Within fifteen seconds, I saw someone with an orange face come barreling toward me. Yowtch. It was Hubert with his signature "tan."

"Hi, Justin," he said when he got close.

"Hi, Hubert," I said, remembering and resenting the fact that the *t* was silent.

He spoke very quickly. "Thanks for getting this done so fast. I'll take the scarf off your hands."

I wondered why he was suddenly being helpful. Not that the scarf was heavy to carry, but it was a nice offer. I handed him the scarf and used the opportunity of having both hands free to pull my hat over my ears.

"It's so cold!" I said. I wanted to ask him why he was lying about my availability to Chase but knew I shouldn't have a fight with him before I was safely in rehearsal. I decided to make conversation using the most neutral topic of all—the weather.

"It is cold!" He held up the scarf. "That's why I needed this. They're about to break for lunch and Chase has to keep his neck warm."

Oh! That was the big rush. But . . . if there was such a rush on getting the scarf, why weren't we racing back to rehearsal? Hubert was still standing in front of me. I then noticed he had an envelope.

"Here ya go," he said, handing it to me.

"What's this?" I asked, hoping it wasn't what I thought it was.

"It's a few more things I need you to do this afternoon."

It was what I thought it was. Argh! The whole reason I rushed this morning was so I'd have a chance to be in the theater this afternoon. "Can I do it after rehearsal?" I asked.

"I need it ASAP." By the way, he didn't say "as soon as possible," which would have been preferable. Nor did he say A-S-A-P, which I find irritating. Instead, he pronounced it the most annoying way: "A-sap." Whenever someone says that on a TV show, it's always the person who thinks other people exist only to do his or her bidding. I guess that describes Hubert down to a (silent) *t*.

Without saying goodbye, he started walking toward the theater. And it was obvious he didn't want me to come along.

I ripped open the envelope and saw a brand-new list of tasks. One of them involved going to expensive Gracious Home and getting things like soap dispensers and towels. Wow. It seems like Chase had accounts set up at every store in New York. There was a handwritten note on the list: *Please take photos of all bathroom items and text them to me for approval. The dressing room is blue, so keep everything within a similar color palette.*

I guess I was in charge of decorating Chase's dressing room bathroom instead of going to rehearsal.

Was this going to be my whole internship? I would have been more involved with theater if I had stayed at Big Noise Media. For a second, I considered quitting to go there, but how would I explain deserting my family in their time of mourning?

This was it. Either Hubert let me into rehearsal or I told Chase everything.

I started running down the block toward him.

"Hubert! Hubert!" I yelled. I felt like an idiot calling out words that made it sound like I was excited to see a grizzly. (Oo! Bear! Oo! Bear!)

He turned around and saw me. Then briskly walked back up the block to where I was standing.

"Yes, Justin?" he asked, clearly annoyed. "Is there something you don't understand?"

"There actually is, Hubert. I was offered this internship by Chase."

"Yes?" he asked haughtily.

"And I ran into him last night and he seems to have some wrong information about my availability."

"Does he?" Hubert asked.

"Yes, and I plan to set the record straight." I turned to walk past him and he put his hand on my arm.

"Why don't you take a moment first, Justin?"

"For what?" I asked, not interested in his excuses.

"Well . . ." He put his arm around me (gross) and walked me over to Shubert Alley. I knew it was to place us out of the view of anyone exiting the *Thousand-Watt Smile* stage door. "I wasn't planning on you running into Chase last night, so I didn't share this with you right away. Quite frankly, I was waiting until a moment like this to fill you in on your 'availability.'"

"You're filling me in on *my* availability?"

"Yes, Justin." He gave his version of a smile. "Let's be honest. *I* wasn't interested in you interning for Chase. I handle everything for him." His eyes flashed. "And I mean *everything*."

What a control freak.

"But I soon discovered I would need some help right about now for personal reasons and it worked out perfectly that you were available."

"I *am* available. But I was planning on being at the theater. And I'm sure that's what Chase would want." I started to walk away.

"My point is," he said in a loud voice that stopped me in my tracks and brought me back to him, "I was at a lovely Christmas party recently and ran into Sophia, the head of Big Noise Media. People in the theater socialize with each other at various events and I know her quite well. Lovely woman."

"Yeah?" I said. What was his point?

"I remembered that you were planning on interning with her until Chase asked you to help out."

Uh-oh.

"I hadn't yet confirmed your internship with us and I planned on asking her if she would make sure you stayed at Big Noise."

Where was this going?

"Yes?"

"Well, I mentioned that I had met their newest intern and was surprised to find out that you suddenly weren't going to be available for them . . . because of the recent death in your family."

Oh boy.

He went on. "I expressed my deepest sympathy." He put on a concerned look. "Not only for you but also for them. It seems they were relying on your help because they are struggling." Then he added, "And you left them quite abruptly."

The same feelings of guilt I felt when I dropped them came flooding back.

You had a commitment and you broke it. Even worse, you broke it with a lie.

Shut up, Spencer!

"Anyway," Hubert said with a condescending smile, "I didn't tell Big Noise Media that you might not be staying with your family on Long Island during this time. I didn't tell them that you might, indeed, be in New York City. I didn't tell them that, perhaps, your family isn't in mourning. But," he said as he leaned in, "I could."

We stared at each other.

I was stuck. If he told Sophia, she would tell her father, who would tell my dad. How would I explain letting down his friend who pushed for me to get the internship? I'd probably get grounded, which would mean I couldn't do the spring musical. Also, Hubert would probably tell my school and I wouldn't get credit for JobSkill!

And, worse than all of that, Spencer would find out. He wouldn't even have to say anything. I'd know how disappointed he'd be in me. Any chance I had to fix our friendship would be ruined. I'd proved how selfish I was.

I kept staring at Hubert. I had no choice. I'd have to do the internship his way.

"OK," I said finally. "I get it. I'm off to do errands."

"Exactly. You help me out and I'll help you out."

Help me out? He really means he won't rat me out.

I watched Hubert walk out of Shubert Alley toward the *Thousand-Watt Smile* theater.

When he got nearby, people started exiting the theater. And there was Chase! Hubert walked over to him and then walked toward Eighth Avenue.

"No lunch?" Chase called.

Hubert waved to him. "No time! I've got to run some errands for you!"

The nerve. *I* was the one running errands for Chase.

The thought of walking back to the subway and going back uptown felt overwhelming. I hadn't bought lunch today, so I decided to spend money on a cab.

I hightailed it to Gracious Home and got some beautiful stuff. Taking photos and texting them was arduous, but Hubert must like my taste. I finished pretty fast.

Ding.

Forgot to add something to the list. Too long to text. Call me.

What choice did I have?

I walked out on the street and dialed. A loud fire truck went by as it started ringing but I put my finger in my ear so I could hear. Hubert picked up after two rings and I heard the same fire truck from his side of the phone call. What the— He must be right nearby. I started scanning the street as I asked him what he needed. He told me he was putting me on the list for an exclusive leather store in the Village and he wanted me to pick out an ottoman. He was almost done describing the various leather textures and colors he was interested in when I suddenly said, "Aha!"

"What is it?" Hubert asked.

I see you across the street from me, you secretive person! I almost blurted out.

Instead, I said, "Aha! I know exactly what you'd love. I'm on my way."

"ASAP," Hubert said as he hung up, and I saw him put his phone away. He was standing with another man. The guy had short, bright red hair (not like Spencer's orange hair). And he was wearing a ski parka. Hubert is so deceitful that I wondered if they were up to something he wouldn't want Chase to know about. How cool would it be if I saw them doing some illegal activity? I'd have something to blackmail him with so I could start going to rehearsals! I decided to follow both of them. But first I ran a block ahead so I could discreetly turn around and get a clear picture of them facing me. I didn't watch a twelve-hour marathon of *Law & Order* on Christmas Day for nothing.

Well, I followed them for a while, but not only did they do no illegal activity, they only did boring activity. After an hour and a half, I figured they're just friends who were spending the afternoon visiting other friends because first they went into a luxury building and stayed there for a while. They finally exited and walked uptown. I stayed a safe distance behind. I hoped they would go into a store and shoplift something, but all they did was enter another building. The only difference this time was the building was a brownstone. I waited around the same amount of time and when I saw them cross the street and go into yet another apartment building, I gave up. Even if they were doing something illegal, I couldn't follow them into an apartment and video them. Thinking about video made me remember the photo of them. I thought I could maybe use it for evidence one day if I did find out something nefarious, so I decided to email it to myself in case I lost my phone (which is what happened to one of the crime witnesses midway through the *Law & Order* marathon). Well, right after I sent it I checked my email for the first time that day and . . . there was a message from Devon!

Who cares about following Hubert anymore—my soon-to-be-possible boyfriend had finally contacted me! I saw from the time stamp that he had actually sent it hours ago. He wrote that he hates text messages because you have to limit how many letters you use, so he decided to send an email instead. Why didn't I check all day?!?! He knew he'd have very little homework this weekend and wanted to know if I'd be cool getting together. I immediately gave up on stalking Hubert and wrote back that I intern during the day, but I could meet him Friday for dinner.

Yes!

My first date with a real New Yorker!

Take that, Scotty. And Spencer.

And both of your S's!

Well, after a week and a half of nonstop errands, I've simply accepted that this internship will not be what I expected. As a matter of fact, it's worse than what I imagined. It's one thing to be bored at a publicist office, but at least it's related to theater. Instead, I spend every day (including the weekend!) running around the city doing Hubert's bidding.

And my whole fantasy of seeing Broadway shows every night never happened. I have so many errands that I'm usually not done till after eight p.m. . . . just late enough so I can't make curtain time. It's almost as if Hubert has planned to ruin my time in New York. The only good news is, Devon is looking more and more like my New York City boyfriend . . . even though no smooching has happened yet.

On Friday, I met him at The Cottage, a delish Chinese restaurant on Seventy-Seventh and Amsterdam where we spent the whole meal comparing Elphabas from *Wicked*. It was so different from a date with Spencer. Yes, we'd spend some time talking about Broadway, but then the conversation would switch to some world event that Spencer wanted my opinion about, or a book I wanted him to read, or the forceful letter Spencer was about to write about some political injustice, or something hilariously crazy my parents did. With Devon, it was so refreshing being able to focus solely and completely on Broadway instead of going from random topic to random topic. He walked me home and as we stood in front of Grandma Sally's brownstone, I prepared for a little good-night kiss. I popped two pieces of extra-strength spearmint gum in my mouth to counteract my tofu with garlic sauce, but we were so intensely discussing our favorite Tony Awards that it seemed weird to interrupt him for a smooch. I was going to suggest a walk in the park to prolong our date, but then I figured the longer we held off kissing, the more exciting it would be when we finally did it. Also, even though a walk in the park at night sounds like a romantic idea, I realized we weren't on Long Island. In other words, romance is usually lost after a mugging.

On Monday, Grandma Sally had to cancel her weekly dinner with Devon due to the last remnants of a cold she'd had all weekend, so he invited me to have dinner at his apartment! I had spent the whole day in Brooklyn in a special coffee store where I had to wait for Chase's personal blend of coffee to be roasted over a slow fire. Then I had to carry the enormous five-pound bags back to the Dakota. It didn't bother me, though, because I kept thinking about what it would be like that night to meet Devon's rich parents (they both worked on Wall Street) and be asked to go on vacation with them to Switzerland (he had mentioned they have a chalet that's a time share).

Well, I did have dinner in his apartment, but his parents were nowhere to be seen. Turns out they always work too late to have dinner with their kids. His regular dining companions are his three-year-old sister and her nanny. His sister's name is Lucinda and her favorite sentence is "I want!" That's it. Just the two words. You're supposed to figure out the noun she's referring to by following the direction her finger is pointing. Her nanny is an overweight British woman whose teeth have seen finer days, and throughout the entire meal, I only heard her speak two words: "Lucinda" and "no." I guess the creative part of her job was figuring out how to use them in every combination:

There was the plain *"Lucinda!"* and *"No!"*

The combo *"Lucinda, no!"* and *"No, Lucinda!"*

And at one point she really thought outside the box and came up with *"No, Lucinda! NO!"* Devon and I barely got a chance to get out three sentences before Lucinda would break/throw something and the nanny would let loose with her two signature words, cutting off anything we were saying. I had a splitting headache from the nonstop cockney reprimands so I fled the apartment right after dessert and went back early to Grandma Sally's. Speaking of which, I guess that's why Devon's so willing to have dinner with her once a week. Yes, Grandma Sally's a cranky ass, but she lets Devon have an actual conversation, unlike Lucinda and her nanny. And Grandma Sally has more teeth than both of them combined.

Tuesday and Wednesday seemed like the same day to me since I spent them in Queens waiting for a custom-made end table to be sanded and stained. On Thursday, I visited various high-end furniture stores all morning and picked up swatches, which I then dropped off at the Dakota for Hubert to peruse. We met briefly on the corner of Seventy-Second Street and Columbus, where he told me that he was in the final stages of helping Chase redecorate his apartment. Since he had narrowed it down to various pieces, it was up to me to go to the stores, take photos of the pieces from all different angles, and text them to Hubert. He then made the final decisions and I purchased them for him with the corporate credit card he gave me. The worst part was the afternoon, which I spent food shopping. Movie stars have very particular tastes. Suffice it to say, if I were ever on *Jeopardy!* and the answer was "An obscure, tiny bakery deep into Brooklyn that is only accessible by taking three different subways," I would respond, "Where can you get artisanal handcrafted gluten-free donuts?"

I arrived home exhausted and looking forward to one of Grandma Sally's enormous meals, but when I walked in, she had a face full of makeup and was putting on her rain bonnet. She told me she was on her way to the senior center monthly meeting.

"If I don't get over there and vote," she said, while tying the strings of her bonnet, "those sons of b's will approve something as dangerous as Three Mile Island and dumber than Loni Anderson."

I didn't have the energy to Google her references, so I just nodded.

"I didn't have time to make dinner, so why don't you go out

tonight?" She paused for effect. Then she finished her phrase. "With your boyfriend."

Was she psychic? Did Devon say something?

"He's n-not . . . ," I sputtered. "I'm not—"

"Well, if he's not and you're not, you must be very disappointed."

"Why would I be—"

"Spare me, Grandson. Even with cataracts in both eyes, I could tell you were practically drooling last week when we all had dinner together," she said with a wave of her hand. "And I don't think it was because of my lasagna," she added with a wink. A long wink.

When her wink failed to resolve itself, I realized her eye had involuntarily closed because of a clump of mascara stuck in it.

"Cheap-ass Maybelline," she muttered with one eye still closed, and went off to the bathroom.

I stood in the hallway in shock. I didn't even know my grandmother knew I was gay. It was a subject I didn't want to ever bring up with her. Not because I was afraid she was homophobic (she was an old-school New York liberal), but because I didn't want her to poison my mind against someone I was interested in. My dad still jokes about the nicknames she called all of his high school girlfriends: La Unibrow, Bessie the Moo-Cow, and Madame Chafing Thighs.

I don't think Grandma S necessarily had anything against them. I just think she doesn't want anyone to be a couple. When she was pregnant with my dad, her husband deserted her, which left her with the desire to see everyone else's relationships fail. And this applies to fictional characters as well. I've noticed that every time I'm visiting and *Titanic* comes on TV, Grandma will watch it up until the Leonardo DiCaprio character dies just so she can say, "Finally!"

The water ran for around two minutes and I asked how her eye was. "It still burns a little!" she yelled from inside the bathroom. Then, "Aha! I'm glad I still have this from my last bout with conjunctivitis. . . ."

The next thing I knew, she came out wearing an enormous eye patch. Before I could comment, she put her coat on and yelled over her shoulder on the way out.

"Have a good time with Mr. Straw Hair!" She closed the front door.

Wow. She was able to stir up trouble even while looking like an aging she-pirate.

Well, she wasn't going to ruin my new relationship.

Even though she did have a point.

Hmm ... I should probably tell Devon to use conditioner every day to help that dryness. Then I remembered I wouldn't be seeing him tonight. I had canceled dinner plans because I was feeling so depressed and didn't want Devon to think I was anything but fun-loving. I was still waiting for that first kiss, and I knew he'd never plant one on me if I was cranky. All day I couldn't help thinking about how bad things had turned out. For weeks I had the secret fantasy of my internship culminating in somehow seeing myself onstage. Instead, it was going to culminate in seeing myself in the checkout line at Home Depot. I decided I'd "take myself on a date," which is a suggestion I see every three months in one of my mom's women's magazines. They're pretty much the same articles recycled every month, but my only other magazine choices around the house are the ones my dad has to read for his practice. Which article would you read if your only options were "Haircuts That Make Your Eyes Dazzle!" or "New Techniques for Bowel Obstruction Surgery"?

I walked out of my grandma's, and because it was cold, I decided to stay close to home and go to Good Enough to Eat. I've eaten there a few times with Spencer because I can order a relatively healthy vegetarian entrée and then reward myself with an enormous piece of their homemade banana cake (with peanut butter frosting), which has all of a 6'5" adult's daily recommended calories.

I got there a few minutes later and luckily there were lots of tables available. I chose a small two-seater and decided I was going to get my mind off my nightmare internship and dedicate myself to some detective work over dinner. I would love to find out that Hubert really was doing something illegal that would totally trump or at least match me lying about my grandmother.

And, speaking of detective work, I still hadn't figured out who was sending me those notes. Yes, "notes," plural. Every few days, I'd arrive home to see another one taped to the front door. They always said: "He's a fake." Who? I saved every one and decided I'd look through the pile tonight at dinner to see if there were any clues hidden in them.

Suddenly I heard a familiar laugh. I looked toward the back of the restaurant and saw Becky . . . sitting with Scotty! So, they really were friends. I tried to lip-read what they were saying to see if Scotty was somehow revealing what kind of boy he likes. The only words I managed to make out were "gym" and "love" and I hoped the rest of the sentence was "I never want my boyfriend to go to the *gym* and hope he has a proud set of *love* handles."

Wait a minute! Sometimes if Good Enough to Eat isn't crowded, they'll seat two people at a table for three to give them more room. Becky and Scotty were at a table for three and I suddenly got an idea. I texted Becky.

Can we be friends again?

I knew eventually we'd make up, so why not do it now when it could also gain me a date with a Disney star! I saw Becky look at her phone and then smile. Yes! She texted back, *Let's talk later.*

Excellent! My plan was now to walk up to the table and say, "How about now?" Becky would laugh and invite me to sit down with them; Scotty would see how great I am and ask me out. I could even help him with some suggestions for his next "No Gay Bullying" ad campaign. "Bullying Stinks . . . with *two* S's!" I'm sure he'd love it and want to discuss it further over lattes.

That's right, Spencer, I thought. *I'd now have* two *guys interested in me!* I put my phone away and picked up my coat to walk over when I suddenly stopped everything. Someone in a winter coat I recognized was going toward the empty seat.

Spencer!

He must have walked right past my table without seeing me.

I couldn't believe Becky! Instead of setting up Scotty with me, Becky had set him up with Spencer? How long had they been dating? I grabbed my phone and tried to figure out if there was a way to retract a sent text. There wasn't. Great. Now she thinks I forgive her, *and* Spencer is about to get a new boyfriend. I got up without them seeing me and left the restaurant. I'd rather sacrifice that delicious banana/peanut butter dessert than see Spencer and Scotty holding hands. I went to The Cottage and ate some tofu with broccoli. I put Spencer out of my mind and tried to concentrate on the mysterious note I got last week. I never did find out who sent it or what it meant. But every time I tried to focus on it, the theme song to *Scotty with an S* kept coming into my head. I'd force myself to think of something else but then my mind would go to Spencer. Then both things I didn't want to think about combined, and I found myself humming "*Spencer* with an S." Ah! Why did his name have to fit so perfectly into the song?

I walked back to my grandma's incredibly frustrated; my internship stank, my boyfriend replaced me, and I was the recipient of random notes that meant nothing and left no clue on how to figure out who they were from. It was Thursday and I'd be back at school Monday with nothing to show for my internship except a platonic new boyfriend and a vast knowledge of furniture stores.

Then to make matters worse, I got a text from Hubert with tomorrow's assignment.

Justin. A friend of Chase's is having some stuff delivered to an apartment. Need you to wait there for the delivery people starting at 1pm and lock up when they leave. 303 W. 82nd Street. Apartment 5R.

This was the grand finale of my Broadway internship? Waiting in an apartment? What a waste!

"Where have you been?" Grandma Sally barked as soon as I walked in. I noticed she had ditched the eye patch, but the sassiness remained.

I told her I had dinner and that I was beat. But before I could say good night, she held out her hand.

"I guess I'm the new mailman," she said as she held out an envelope with my name on it. Then she snatched it back. "And don't tell me about those fancy new names for lady mailmen!"

"Mail carrier" is fancy?

"In my day, they were called mailmen, period," she continued. "And no one cared what they had beneath their underwear!"

"You're right," I said, just to get her to shut up and give me the letter.

She walked into her bedroom and I heard her muttering, "And don't get me started on so-called flight attendants. In my day, they were called 'stewardesses' whether they had a—" Thankfully, her door closed at that moment.

I recognized the handwriting on the envelope and knew it was another note. Grandma got home before me and must have seen it on the front door.

I opened it. Wow! For the first time, it wasn't "He's a fake." Instead, it said:

"You're being scammed!"

Argh! Scammed by *who*?

Or, since I plan on being in AP English next year, by *whom*?

11

I spent the end of Thursday night looking at every note over and over again. Back, side, front . . . nothing! There was no contact information anywhere. And even though this one was different from the others, it still made no sense. I thought maybe it was that old chestnut where the first letter of each word added up to some clue, but what does **Y**(ou're) **B**(eing) **S**(cammed) mean? Then I thought maybe if I held it up to the light, I'd see some secret message embedded in the paper, but that didn't work. Argh! I had so many questions for the phantom note writer, but how could I ask them if he left me no way to respond? I had put that picture on my website as a way to signal him but apparently it didn't work. So frustrating!

I put them all away and then lay in bed unable to go to sleep. Every time I closed my eyes, I saw Becky setting up Spencer on a date with Scotty with an S. How dare she! Hmph. The "S" apparently now stands for sabotage. Around an hour later, I heard my phone *ding*. It was from Becky.

Are you up? Do you wanna do a late-night talk?

Absolutely not! I only sent that text to get an in with Scotty, and Spencer nabbed him first. Well, all three of them were welcome to each other. I deleted the text and went to sleep.

I woke up cranky and, not shockingly, so was Grandma Sally. As soon as I sat down to the breakfast she had made (oatmeal, fresh bialys, and delicious scrambled eggs with onions), she let loose.

"Boy oh boy," she said, shaking her head. "From the looks of you, you were up all night." There was no concern in her voice; she just wanted me to be aware I looked puffy. I pointed to my mouth to indicate that it was full of food and therefore I couldn't answer her. That just gave her license to go on.

"Did you see the ol' fire hazard last night?" She was obviously trying out a new nickname to reference Devon's dry hair. I refused to take the bait and changed the subject instead.

"Thanks so much for giving me that note, Grandma Sally." That was all I could come up with that at least sounded friendly, even though I didn't quite know what I was thanking her for. Not throwing it out?

"What are you thanking me for? Not throwing it out?" Great. Now I had to clarify.

I took a sip of coffee to give myself time to think.

"Well," I finally said, "you could have left it on the door."

"Where? What the hell door?" she asked.

Huh? That was weird. I put the coffee down and looked at her. Grandma Sally is never forgetful. I actually wish she were. Then maybe she'd stop asking me if I was still scared of spiders, which is a reference back to when I was four and terrified of a daddy longlegs slowly crawling up my leg. Unfortunately, I let my fear get the best of me. I won't say exactly what happened but the good news is he eventually crawled off my pants. The bad news is that the reason he did is because, as my grandmother said, "No spider wants to walk on fresh pee."

I spoke slowly to jog her memory. "I appreciate you taking the note off the front door."

She glared. "It wasn't on the damn door."

Oh! That's what she meant by "what the hell door?" She wasn't forgetful . . . just rude. But now I was curious. If the phantom note writer didn't leave it on the front door, where did he leave it?

"Then where—" I began.

"It was handed to me, so I handed it to you."

Oh! A neighbor must have taken it off the front door and given it to her when she got home.

"Who gave it to you? Mrs. Shorofsky?"

"Agnes?" she said with a snort. "We're no longer speaking." She looked away with her chin raised and put two slices of tomato on her bialy.

I didn't ask for details. She and Mrs. Shorofsky have been in an on-again/off-again feud for years. To give you an idea of how long it's been, their first fight happened when Mrs. Shorofsky insulted the debut of Grandma Sally's favorite movie star, Farley Granger. Have you ever heard of him? Exactly.

"So, who gave it to you?"

Grandma looked at me like I was a moron. "He did!"

"Who did?"

"Who do you think?" she asked, completely exasperated. "The guy who wrote it."

What?!?!?

Grandma has met the phantom note writer!

I started sputtering. "Wh-who is he? Have you seen him before? What did he say?"

"Calm down! Anxiety gives you pimples." Just in case I thought she was speaking in generalities, she pointed a gnarled finger right at my chin, where I had started to break out last night.

Ugh! I barely had a mark there. She must have special cataracts that only allow her to see things that make another person feel horrible about themselves.

"If you must know," she continued, "I was coming home and noticed someone standing in front of the doorway with an envelope and some tape. I didn't have time to wait for him to be buzzed in or whatever the hell he was waiting for, so I loudly said 'Excuse me' and went to open the door."

I took a bite of my bialy and swallowed it quickly. "And?" I asked impatiently.

"Slow down!" She pointed again. "Eating fast gives you pimples." Since when? Besides having cataracts that only disappear when she sees a flaw, she also loves to give people helpful hints that aren't really helpful but, yet again, make you feel horrible about yourself. "Well, when I moved by him to put my key in the lock, he somehow got in my way and dropped what he was holding."

Translation: She pushed her way past him and knocked everything out of his hands. "I looked down and saw the envelope with your name on it, so I picked it up. I told him I'd give it to you and he left."

I was chewing, so I made a motion with my hands that said, "That's it?"

She started to point again, but before she could tell me that miming causes zits, I swallowed and spoke. "Grandma Sally . . . what did he look like?"

She looked at me like I was crazy. "How the *hell* would I know?"

How do I answer that? "By looking at him."

"I don't know," she said vaguely while putting brown sugar on her oatmeal. "He looked like a person."

"What does that mean?" I asked. Surely she had some information. "Old? Young?"

"Don't know." She started eating her oatmeal.

"Black? White? Asian?"

"Don't know."

"Dark hair? Light hair? Bald?"

"Don't know."

It was maddening.

"Tall? Short?"

She put her spoon down.

"That I can tell you. Normal height for a guy."

"Why is that all you can tell me? Do you not remember anything else?"

"Oh," she said with a smile. "I still have my memory." Then she added, "Just like I bet you still have your fear of spiders."

She had to bring that up.

"I just couldn't see any features," she added.

"Was it foggy?" I asked.

"Do we live in a seaside community?" she asked with disdain. "No! It wasn't foggy."

"Well, then why—"

"It was freezing last night. He was wearing a long coat and gloves, and he had on one of those winter hats that cover your whole face . . . except for those little holes for your eyes and nose."

Creepy. A winter hat that looked like a mask. Wow. He was like the Phantom without the opera.

"What did the note say?" she asked.

Uh-oh. I didn't want to get her involved. What if she told my parents that someone was leaving me cryptic notes and they made me come home before I made my Broadway debut? And yes, even though I have to go home Sunday night, I'm still somehow hoping to be on a Broadway stage.

Thankfully, before I could answer, I got a text. "Sorry," I said, leaving the table, "gotta take this."

Of course, "gotta take this" makes no sense because it's not a phone call, but anyone over sixty usually doesn't understand the way texts/tweets/cell phones work, so I knew she'd buy it. I grabbed my coat, headed outside, and read it on the street. It was from Hubert.

Meet today at noon. At the theater.

Huh?

I wrote back. *What about friend's apartment I'm supposed to be at?*

He wrote back right away. *You were sent the wrong text. Come at noon to theater to watch rehearsal.*

I reread it three times. He was asking me to come to the theater! And apparently enter it! And stay there! Ah! I couldn't believe it! I was finally going to witness a real live Broadway rehearsal.

I'm sure Hubert is somehow benefiting from the change of plans, but it doesn't matter because, after almost two weeks, I'm getting what I hoped for! I don't even mind that Spencer is probably spending the morning planning another date with his boyfriend. Speaking of which, I still need to solidify Devon as my boyfriend. We haven't even had our first kiss yet and my time in New York is almost over. I need to move things along, especially since Spencer is trying to trump me in the new boyfriend department by nabbing someone famous. I sent Devon a good morning text, and he wrote back asking if I wanted to meet for breakfast! Yay! I had already eaten but, of course, I was already hungry. It wasn't until I sat down at the diner above Fairway that I realized Devon should have been at school. I'm so used to running around the city all day for this internship that I've forgotten other kids my age don't have that kind of freedom.

Devon was already sitting at a table when I got there. We were seated near the window and his blue eyes sparkled every time the sun hit them. Dry hair or not, he was cute!

"Are you home from school today?" I asked him as the waiter served us coffee.

"No, I'll just go into school late," he said as the waiter put down the skim milk I requested.

"Won't you get into trouble?" I asked as I sadly poured the skim milk into my coffee. I didn't want Devon to know I used tons of half-and-half with every cup I drank because I'm trying out a theory that if I eat like a skinny person in front of him, he'll think I actually am a skinny person. The only problem with my theory is that skinny people eat food that's disgusting. I stared at my coffee, which had barely gotten any lighter from the skim milk I had poured in, and continued my assault on decent eating by adding two packs of Splenda.

Sigh. That cup of coffee was going to remain untouched.

Devon didn't even notice what I was putting in my coffee because he was answering my question the whole time. "I can come late because my mom wrote an excuse note for me months ago when I went to the doctor's really early in the morning in case my appointment went long, which it didn't." He picked up the small container of half-and-half. "I saved the note, which thankfully doesn't have a date, and I'll use it today."

"Better be careful you're not caught," I said. Huh? Since when did I warn people to be careful? I faked a laugh to show Devon I wasn't serious, but he didn't seem to care either way because he was busy pouring half-and-half into his coffee. He then added two

119

big tablespoons of sugar. So unfair! He doesn't have to pretend to eat skinny in front of me because he is skinny. He dropped his napkin, and when he ducked under the table to get it, I used that moment to quickly reach across the table and drink from his cup. Mmm. Stolen deliciousness. I put the cup back in the saucer and put on a blank face.

While he drank (what was left of) his coffee, I thought about how saving an excuse note for later use was very similar to a stunt I would pull. Of course, Spencer would warn me that I was taking a big risk and ask me what I would do if the school called my parents before I showed up with the fake note. I'd tell him he was uptight, but then would wind up changing my plans and coming back to school an hour earlier than I intended in case he was right. Well, now Scotty would have to deal with Spencer's nonstop warnings and admonishments.

When our meals came, Devon went on a tirade about the Tony Awards only being three hours on TV. He felt they should be held over two days to really give Broadway its due. It was just the kind of unrealistic thing I'd rage about with Spencer, who'd then tell me that television shows depend on ratings and if the Tony Awards already get low ratings for one night, there's no way a network would add a second night. I told Devon that very thing.

Oy! When did I become such a downer?

Of course, Devon did just what I would do and waved me away, saying, "We'll see what happens after I start an online petition."

Wow. It's amazing how similar we are. The only difference is how cute he is. Great teeth and eyes and a naturally fit body. I decided to stop placing myself in the role of schoolmarm and to take a picture of us instead, which I would then immediately upload to my website. Nothing makes someone (Spencer) more jealous than photographic evidence. The waiter came to refill our coffee cups (really just Devon's since mine remained untouched), and I asked if he'd take our picture. I handed the waiter my phone and ran to Devon's side of the table. I decided to boldly put my arm around him and it paid off because he then put his head on my shoulder.

It was such a boyfriend pose. Excellent!

This was sure to send Spencer into jealousy overdrive. Devon and I split the check and as we were leaving the café, I began to think of how to ask him out tonight so I could finally get a kiss and solidify our dating status. For all I knew, Spencer had a make-out session after dinner last night and was meeting Scotty for lunch today. I couldn't let him beat me in terms of getting a new boyfriend. Devon and I walked to the street and he turned and told me he had to get to school. Oh no! I knew I'd be stressed out all day if we didn't have a definite date scheduled. I had to ask him right then.

"Devon," I began, but never finished my sentence.

How could I when I couldn't talk?

That's right . . . Devon kissed me! Right there on the corner of Seventy-Fourth Street and Broadway.

The kiss lasted ten seconds and I don't know what was going through his head, but I know what was going through mine.

Wait till Spencer hears about this!

12

Well, the last day of my internship was off to an amazing start! Not only did I have a picture of me and Devon on my website looking like we were boyfriends, but I actually received a real boyfriend-style kiss from him that solidified it. I just needed to spend some focused time figuring out the best way to get the news to Spencer without him knowing I spent some focused time figuring out the best way to get the news to him.

I decided to wait until after rehearsal to think it through and hopped on the subway to Forty-Second Street. It was the express train, so I got there in five minutes and followed the crowd exiting the train. We went up the stairs, through the turnstile, and up another flight of stairs until we were in Times Square. As soon as I started walking up Broadway to the theater, I mentally prepared myself for Hubert pulling a fast one and blocking me from walking down the street, but when I got to the stage door, he was waiting for me outside. Well, not waiting for me specifically; he was actually waiting for Chase, whose car arrived as I walked up.

"Hi, Justin!" Chase said, stepping out of the backseat of a black Lincoln Continental. There was a driver in a gray suit who was holding open the car door. So fancy! Hubert and the driver went to the trunk and started getting some of Chase's stuff out. I knew I should probably offer to help, but I suddenly went into a trance because I had turned away from the street for a moment and saw the stage door.

I've been to many Broadway theaters, but I've only entered through the doors that the audience member goes through. The stage door, however, is the entrance that all of the actors use. And not just the actors, but also the stage managers, orchestra members, dressers . . . anyone involved in the show. If you walk through the stage door, you're no longer just a random audience member. You're on the inside.

Hmm . . . I better clarify because I guess either door will lead you inside the theater. When I say "you're on the inside," I mean you're an insider, not simply standing inside the building. And I want to be an insider!

I stared at it. It actually had a sign that said STAGE DOOR.

Was today the day? Or would Hubert think of some last-minute errand I had to do in southern New Jersey? I watched him pick up Chase's backpack and leather messenger bag from the trunk and then he and Chase came toward the theater. Hubert walked by without giving me an order to hop on a subway. So far, so good.

Because Chase wasn't carrying anything, he opened the stage door and gave Hubert space to walk by him. I stood on the sidewalk among the last vestiges of snow on the ground and looked inside the doorway. It was dark, but I knew that a Broadway stage lay just a few feet away from it. I guess I could have made a mad dash through the door, but simply entering through the door wouldn't make me an insider. I was like a vampire outside a victim's house; I knew I had to be invited in.

"What's the holdup?" Chase said with a smile as he held the door open. "You want everyone in the theater to freeze?"

Could it be? Is this it? It wasn't an official invitation, but it was close, wasn't it?

"Justin!" I heard Hubert yell from inside the theater. "Get in here ASAP!"

Yes! No one ever said a rude invitation didn't count. This was it!

I started walking toward the door and thought to myself, *I am sixteen years old and crossing the threshold from outsider to elite.*

As I approached, Chase opened the door a little wider and I walked through.

Wow!

I'm not going to say I felt an actual bolt of electricity go through my body, but I'm not going to say I didn't. Suffice it to say, something went through my body and it was thrilling. The air was magical.

And smelly.

P.U.! When was the last time the inside of this theater was washed? Or how about just an ample spritz of Glade? I breathed through my mouth and took in my surroundings. To the left was a board with papers tacked to it. It must be the call-board! There was one sheet of paper up that had all the cast members' names on it and a check mark next to each one. That must be the sign-in sheet. Cool!

I turned to my immediate right and saw an old guy in a Yankees sweatshirt sitting inside a little tiny room, watching a football game on TV. The stage doorman! Just like in movies. Then I saw him spit something out into an old, broken-down garbage can. Whatever it was looked wet and brown. I sniffed again and then put two and two together—chewing tobacco. Gross! He was chewing and spitting tobacco into the garbage can. That's why it smelled like I walked into a pack of cigarettes that had been stored in somebody's old sneakers.

Yet a part of me liked the horrible stench. It made me feel like I was in a real old-time Broadway theater with tons of history. Which I was! As well as a real old-time Broadway theater with tons of disgusting smell molecules in the air.

Speaking of disgusting things, Hubert walked into my line of vision. He was more orange than usual. I guess he had extra time for tanning since I was doing all of his work.

"Justin," he said in his version of a friendly tone, "I'm about to leave, but I'm glad you were finally available to come to the theater."

Finally available? More like finally invited.

He did a small bow. "I want to thank you for helping Chase today."

"Sure," I said slowly. I knew his appreciation wasn't real, and I was wondering what he was leading to.

Then Hubert wagged a finger at me with a big, fake smile. "And make sure you don't bother Chase with a lot of chattering. You know that old Chinese saying, don't you?" He leaned in and spoke very distinctly. "Too much talking brings out grandmother truth."

He was using a fake Chinese proverb as a threat?

I couldn't call him on it. I simply nodded and said, "I understand."

"What does that mean?" asked Chase with a confused look.

Hubert was silent.

Great. Now I had to cover for him. "It means that . . . asking a lot of questions . . . can sometimes make people tell old wives' tales."

"Exactly!" Hubert said as he buttoned his coat. "Chase, I'll call you from the airport."

Airport?

Before I could ask where he was going, he opened the stage door and left.

"Hank, this is Justin," Chase said to the chewing tobacco guy. "He's going to help out today."

"Hi, Hank," I said. I also said it with as little air expelled as I could manage so I could stave off having to inhale as long as possible.

"What about Hubert?" Hank asked without lowering the volume of the TV or taking his eyes away from it.

"He needs to take off the next week, so Justin's going to be my right-hand man."

Wow. I *was* an insider.

Ahhhhh. I let out a deep, satisfied sigh.

Uh-oh.

I never should have sighed! I needed oxygen. But I didn't want to inhale the stench that was mixed with the oxygen. Mustn't. Breathe. In.

"Let me show you my dressing room," Chase said, and I nodded with my eyes bulging.

"You'll get used to the smell," Chase said quietly as he walked ahead of me.

I followed Chase as we walked farther into the theater and finally inhaled. I was excited to breathe again *and* because I was about to see a real Broadway dressing room! I was most excited, however, to see his bathroom. After all, I was the one who picked out all his towels, soap dispensers, and the shower curtain! Well, not really picked them out. Hubert told me exactly which ones to buy, but it would be nice to see some results of my internship.

I knew his would be on the main floor since Chase is the star of the show. I've read that a dressing room's distance away from the stage is in direct proportion to the size of the role. In other words, I'd only be visiting the male chorus members if I could build up the stamina to climb six flights of stairs.

He opened a door that had his name on the outside, just like

I've seen in books about Broadway. I walked in and it was the classic Broadway dressing room: lights around a big makeup mirror, a vase of roses, a big glass jar of cough drops, and a little couch with various shoes lined up underneath it.

"This is it," Chase said with a sweep of his hands. "Small but cozy." It *was* small, but probably giant compared to the other dressing rooms.

"Where's the bathroom?" I asked excitedly. I wanted to see the actual fruits of my internship.

Chase pointed to a small door on the left and I entered.

I turned on the light and looked around.

What the—?

The bathroom had two white towels that looked like they were from the five-dollar bin of some cheap department store. They certainly weren't the luxurious ones I bought. And the shower curtain! It looked like it began its life as white long ago but was now beige. And the whole thing was dotted with mildew stains that probably started forming when Ethel Merman was a young starlet. At least the bath mat was new, but instead of the thick, plush Ralph Lauren one I distinctly remember buying, it was like a cloth version of a Hollywood star in her early twenties (incredibly thin). And underneath the sink was a wastepaper basket that was obviously the same one the theater owner placed in every room because it was the same crappy one the doorman had.

This was bizarre. Where were the two-hundred-thread-count

bamboo towels I bought? The modular wastepaper basket based on a design by Frank Lloyd Wright? The Jonathan Adler shower curtain? The teal-colored super-absorbent bath mat?

Hmm ... I remembered that Hubert told me to buy everything but have the stores hold it all until he got the exact address of the theater. I guess he could have forgotten to call in the information and therefore none of it's been delivered yet.

I walked back into the dressing room and saw Chase starting to shave while standing over the small basin directly next to his makeup mirror.

"When do you get all your bathroom stuff?" I asked loudly, trying to be heard over the running water.

"What do you mean?" he asked as he looked up with his face covered in shaving cream. I momentarily didn't answer because I was taken aback by how the whiteness of the shaving cream made his eyes appear brighter. No wonder he was consistently on *HOT* magazine's "Hottest Guys with the Hottest Eyes" list.

"Are the towels missing?" he continued. "They probably just fell on the floor."

I snapped myself out of my trance and was about to tell him that he paid for tons of bathroom stuff that's not here but then stopped. I'd gone almost two weeks without my grandmother lie being exposed, and it wasn't worth ruining everything this late in the game. Yes, perhaps Hubert was ripping him off somehow, but I need school credit for doing JobSkill. And I don't need my parents to ground me, which would make me lose out on the chance to do the spring musical. And I especially don't need to see Spencer's head shaking in disappointment.

The fact is, Chase is rich. So what if he spent some money for things that never got delivered? He can just make more money and buy it again.

I had to backpedal. "I just thought, you know . . . maybe Hubert was going to get some fancy-schmancy bathroom stuff for you."

He gave me a thumbs-up with his nonshaving hand. "You totally know Hubert's style. He loves his hotel-quality this and organic cotton that."

I tried to answer without revealing how much I disliked him. "Yes, he seems to be very . . . particular." That's the only word I could think of because all I wanted to do was say "hateful."

Chase let out a big laugh. "He's *very* particular! About every aspect of his day." He started listing them. "He'll only eat green olives and *only* ones from Gristedes. Every night he has to have his martini at the W bar. Every morning he must have his double espresso at Le Pain Quotidien. . . ."

Typical. Hubert would insist on getting coffee at the only restaurant whose name is as pretentious as he is.

"Anyway," he finished, "he's been so busy running errands for me that he didn't have time to class up my bathroom."

"That's too bad," was the half sentence I spoke. The full sentence being "That's too bad he's continually lying to you."

"He's like Superman. He'll watch rehearsal, give me some great feedback, run out and do some heavy-duty assisting stuff, and then be back at rehearsal for more feedback."

"What kind of assisting stuff?" I asked, just to see if Chase would list everything I've done this week.

He did.

"You know," Chase said as he shaved his left cheek, "picking up dry cleaning, mailing out autographed photos, getting my dressing room stocked up for a long run with my fave foods . . ."

Yep. I listened as he named all the errands that I had done. I started to obsess: What was Hubert doing when he claimed to be doing everything I was doing? Visiting friends on the Upper West Side with that redheaded guy? Why so secretive? Was the guy his boyfriend and he was hiding it for some reason?

And I still didn't understand why I was finally allowed at the theater and where Hubert was off to.

Well, I could find out some of that information.

"What's Hubert doing now?" I asked.

"He's flying to Kansas tonight to visit family, so I gave him the rest of the day off. It worked out perfectly that you were *finally* able to get to the theater today."

"Well," I said, just to see what Hubert told Chase, "I probably could have come a few days ago. . . ."

Chase shook his head. "I wouldn't want you to have gotten in trouble. Hubert told me that your school made you do that New York orientation all last week." What a liar. "And then he told me how out of the blue they decided a Broadway internship wasn't academic enough."

He kept talking as he shaved his upper lip. "I know people think theater is all fun and games, but I believe you can learn a lot from being here. You must have been so upset when they told you to come back to school and resume your regular classes this week."

Wow. I was speechless from all the maneuvering Hubert had done to keep me away.

So why was I here?

"Well, I'm glad it worked out. It was . . . unexpected." I wanted to hear what he thought happened.

"Well, you may not know it, but you can thank Hubert for that."

"I sure will." *Never.* "Why?"

"Well, I found out from the stage manager what school you went to and was just about to call and give your principal a piece of my mind when Hubert came through."

"He did?" I asked.

Chase beamed. "He's so great. While I was rehearsing, he beat me to the punch and called the school. He said he pleaded with your principal and told him how important it was that you spend at least one day at the theater. That's why you're here today!"

In other words, Hubert knew his cover would be blown if Chase called the school, so he had no choice but to make up a story and let me come to rehearsal.

But how odd that he suddenly was out of town.

"When did he decide to go see his family?" I asked innocently.

"A cousin of his *just* gave birth. It's real premature. I never even knew she was pregnant." *That's because she doesn't exist,* I thought. "He felt he needed to be there for support." He gave me a classic Chase smile. "I'm glad you're available today. It was very last minute."

Last minute indeed. I'm positive that his decision to go out of town has something to do with me being at the theater.

So much mystery. So many lies. And why was Chase so dedicated to him? Did Hubert also know some horrible secret about him that he was threatening to tell?

"That's very caring of him," I said, trying to sound believable.

He turned away from the mirror and looked at me. "I know Hubert can be hard sometimes, like when we met you at *Phantom*, but he's just doing it because he cares a lot about me."

"He does?" I meant that to sound like, "Yes, he does." But it came out as a question.

"Yeah, he does." Then a cloud seemed to pass over Chase's face. "He was really there for me after my mom passed away four years ago."

I had read that he lost his mother in a car accident. She had raised him as a single mom and the loss must have been devastating. Hubert had obviously helped him through that and Chase was thankful. But thankful enough to deal with Hubert's awful personality every day? Even if Hubert put on a nice-guy act around Chase, didn't Chase's other friends tell him how horrible he was?

Chase turned back to the sink and washed the shaving cream off his face. "I was pretty messed up after I lost her. We were really close." Chase reached for his towel. "Hubert helped me out and wound up completely changing my life."

"Oh?" I said noncommittally.

"Oh yeah! Before I met him, I had a *whole* team of people working for me."

"Where are they now?" I asked.

"Gone. Hubert made me realize that they were out for themselves and not for me. And turns out, he was able to do their jobs better than they were!"

Wow. It's pretty clear that Hubert got rid of any naysayers and now controls everything in Chase's life.

He nodded a few times. "I trust him more than anybody."

Chase dried off his face with the towel that looked the most dry and scratchy and actually said "ow" at one point.

But back to the basic question: What was Hubert hiding and why? For instance, why tell me to buy the most expensive bathroom stuff and then give Chase sandpaper towels? Was it a surprise for later? If so, when is he gonna spring it on him? Chase already moved into his dressing room. And, now that I think about it, how could Hubert not know the theater's address for delivery? He texted me the address days ago!

Something severely strange is going on. I had given up on finding out what Hubert was up to. But Chase was being so nice to me. If Hubert was somehow scamming him, he deserved to know. I decided to figure out what Hubert was up to. And somehow keep my secret safe.

A few minutes after Chase finished shaving, I heard a voice over a loudspeaker calling all the actors to the stage. Chase told me he'd be out in a minute and ran into the bathroom. I stood alone in the dressing room. *One day I'll be in a dressing room just like this getting called to the stage.* I looked at the row of Chase's costumes and thought about what it would feel like to wear one of them under the stage lights.

The voice came over the loudspeaker again. "Once more, all actors to the stage."

All actors.

I wondered what it would be like when that announcement pertained to me. I checked my hair in the dressing room mirror, then hummed a little to see if my voice was in shape to sing. I ignored my fifteen-second coughing fit and decided I was warmed up. Then I stretched my hamstrings and my calves. Of course, that made my lower back have a spasm, but I still felt like I was ready to go onstage. I heard the other cast members making their way downstairs from their dressing rooms, and for a minute, I felt like I was a real Broadway actor.

"Here we go," Chase said as he pocketed a couple of cough drops.

We walked out of the dressing room and I waited for him to open the door that led to the audience area and for me to become just another observer. Instead, we walked right past the door . . . and onto the stage! As soon as we stepped past the wings, I could hardly breathe. There I was, standing in the exact place I've always dreamed of. Well, truth be told, we were on the right side of the stage and I've always dreamed of being directly in the center, but nonetheless I was on a *Broadway stage!* The perspective I was used to was totally reversed; instead of sitting in a seat and looking at the stage, I was on the stage looking at the seats! Theater people were all around me; the dancers were on the floor stretching and everyone else was either standing or sitting on various set pieces. It looked like there were around twenty people in the cast and they all got quiet when Chase clapped his hands.

"Hey!" he announced. "This is my friend Justin Goldblatt!"

How cool that he called me his friend!

"He's going to assist throughout rehearsal. . . ." *And one day be on this stage with all of you,* I wanted him to add, but he didn't.

"So," he finished, "everyone say hi!"

Everyone waved and said hi, and I waved back. It was so cool! People in an actual Broadway show now knew who I was! I realized there were probably producers in the audience as well as the director and choreographer, and I suddenly thought about all those stars who were first spotted by casting agents while walking around a mall or at a coffee shop. I was on a *Broadway stage*! What better place to be discovered? I scanned the crowd, hoping I would see someone running up to me and giving me a contract.

I turned to my right . . . and there was someone running up to me! Yes! It was a bald guy who was carrying a clipboard. Perhaps to write down my information! Do I give my home number? My agent's number? Don't I first need to have an agent in order to give out his number?

"Can I help you?" I asked in a singsong manner, adding a little vibrato on the last word to show what a great voice I have.

I waited for the "You're the exact type we've been missing from this show! When can you begin performances?" Instead, I heard, "Jared, we're about to begin, so you'll need to leave the stage."

Leave the stage?

Jared?!

"It's Justin," I said, disappointed.

"Oh, that's right! Justin," he said with an embarrassed smile. He put out his hand. "I'm the assistant stage manager, Gary."

I shook his hand and let him lead me off the stage.

When we were in the wings, he looked at me again. "You're with Chase today, right?"

"Yes," I said with a big smile. "I'm here to help!"

He looked away and muttered, "Well, he needs help."

I was about to ask what he meant, but then an actor in a sheriff's uniform called Gary's name and he started walking away. "That door will take you right to the audience," he said as he pointed over my shoulder. I had no choice but to leave.

Hmm . . . Chase needs help? How? Because Hubert is devious? Or for some other reason?

Unfortunately, I soon found out.

First, I went into the audience and noticed I could pretty much sit anywhere. Finally, I could get a great seat on the aisle and not have to babysit for six weeks to pay for it! Then I noticed that around fifteen rows back, across a whole row of seats, there was a makeshift table set up with people sitting behind it. I casually walked by and right away recognized Peter Geraci, who was sitting right in the middle. He's very recognizable because he has black hair that's obviously dyed and a full silver beard. Why try to pretend you're young only above your eyebrows? Peter is British but has been directing on Broadway for years. However, all of his hits have been plays. When it was announced that he was going to direct *Thousand-Watt Smile,* all the people on the theater message boards went crazy because Peter's so British and the show is so American. *And* it's his first musical. I could tell just by looking at him that he was feeling stressed. I don't mean to imply I had some sixth sense that picked up on his tension level. I literally could tell by looking at him. The theater was freezing, but he had two enormous sweat stains under his arms and was continuously wiping his forehead with a handkerchief. I assumed that the other people around him were the choreographer and lighting/set/costume/sound designers as well as the stage management team. Like Peter, they also seemed to be severely tense. Yet again, no sixth sense was needed on my part. All I needed were two ears because without even using my signature eavesdropping technique, I was able to make out parts of conversations with the following phrases: "What the hell are we supposed to do?" "I'm freaking out," and "Shoot me now."

What was everyone having a breakdown about?

I heard a British accent fill the air. "Hello, lads and lasses! Let's settle down."

I turned and saw Peter had a microphone and was speaking to the cast from the table area.

"We're going to start with the opening number. Let's take our places, shall we?"

Everyone left the stage except for Chase.

"Don't forget," he said, sounding nervous, "there's a full orchestra underneath you, so I need you all to sing out."

I could see the conductor standing in the orchestra pit and hear various instruments warming up.

"So, yet again," Peter continued, "I need you to *sing out*." He already said that. "Did you hear that, Chase?"

"Yes, Peter!" Chase called from the stage in a loud voice.

"Well, I told him," I heard Peter say, not using his microphone.

"OK, Chase, old chap," he said into his microphone, "let's start right when you begin singing."

"Gotcha!" Chase called back.

"Light cue eighteen . . . *go!*" someone behind the desk said, and all the lights changed to just a small spotlight on Chase. The orchestra began playing an introduction and soon Chase started singing. Or at least, I think he did. I mean, I saw his mouth moving, but boy, it was hard to hear him. I was sitting around seven rows back, so I figured I was too far away to hear him. I decided to move closer and tiptoed down to the front row. Wow. Let me just say that my tiptoeing was actually ten times louder than Chase's singing. What was happening? He had a mic on, but it seemed like he was testing how well it worked by singing in a whisper. I didn't get it. Was the whole musical being sponsored by a hearing aid company and this was a tactic to boost sales? Was the song supposed to be quiet? I didn't think so since I could see the music sitting on the conductor's podium and the title was "Loud and Proud."

Maybe the people behind the table had some special speaker system set up? I walked up the aisle and right when I got near the table, I heard Peter's voice boom through the theater.

"Cut, please!"

I sat down right away in the row behind the table and Chase stopped singing. Not that I heard the sound end, I just saw his mouth stop moving.

"Chase?" Peter was talking into his microphone and his voice filled the theater.

"Yes?" Chase responded. *That* I heard. Chase's speaking voice was a thousand times louder than his singing voice.

"Can you please sing out?"

"Peter! I'm singing it how I'm going to sing it in the show." He smiled. "After all, I'm wearing a microphone."

"Yes, but . . ." Peter moved his microphone away and spoke to the people around him. "Yes, but a microphone can't pick up *whis-*

pering! Chase, dear," Peter said back into the microphone, "you really need to sing in a louder voice."

"I don't think my character would sing any louder," Chase said with a shrug.

"But—"

"Look, Peter," Chase said soothingly. "Let me try it during previews. If it doesn't work, we can change it then."

"Hold, please," Peter said, and then huddled with the people behind the table. I was sitting low in my seat and the theater was still dark so they couldn't see me.

"What do we do?" Peter asked while mopping his forehead with what looked like a soaking wet handkerchief. "We can't force him to sing louder."

"We can't force him to do anything!" said a man with a Texas drawl and a big belly. From his cowboy hat I assumed he was Jim Bob Wheaton, the country star who wrote the script, music, and lyrics to the show. And from the various stains on his shirt, I also assumed he used an ample amount of ketchup this morning. "He's been hacking away at my script more than a beaver tears through a tree."

Chase has been cutting up the script? How? I was about to ask him to clarify when I realized I was eavesdropping and needed to keep my trap shut.

Jim Bob stood up and pointed at Peter. "Why the hell did you hire him?"

Peter tried to keep his cool. "You were at his audition. He was fantastic. And he's been fantastic."

Jim Bob piped up again. "*Been* is right! For the last two weeks he hasn't sung louder than a breeze in a meadow! I thought at first he lost his voice."

"Me too! How on earth were we to know he was choosing to sound like that?" Peter said.

Jim turned the other way and pointed to a well-dressed woman with her designer glasses and her gray hair in a French braid. "You're the damn producer! Why did you give him complete control of my show?"

"Jim Bob, keep your voice down," the woman said in a whisper, which incidentally was much louder than Chase's singing voice. "I didn't give him complete control of the show." She paused. "I gave him final approval of his material . . . and how he performs it."

"It's the same dang thing! He can say whatever he wants and sing however he wants!" Jim Bob hissed.

"Regardless, that was in the contract he had on *Vicious Tongues* and that's what he now requires. He seemed so excited to be doing a Broadway show that I never thought he'd use his final approval to—"

"Make my show a crapfest?"

"Hey, Peter!" Chase called from the stage. "Can we keep going? I've got some new ideas for the opening scene I want to try out."

I've never heard so many people at once mutter, "Oh no."

"OK, Chase," Peter said into his mic. "Resume, my good man." He looked at the stage hopefully, but I think we all knew what was about to happen. The orchestra played the intro and once more we watched a silent movie starring Chase.

Suddenly, my phone lit up with a new text. Ah! Luckily, I had turned off the sound or else my cover would have been blown. I bent down underneath the row of seats to read it and happily saw it was from Devon asking to meet for dinner! I wrote back that I didn't know how long my rehearsal would be, but I would text him the minute it was over. I was excited to have our first date since our first kiss, but more excited because I had a feeling he'd share in my penchant for nosiness. This Hubert mystery coupled with the Phantom note writer has gotten so bizarre, I've decided I need a right-hand man. And what a bonus to get one with snooping *and* smooching skills!

14

After I got Devon's text, I watched more tech rehearsal, which was incredibly exciting.

For the first three hours.

At first it was fascinating because I was seeing real Broadway professionals in rehearsal and there was so much skill involved. Not just the great voices and brilliant dancing, but I was most riveted by the problem-solving skills so many of them had. I've only seen Broadway shows after they've opened and everything has already been worked out. It was so much cooler to witness what seemed to be an insurmountable problem and then watch it be solved. At one point, Lisa Clark Oliver (whom I remembered seeing in *Chicago*) is supposed to run offstage in tears. Then, seconds later, she's supposed to enter (as her twin!) from the other side. Lisa thought she'd have enough time to exit and then run backstage to the other side for her entrance, but it took so long that the effect of seeing her come on as her twin didn't have any magic. So, she and the director came up with this amazing idea where she starts running offstage but right away passes behind one of the trees on the set. Turns out, hiding behind the tree is a girl dressed just like her who runs offstage right while Lisa passes behind the tree. It happens so quick that it looks like Lisa passes behind the tree and continues running. As the fake Lisa runs offstage one way, the real one runs the other way, with a crowd blocking the audience from seeing her. She's then able to reenter as her twin two seconds later. It looks amazing!

But for every exciting theatrical moment like that, I had to sit through dozens and dozens of incredibly tedious one. I hereby want to change the expression "God is in the details" to "Boringness is in the details."

Essentially, 95 percent of the day consisted of a scene starting and then two minutes later everything stopping so one light could be adjusted. The adjusting would take five minutes; then they'd start again. Twenty seconds later, the choreographer would run onstage and move everyone a few inches to the right so they filled the stage more evenly. They'd start again but immediately stop because the lights would have to be adjusted once more due to everyone moving a few inches to the right. During a merciful break, Gary walked by my seat and told me that watching tech rehearsal is like watching someone with obsessive-compulsive disorder clean their house.

The nice part is Chase would come find me in the audience during breaks and ask me how I thought it was going. I started to tell him it was a little hard to hear him during the opening number, but he cut me off and told me it would all make sense when I saw the entire performance.

. "My character comes into his own and finds his voice at the end of the show." He smiled. "Get it? I'm gonna start the show with hardly any voice and then I'll 'find it'"—he added a few winks to make his point—"at the end of the show. Get it?"

I did get it. And it was stupid.

He ordered in lunch because he had a phone interview scheduled, but he invited me to stay in his dressing room till the interview began. I wanted to ask him all about *Vicious Tongues* and find out the story about who he was really dating. I've read that he's been dating the lead girl off and on for years. But I also read some really dishy stuff about him being a so-called playa. However, I'm not sure if that's true because I read that in my dentist's office in *People Español* and I don't speak Spanish. I based my conclusion on the photos and the amount of exclamation points. I was about to ask him the juicy stuff, but instead he asked me about myself.

"Justin," he said as he sat on the couch, "have you thought about what you're going to do after this internship?"

"Well, I have to go back to school."

He shook his head. "I meant this summer."

"Oh! I guess I'll go back to musical theater summer camp."

He looked disappointed. "After being on Broadway?" he asked.

"Well, I'm not actually *on* Broadway," I said with a wistful smile, "but it is my wish more than anything."

"Then why don't you stay here in New York for the summer?

Audition for some professional shows! See what it's like to be an actor in the city."

Wow. I never thought of that. Hmm . . . I would be in the oldest group at camp this summer. Maybe too old?

But where would I stay? Every year, Grandma Sally's sister comes for the whole summer and there's no way I'd stay with them. Not only would there be no room, but there'd also be no peace. Every time I think there's no one worse than Grandma Sally, I think of Great-Aunt Rhoda and realize how lucky I am to only have to see her at Passover.

I definitely had some money saved I could put toward rent, and my parents would help me out. But where? Could I get a place for just a few months?

"Where would I stay?" I asked out loud, and then immediately regretted it. It sounded like I was asking him to give me one of his rooms in the Dakota. "I mean, I'd definitely rent something," I said firmly, "but I wouldn't know where to begin."

Chase dismissed me with a wave. "It's not hard to find a sublet for the summer. But the bigger question is, what about after high school?"

I got nervous we were talking too long. "Don't you have to do another phone interview or go over your lines?"

He laughed. "Look, I asked you to intern because I think it's important that young people have someone older to help them out." He patted the seat next to him on the couch.

What a great guy. He's about to open in his first Broadway show and he's taking the time to talk to me about my future.

"Well," I said, sitting down, "I thought I'd get a college degree in acting and go right into, you know . . . *the business*." I felt stupid calling it "the business," so I did air quotes. Then I felt stupid because I did air quotes.

"An acting degree?" he asked. "What if you don't get cast your first few years out of school? How are you going to make money?"

I never really thought of that. I'd assumed I'd be starring in a Broadway show the day after college graduation.

"You mean, I'd need something to fall back on? Like being an accountant?"

"Accountant?" He laughed. "You could make money playing the piano. It doesn't have to be something boring."

Aha! I tried to use my ESP to relay the thought, *That's right, Spencer! I'm not the only one who thinks math is boring.* I waited for an ESP response but got nothing.

Chase stared at me. "What are you thinking about?"

Busted! I forced myself back into the moment.

"I was thinking . . ."—*think of something!*—"that you never have to worry about an acting job because you can always make money from modeling."

He nodded. "You have a point, but once you become known as an actor, I think it's bad for your career if you freelance as a model." He whipped his head away from me and then whipped it back and gave a half smile.

"That was my famous look," he explained.

So cute!

"I can still hit that half-smile even though I haven't modeled in years."

"But you haven't left GlitZ, right?" Maybe he had some pull there and could use it to get Spencer a better internship for the summer. It would be nice if we were both in the city for July and August. I could be auditioning for shows and he could do actual accounting.

"Sort of," Chase said. "I mean, I'm still signed with them in case I ever go back to modeling one day. . . ."

"So, would you have any influence there?" Maybe Spencer and I could even sublet an apartment together. Becky, too!

Once they apologized, that is.

"Influence? Not at all! All agents really care about is money and I haven't made any for GlitZ in years." He looked away dreamily. "I do miss that easy cash, though. Stand, smile, gimme a check." He shrugged. "No more."

It was so cool sitting and talking with someone I've seen on TV every week. I had so many questions to ask but didn't want to seem like any other fan. My resolve lasted ten seconds.

"So, are you really dating every girl on the show?" I asked eagerly.

"What?" he said. Then he wagged his finger at me. "Do you pay money for those trashy fanzines?"

"Of course not," I said.

I make my mom pay for them.

"Why don't you ask me something about working in show business? Maybe I can help you."

I instead asked what I was dying to know. "Are you going to do the *Vicious Tongues* spin-off?" Then I pathetically added, "Please?"

He laughed. "You sound like Hubert. He really wants me to go back to L.A. and do the spin-off."

Hubert wanted it? Now I no longer did.

He continued. "I mean, a part of me thinks 'who am I to turn down such great money?' But . . . I never wanted to do TV. I always wanted to do Broadway. Ever since high school. Like you."

"Why'd you do the TV show in the first place?"

He rubbed his fingers together. "Money, man. You can't imagine the cash actors get for TV." His eyes got big. "I'm taking a huge pay cut doing a Broadway show, but I don't care." He laughed. "Most of the time."

"Who's doing your part on the spin-off?" I asked. Not that anyone could ever replace him.

"I don't think they've found anyone yet." He shrugged. "Maybe they'll write my character out of the show. What else do you wanna know?"

I had something on the tip of my tongue I wanted to ask, but instead I went for the obvious question.

"Uh . . . who's your favorite composer?"

"Stephen Sondheim. You already know I worship him."

"Oh, right. Me too."

Silence.

Ugh! I did have something I really wanted to talk about, but it wasn't showbiz related.

Chase wasn't really the right person to go to, but . . . I couldn't ask advice from hostile Grandma Sally or my meddling parents and I certainly didn't want Devon to know how bad it was with my two best friends.

Chase was being so nice, though, I decided I would take a chance and talk to him.

"This is kinda off topic, but . . ." Should I relate it to show-biz? "Well, it kinda reminds me of the episode on *Vicious Tongues* where you make your roommate move out."

"What does?"

I sighed.

Then let loose with a stream of words. "I have a friend. Two friends, actually. Well, one's an ex-boyfriend."

"Ex-boyfriend? The one you were dating when we met at *Phantom*?"

Wow, he remembered! "Yes! He's great. Well, he was great. My point is they're both mad at me. And I'm mad at them. And we're not speaking right now. Or maybe never again and—"

"Stop right there. When did this all happen?"

"Last week."

"Then apologize right now," he said firmly.

"But they—"

"I don't care who was wrong. You need to do everything you can to keep your friends." He looked at me seriously. "Right now Hubert is my closest friend." *Then why am I taking advice from you?* "But before Hubert, I had a"—he looked away sadly—"really close friend and we had a stupid fight. I probably should have apologized, but I didn't. And now things have gotten so bad between us, it's too late to fix it."

"So . . . ?" I didn't want him to say what I knew he was going to say next.

"So, I'm telling you to fix your relationships now before they become unfixable."

Ugh! Why do *I* have to fix it?

The phone rang and I knew I should go do some interning.

"There's my interviewer." He handed me a piece of paper. "Can you handle this for me?"

I nodded and left.

The errands were easy: a caramel Frappuccino from Starbucks and two croissants from a delicious bakery called Amy's Bread on Ninth Avenue.

While I got Chase's food, I thought about what he said and decided that maybe, *maybe* I would apologize to Becky (for real this time), but I was definitely and absolutely *not* apologizing to Spencer. He broke up with me! Asking for his friendship back would be one step away from asking him to be my boyfriend and that would make me look pathetic. And I wasn't interested in that. I had Devon.

I know Spencer will eventually apologize, so the healthiest thing for me to do is force that to happen sooner rather than later. I simply have to work harder to make him see how amazing my life is without him so he'll say he's sorry and ask to be a part of it again. Once he offers an apology, I shall accept it.

But I will definitely not offer one first.

Hmm . . . how to ratchet up Operation Jealous? I dropped off the stuff for Chase in his dressing room while he was still talking and went back outside the theater. I decided the first step was a shot of me in front of the marquee that I could post on my website. Spencer needed to know that I was living it up on Broadway. I mean, I'd been writing (lying) about that every day, but now I could finally back it up with photographic evidence. It was the last afternoon of my internship, so I needed to get as many shots as I could. I went out through the lobby doors and ran into Peter, the director, who was standing by himself, smoking. He seemed lost in his own world as he stared toward Eighth Avenue.

I thought a picture with a big-time director would be sure to make Spencer envious. I didn't want to walk right up to Peter and ask him to pose because it seemed like he wanted to be alone with his thoughts. But I wanted that photo! I decided to make him notice me in a low-key way, so I casually walked past him and then bent down to tie my shoes right in his line of vision. I then realized I was wearing shoes without laces, so I quickly changed my tactic and pretended I had bent down to pick something up. Thankfully, I saw a receipt someone had dropped.

"There it is!" I said loudly as I picked it up. Of course, it had been on a New York City sidewalk for who knows how long and I immediately noticed it was encrusted in dirt and old food. And why were parts of it red? Gross! I feigned putting it in my pocket but let it fall to the sidewalk.

"You dropped something," Peter said.

I turned around and saw he was pointing to the ketchup/blood-laden receipt.

Argh! What choice did I have? I smiled, bent back down and slowly picked it up again, trying to use only the top two centimeters of my thumb and third finger.

"Thanks," I said as I put it in the pocket of my jeans that are now at the bottom of Grandma Sally's garbage.

Peter let out a stream of smoke. "You're the intern lad working with Chase, aren't you?"

"Yes, I am," I said with a smile. Wow! A big Broadway director knows who I am!

"He is a . . . nice fellow," he said slowly.

Yowtch. That was the blandest compliment I've ever heard. I'm sure Peter was being driven crazy by Chase's horrible singing/ acting/ideas.

"I'd love to have a picture of us together if that's OK," I told him.

"Of course," he said, and stomped on his cigarette.

I took out my phone and he immediately grabbed it. I guess being a director means he likes to be in control. He held it above our heads, we smiled, and he took the picture. Unfortunately, he's also one of those "I'm over sixty and barely know how to use anything electronic" people, so he didn't reverse the camera image. He just estimated and held it at an angle where he thought we'd both be in the pic. He handed the phone back to me with a smile and a "Cheerio" and walked back into the theater.

I looked and saw that my picture with a famous director that would make Spencer envious was actually a blurry photo of the top of Peter's head with the only clear images being of two home-less people who were in back of us, leaning against the theater.

I figured I'd instead get a shot of me in front of the marquee and was about to ask a random tourist to take it when I saw Gary coming back from lunch.

"Hey, Justin! Glad to see you in the outside air instead of the darkened theater."

"Gary!" I was glad to see him, too. "Would you mind taking a picture of me in front of the big *Thousand-Watt Smile* sign? It's for my website. I want my high school friends to see what I'm up to."

"And be green with envy."

Was I that transparent?

"Kind of," I said.

"Sure!" Then, "Wait! Any tourist can get that picture. Don't you want one that says you're a part of the show?"

"Yes!" I said eagerly.

"OK," he said, and led me to the stage door. "I'm gonna go inside and take a shot of you entering. That'll show everyone back home what you're doing."

"Thanks, Gary!"

He opened the door, walked in, and turned around to take the photo.

"OK, Justin," he said with my phone up to his eye. "Start walk-ing through and I'll take the shot."

I started walking in right when the stage doorman spit out a hefty dose of wet, smelly tobacco. The combination of the sound and smell was so disgusting I couldn't control my facial expression and the flash went off at the height of me looking completely repulsed.

I was about to beg Gary to take another picture when the stage manager came on the speaker. "All actors to the stage. All actors to the stage."

"Here you go, Justin," Gary said, handing me my phone. I looked at the photo and reluctantly posted it, hoping that Spencer's jealousy of my amazing life would override his certainty that he made the right decision in breaking up with someone whose face was capable of distorting into that position.

I heard everyone gathering on the stage so I went back to my seat in the audience. It was my first day in a Broadway theater, but the thrill of watching rehearsal was over. I was almost hoping for one of Hubert's crazy lists, but I hadn't heard from him all day.

By 6:00 p.m., they had only gotten through half of the first act. Even though I was bored, I didn't want my internship to end. During the break, Chase came into the audience.

"Listen, Justin. There must be child intern laws in the books somewhere. You should go. I appreciate all the help you've given me today."

I was torn. It was definitely cool watching a real Broadway rehearsal. But after a while, it was killing me to see the same one-minute section run over and over just so the stagehands could practice moving a small piece of the set.

Plus, I wanted to meet Devon for a date and hoped to jumpstart a team investigation. How cool would it be to somehow solve the Phantom mystery *and* get Hubert busted!

But, I thought . . . this is my last official day of my Broadway internship. Is my last memory destined to be of me leaving a rehearsal in the middle, even if it's more boring than one of Spencer's yoga DVDs? Hmm . . . I could stay at Grandma Sally's this weekend and take the Long Island Rail Road to school Monday morning if Chase would keep me as an intern this weekend. After all, they'll be doing full run-throughs starting tomorrow, which are bound to be more exciting than this boring tech rehearsal and maybe I could even get an invite to the first public performance on Sunday night!

And, I must admit, there's a small delusional part of me that's still holding on to the hope that I'll somehow see myself on Broadway before these two weeks end.

"Well," I said, standing in the aisle, "it would be nice to get some dinner, but I'd love to see more rehearsal this weekend if at all possible. Do you think—"

"That would be great!" Chase said. "Hubert's away so I could totally use the help."

Yay!

"And besides," he said as he ruffled my hair, or to be clear, rearranged my Jewfro, "I like talking to you!"

He waved and walked away.

I texted Devon, telling him to meet me at seven.

It was time for dinner and a date.

And some heavy-duty detective work!

Since my parents had given me a charge card to pay for stuff I needed for my internship (which I had barely used), I told Devon I was buying him dinner. If we ate at either of our apartments, we'd never be able to talk freely because our families would be around. I wanted to tell him everything that had been happening with Hubert, Chase, and the Phantom note writer, and I didn't want his sister's brattiness or Grandma Sally's crankiness interrupting me.

And, quite frankly, I wanted to eat in a restaurant so we'd be seen.

By Spencer.

I knew I needed to amp up the jealousy so I'd get an apology before we went back to school. What better way to do that than by him seeing me on a date with a super-cute boy? I chose Good Enough to Eat because I thought maybe Spencer would take Scotty to dinner again and I would casually start an enormous make-out session with Devon when they walked in. And even if he didn't show up at the restaurant, there was a good chance I'd see him walk by since the restaurant is directly between the subway and his apartment. Yes, I did some Google map work.

I got to the restaurant at one minute to seven and luckily there was a seat right by the window. Perfect! I could talk to Devon *and* keep an eye on the street in case you-know-who walked by. Devon walked in a few minutes later and gave me a huge smile when he saw me. Whoa. He really is cute. Different from Spencer cute. Devon is more perfect-face-cute and Spencer is more . . . I don't know. Something else. That's not the point. The point is Devon walked in, smiled, and immediately planted one on my kisser. I looked around the room to see if anyone happened to witness it, but annoyingly the restaurant was pretty empty. The waiter came over and filled our water glasses and Devon barely took a breath before he launched into a story about someone at school he was "acquaintafriends" with. He quickly added that he and his friend Colin made up that word, which is like "frenemy" but different because it's a combination of "acquaintance" and "friend." He told me "acquaintafriend" means someone you know but you're not totally friends with. I don't know why they needed to make up that word since acquaintance means the same thing but I smiled and listened to his story. Well, I listened but I didn't understand. The whole thing reminded me of one of the lengthy/convoluted stories I'd tell Spencer, during which he'd smartly interrupt every two minutes in order to clarify a detail. I've never been on the Spencer side of one of those tales and by the time I realized I should interrupt to clarify, too many minutes had passed for me to even try to figure out what needed clarification. The only upside was that Devon never took a break from talking, so I had no competition in the bread basket department and was able to finish the entire thing by the end of the story. Delish!

After he finished his story, he took a sip of water. "OK, OK . . . ," he said with a laugh, "enough of high school drama about water fountains." *That's what the story was about?* "Tell me about your day."

He reached for my hand. I did a quick scan of the restaurant (still no Spencer) and launched into the Hubert/Phantom/Chase details. I ended with a recap of today's whispering tech rehearsal and after I finished, Devon sat there silently. Finally, he spoke.

"So, you think that all these things are related somehow?" Devon asked while reaching for the bread basket the waiter had thankfully refilled.

"Exactly. It's too peculiar that the Phantom should randomly appear right when I began interning. They've got to be related somehow."

"One thing doesn't make sense, though. Why don't you just tell Chase that Hubert has been lying to him?"

"Well," I said, not admitting the real reason, "I don't think he'd believe me if I did. It's like Hubert has some kind of hold over him." It seemed like Devon bought that explanation and I didn't have to reveal that Hubert has a hold over me as well.

I did another quick scan of the restaurant and street and something caught my eye . . . Spencer! He was walking right past the window. I'd recognize that orange hair anywhere. Even shoved underneath a cap.

"Uh, wait right here," I said to Devon. "I have to run out for a minute."

He looked completely perplexed. "Huh?"

I reached across the table and wiped some crumbs from his chin. He needed to look cute when Spencer saw him.

"What was that for?" he asked, but I ran out without answering him.

"Spencer!" I yelled when I got to the street. He was halfway up the block and didn't hear me. "Spencer!" I yelled again and ran toward him. He turned around.

"Hi!" he said with a big smile, almost as if he had forgotten we broke up. The smile went away in a second and he looked uncomfortable. "What's going on?"

"Oh," I said casually, "I was just on a date and saw you through the window and wanted to say hi."

"Oh," he said. "Hi."

"Don't worry," I said, trying to add a laugh, "he's not the jealous type."

"Don't worry about what?" Spencer asked.

"Uh . . . don't worry . . . you know, that he'll . . . you know, be annoyed I'm talking to my ex. He's not going to run out here and try to beat you up."

Spencer looked at me without speaking. Finally, "Justin, are you really on a date?"

"Yes!" I said, sounding a little like the four-year-old I babysit when I asked her if she really had a pet unicorn.

"OK," he said, and then the conversation stopped.

It was freezing and I had run out with my coat open. I pulled it around me. "How's Scotty?" I said as casually as I could. "I saw another one of his 'Don't bully gay kids' posters in the subway. Someone drew a mustache on his face." I could feel myself smiling, so I added, "Not cool."

"He's fine," Spencer said slowly.

I couldn't take it anymore. "Are you dating him?" I blurted out. I was mortified at my lack of control, but I couldn't stop myself.

The good news is he didn't say yes.

Unfortunately, he also didn't say no.

"I can't talk about any of that." *What?*

"Why not?" I asked.

He lifted his chin. "Because I promised."

Argh! Of course Spencer keeps a promise. Typical.

"Justin, don't you need to get back to your date?"

I sighed. "I guess."

Silence.

Where was the apology from him? He had to have seen the Scotty photo *and* the picture of me at the stage door. Where was the begging to be part of my madcap life?

Nothing? Really? Have I put all this work into making him jealous for no results at all?

I thought about what Chase said. What if Spencer got annoyed at all my obvious jealousy-inducing schemes and instead of apologizing, he completely closed off from me? Yes, we were in a fight now, but I knew it wasn't a permanent one. What if we lost contact in the future like Chase and his friend? Should I take Chase's advice?

"Spencer," I finally said, "I think it's great that we stopped dating." He nodded. Then I couldn't help adding, "Especially since I have an incredibly cute boyfriend now." *Too far?* "But . . . can we be friends again?"

Once I said it, I realized how much I missed him.

And Becky.

Yes, Devon was really cute and smart and funny, but I missed having friends who knew me so well I didn't have to keep explaining basic things about me. Every minute I felt I had to tell Devon things like "Oh by the way, my dad is a doctor" or "I did great in algebra but had to get a geometry tutor" or "Just so you know, I don't allow the word 'mash-up' to be used in my presence. It's called a medley."

Spencer smiled. And this time it didn't fade away two seconds later. "Yes, Justin, we can. I've been thinking a lot about that day at Starbucks and how stressed Becky and I were. I know we shouldn't have blamed you for our internships." He paused. "I'm sorry."

Yay! He *did* apologize first! Chase is a genius!

I knew Spencer was waiting for a response. "I'm sorry, too," I finally said.

Spencer gave me a hug. It wasn't the kind of hug we had when we were dating, but it still felt nice.

"It was hard not calling you this whole time," I admitted.

"For me, too," he said. "How is the internship?"

I told him a truncated version of what was going on. And by "truncated," I mean I left out Hubert's threat to expose my lie.

"Mysterious notes? Be careful, Justin."

"I'm not scared of the notes. The only thing I'm scared of is Hubert texting me from Kansas and making me go back to Staten Island this weekend!"

"Oh, please. Your internship is officially over. He has no real power over you."

Uh-oh.

"You're right," I said, averting my eyes in case Spencer was using his "I know when you're lying" powers.

He then looked like he was going to start saying something a few times but kept stopping himself. Finally, he spoke. "Tell me the truth—did you come by GlitZ that day to apologize and then chicken out?"

He knows me well! But this time he was wrong. I shook my head. "Actually, that GlitZ trip was part of my internship."

"Oh." He looked disappointed. "I had seen your name on the GlitZ guest list and thought maybe you came up with some scheme to 'accidentally' run into me in the building." A downtown bus pulled up next to us and a few people got off. "I actually stayed late, waiting in that horrible accounting department till after six."

"Aw! I'm sorry you waited for me. And . . . I'm sorry you got stuck at GlitZ." Wow! I was getting good at apologizing. Thank you, Chase!

Spencer shrugged. "It's a nice credit for my résumé. I mean, everyone's heard of GlitZ." He smiled. "After all, they discovered Chase Hudson!"

I nodded. "Chase was reminiscing with me today about how much he misses his modeling days."

"What?" Spencer said, surprised. "He's on Broadway! Why does he miss modeling?"

"Well," I said with a laugh, "modeling's not exactly what he misses. He admitted it was all about the checks for him. He used to make a mint! But"—I shrugged—"that was years ago. No more checks, no more easy money for doing *this*." I tried to imitate Chase's model pose but slipped a little on the icy sidewalk and Spencer grabbed me.

We both looked at his hand holding my arm.

I heard a *ding* and took my phone out with my other hand to see a text from Devon: *We need to order.*

"That was from Devon," I said, and Spencer let go of me. "I guess I have to get back."

"I'll tell Becky we made up when I get home," Spencer said, brushing some snow off his pants. He suddenly got a huge grin. "Why don't we have dinner tomorrow and really catch up? I want to hear more about this mystery."

"Sure," I said. "Can I bring Devon?" *Aka make you jealous?*

"Absolutely."

"Great," I said. And then I forced the next sentence out of my mouth. "And Scotty should come, too."

Spencer looked taken aback. But then nodded. "Good! Let's meet at Becky's cousin's apartment at seven-thirty. I'll cook."

"I'd . . . *we'd* love that," I said.

Spencer and I stood looking at each other. Spencer took a step backward and waved. "See ya tomorrow!" he said, and walked off.

I felt as if an enormous weight had been lifted off my chest. I had to thank Chase. Unfortunately, Chase is one of the stars who doesn't do any social media, and since I never got his cell number, I had no way to reach him. I decided to do the next best thing. I took out my phone as I walked back to the restaurant and logged onto my website. "Yes, Chase is a big, gorgeous TV star," I typed into my status. "But he's also a great guy with a good heart. Thank you, Chase Hudson, for making me happy again!" Hopefully he'd see it one day.

"What happened?" Devon asked as soon as I sat down.

"Oh," I said, "I saw a friend walking by and was so surprised I had to say hello."

"A friend from high school?"

"Actually," I said casually, "he's my ex. But we're totally friends now. As a matter of fact, he invited us to dinner tomorrow night. I'm sure I can leave rehearsal early. Are you free?"

Devon looked excited. "Yeah! I'll get out of dinner at my apartment again." Then he looked serious. "But are you sure there's going to be rehearsal?"

"What do you mean?" I asked, and he solemnly handed me his phone. One of the dishiest theater websites was open on his browser: BroadwayBitchery.com. There was a long thread that began with a posting by "ThousandWattInsider." I couldn't believe what I was reading. It talked about how horrible Chase was in the role and how he couldn't sing! It specifically mentioned how he was asked to sing out during the opening number and refused. I was in shock! This had to have been posted by someone at the rehearsal. But who?

"Do you think I could contact the site and ask them to take it down before any of the big gossip sites pick up on it?" I asked.

"Too late. I've been scrolling through them all the whole time you were gone."

I went to his history and saw EntertainmentWeekly.com. The top headline was "*Vicious Tongues* Star Gives Broadway a Vicious Headache."

Oh no!

"Devon," I said, leaning across the table, "something really weird is going on and it's bigger than I thought. This kind of thing could ruin the show and put all of those people out of work."

I grabbed his hands. "We've got to do something."

He nodded seriously.

It took two desserts (both for me), but we came up with a plan.

I went back to the theater this morning and immediately high-tailed it to Chase's dressing room.

"Chase!" I said after I knocked. "I'm so sorry about the gossip sites."

He actually smiled. "Oh, Justin. There's been so much gossip about me throughout the years that it's pretty easy for me to ignore it all."

Maybe he didn't know how specific the gossip was. I didn't want to hurt his feelings, but perhaps he'd stop stinking up the joint if he really knew what they were saying about it.

I took a deep breath. "Chase, they're saying you can't act. Or sing."

He shook his head. "Justin, there will always be people who challenge artistic choices. It doesn't bother me."

How could he think his whisper singing and unfunniness were artistic choices?

I left his dressing room and headed into the theater. There was a different energy in the air. Yesterday, even with all of Chase's annoyingness, people were laughing during the breaks. Today, every time the stage manager yelled, "Take ten!" people seemed to keep to themselves. ThousandWattInsider had spread a pall over the theater.

Not surprisingly, Chase made the same bizarre choices as yesterday. However, I'd say today's were even worse. For instance, Chase had a witty line at the top of Act Two and he got a big laugh on it from me and the creative team because the face he was making was hilarious. After lunch, the director started the scene again and this time Chase delivered it with his back facing the audience! Yet again, he said he wanted to "try it during previews." It was maddening! Why would he try such a stupid idea when it was so obvious it wouldn't work?

I was loving watching the cool parts of rehearsal, but I was also working feverishly on my laptop during the boring parts. My assignment (which Devon gave me last night) was to write down everything that had happened since the internship started and then make a list of all the unanswered questions that were driving me crazy. For instance, where is Hubert? Last night, Devon and I concluded that there's no way he's helping his mysterious cousin in Kansas. But is he out of town somewhere else? Or is he hiding somewhere in New York?

We wracked our brains trying to figure out a way to track him when I remembered something Chase said yesterday in his dressing room. When I had mentioned how particular Hubert was,

Chase agreed and told me that Hubert *had* to get his coffee at Le Pain Quotidien every morning. I found a picture of Hubert online so Devon would know what he looked like (essentially a navel orange with blond hair), and Devon planted himself at Le Pain Quotidien in the early morning.

He texted me right when rehearsal began at ten. However, all it said was *SS*.

I texted him, *What does SS mean?*

Devon immediately wrote back. *Will respond later. Don't want to leave paper trail.*

I wrote back. *Devon. Texts aren't on paper.*

No response.

Finally, I called him on a break and he explained his first text of the day, which, I was relieved to find out, was not a reference to Nazi storm troopers. According to Devon, it was code for "Subject spotted."

Really? Why not just write "He's here"? It's just as mysterious to outside eyes but also actually makes sense. Devon claimed he had no more time to talk because "the subject is mobile." I guess that meant Hubert was walking. After that phone call, I had to focus intensely on nonstop code translating. After much guesswork, I figured out that *S@BBB* meant "Subject at Bed Bath & Beyond," *SonPTrsport* meant "Subject on public transport" (subway), and *S@ZBRS* meant "Subject at Zabar's." Once, it took me twenty minutes to realize "eeoINr" was the result of Devon sitting down while his phone was in his back pocket.

During lunch, Chase came over and asked me to do some

quick errands. While I was getting him some fresh flowers at a florist on Eighth Avenue to liven up his dressing room, he texted and asked me to bring him back two packs of sugarless bubble gum. The text came from his actual cell phone, so I now have a celebrity number in my phone!! Ah!

I did some more errands and dropped everything in Chase's dressing room right before lunch ended. I sat back in the audience when rehearsals began again and tried to focus on why Hubert would lie about leaving New York. What was he doing here? From Devon's bizarre coded texts, it sounded like he was just having a relaxing day on the Upper West Side. So why pretend to leave? This is something that I needed to figure out tonight with Devon's help.

Besides making my list of mysteries and breaking Devon's infuriating code, my other project was keeping one eye peeled to see who could be ThousandWattInsider. I knew that he or she wouldn't be obviously making fun of the show, so I was on the lookout for some discreet negativity, things like lip pursing, deep sighing, or muttering passive-aggressive comments. Unfortunately, that criteria soon led me to conclude that every single person in the cast could be ThousandWattInsider. As well as the entire creative team. The only one I didn't suspect was Chase because he obviously loved the show and was working incredibly hard. He's just a terrible singer and actor.

I had hoped for a full run-through, but yet again it was an incredibly slow tech. Made slower by Chase. I noticed that after every break, Chase would come back to a scene and change something. Sometimes the staging, sometimes a line, always for the worse. It seemed that the stage manager was so busy doing the actual tech that the responsibility for keeping track of all the changes fell to Gary, the assistant. He was constantly typing new lines/staging into his laptop, which he would then print out and distribute to the cast. The wasting of paper was mind-boggling. Chase would make a change and then on the next break, he'd come back and change it again. I barely had any assisting to do, so I volunteered to help Gary and be in charge of carting away all of the old script pages, which kept piling up. Well, by my fourth trip to the paper bin, it was completely filled up. I took out the entire bag of paper and put in a new one. Since it was recyclables, the bag was clear, and when I put it on the floor, I saw something very familiar through the plastic.

He's a fake was written on a small piece of paper.

What?! That was the note *I* got! How did it get here? I opened the bag and found an envelope addressed to Gary in that Phantom's handwriting! Gary got the same note? I ran back to rehearsal with the envelope and note and held them tightly in my lap. Finally, the stage manager called for a break and I made a beeline for Gary. I followed him as he walked to the backstage area where the coffee was.

"What's up, Justin?" he asked as we maneuvered our way past actors in various costumes who were heading either for the coffee machine, their dressing room, the bathroom, or outside to smoke.

"Um . . . ," I muttered as we passed near the stage manager's office, "can we go in here? It'll only take a minute and I promise you can get your coffee."

"Sure . . . ," he said, sounding friendly but suspicious.

It was just the two of us and I closed the door. Then I held out the letter.

He looked at it and then back up at me. "Did that fall out of the bin? Just recycle it."

"It didn't fall out. I took it out. Do you know what it means?"

"Means?" he said. "Yeah, it means that Chase has crazy stalkers."

Aha! "It's for Chase?"

"Well, no. It's *about* Chase. It's *for* the entire cast. We've all gotten them."

Everyone? This was bigger than I thought!

"What do they mean?"

"Who knows? Every couple of days one of the actors or producers gets a note. They all say things like 'Don't believe him!' or 'Everything's a lie!'"

"How do you know they're about Chase?"

He leaned against a desk that had three-hole punches, paper clips, and Scotch tape everywhere. "The first day I got one was the first day we began. It had been sent to the rehearsal studio and the front desk delivered it."

"What did it say?"

He thought for a minute. "I think that one was 'He's not what he seems.'" He shrugged. "Anyway, Chase saw it sitting on the desk and said it was from some silly fan and I should just ignore it. I suggested showing them to the police, but Chase was adamant that I shouldn't." *Why?* "So even though we get them all the time, we all just laugh 'em off. Especially Chase."

So Chase knows about the Phantom . . . but how does the Phantom know about me?

"Did you get one today?" I asked.

He shook his head. "Funny you should ask. Even though Chase told us to ignore them, I've asked the cast to give them to me whenever they get one, in case something changes and they get threatening. Usually, I collect around ten a day. But today, nobody handed me a note."

Why is today different? Another question to add to my list.

Hmm . . . Chase may know more about the Phantom than he's telling Gary. I decided to visit him during the break and try to find out. I thanked Gary and immediately ran to Chase's dressing room still holding the note. I got to the door and saw he was sitting by his makeup mirror, typing on his laptop.

"Knock-knock," I said, and then immediately regretted it. That's something my mother does that drives me crazy! Why is saying "knock-knock" better or easier than actually physically knocking?

Thankfully, Chase smiled at me instead of giving me the reaction I usually give to my mother, which is to glare and ask, "Did you *say* something?" I emphasize the word "say" in order to show that she didn't actually knock.

"Can I come in?" I asked while walking in. Another thing I learned from ye olde mother. Why am I asking permission for something I'm already doing?

"Sure!" he said with a big smile. "I hope you're liking the last weekend of your internship." He turned his chair around to face me.

"Are you kidding me?" I said as I took a seat on the couch. "I'm so glad I'm getting these extra two days to be at rehearsal. It's really educational."

It was. I'm learning how a Broadway show is put together. And how one person can ruin it. "If you need anything, Chase, I haven't forgotten I'm still here to intern for you." Obviously he hadn't forgotten since he had just asked me to do errands, but I meant that I was available if he needed me to run lines with him onstage so I can finally see what it's like to be on Broadway.

That's not what he asked for. Instead, he took out a bunch of business cards from one of his drawers. "Can you scan these and put the info in my laptop? Hubert usually does it, but he's been super busy the last two weeks." *Doing what?* I thought as Chase started putting the cards in a neat pile for me. "I meet so many people and I feel bad throwing them out. And I might need one of these services one day."

"Of course," I said, looking at the cards. "Why, just this morning I was looking for"—I picked the craziest one I saw—"a holistic yoga instructor for dogs, cats, and their 'people companions.'"

He laughed and thanked me.

I somehow fit them all in my pocket and suddenly realized I should be thanking him.

"Chase, I want to thank you for your advice yesterday."

"Really? Did you apologize?" he asked, excited.

"Yes!" I said, smiling.

"And you guys worked it out?" He seemed so concerned. It was very sweet.

"Yes! I actually wanted to meet him tonight for dinner, if I can leave at six?"

"Of course you can!" Then he leaned in a little. "Is it a date?"

"With Spencer? Oh, we're not boyfriends anymore. I'm dating someone new." Chase wasn't the only one who could go in and out of relationships.

Chase looked at me in shock for a second. Then he sighed. "Wow." It was such an odd way of saying "wow." Low energy and almost depressed.

"What?"

He smiled. "I'm thinking about when I first met you at *Phantom*. I was so impressed when you casually mentioned you were there with your boyfriend."

"*Ex*-boyfriend," I corrected him.

"Regardless, I think it's really great how your generation is so comfortable being gay."

We are? "I don't know about that. I mean, I kept it a big fat secret until last year."

He laughed. "Exactly! What are you? Fifteen?"

Hmph. "Sixteen."

"Well, I didn't admit it to myself till I was in my twenties."

Wait.

What?

He didn't admit *what* to himself?

"You're"—I paused—"gay?"

He nodded. "Just like you. But I don't tell everybody."

OMG! "Who knows?" Was I one of the special ones?

"Well, I always tell everyone I work with, of course." I guess I wasn't that special. "But I don't talk about it to the general public or the press." Well, at least he didn't consider me the general public.

I needed more info. "*People* is always writing about girls you're dating."

He looked embarrassed. "I know. I have to keep up that image for *Vicious Tongues*."

"But the show's been canceled," I said while taking a handful of M&M's that were in a bowl next to the couch.

"Right . . . ," he said, and then stopped like he was thinking about it for the first time. "But still, I'll probably go back to TV at some point and the sad truth is . . . it's hard to get straight roles if everyone knows you're gay. But"—he shrugged—"it's also hard to pretend I'm dating different girls."

"Tell me about it!" I said as I feigned moving my phone to the table next to the couch when I was really taking another handful of M&M's. "I pretended I was dating a girl last year and it took so much work. It's much easier now that everyone knows I'm dating Spencer." Uh-oh. "I mean, I dat*ed* Spencer. That's over," I said with finality. This time I didn't pretend I was moving my phone. I just took a handful of M&M's.

Silence.

"Are you dating someone?" I asked, putting the M&M's in my mouth. Since I wasn't the general public, I felt comfortable asking.

"Oh yeah," he said with a big grin. "Hubert."

I almost spit out the M&M's.

Almost.

177

Naturally, I swallowed those M&Ms (I wasn't going to let Hubert ruin my enjoyment of colorful chocolate deliciousness) but still . . . *Chase and Hubert are a couple?!?!?!*

Oh.

No.

Can't.

Deal.

Breathe in. Breathe out.

I had to act like I didn't want to throw up.

"That's so wonderful," I said, using my years of acting training. I quickly stuffed my mouth full of another handful of M&M's to push down my feelings, hoping Chase wouldn't notice even though he was staring directly at me.

"Hubert doesn't like me telling a lot of people about us."

'Cause he knows everyone will try to convince you to break up with him?

"But I can tell you. We've been together for two years."

Do I dare?

"So when is Hubert coming back to New York?" I said, deciding to fish for information.

"Tomorrow night," Chase said, taking three green M&M's for himself. Hmph. So-called healthy portions. "He wouldn't miss my first performance on Broadway."

"And . . . he's in Kansas now?" I asked.

"Yep."

"Kansas the state?"

I asked that just for clarity. I'd hate to find out there's a town called Kansas, New York, that's twenty minutes upstate. Ever since I heard of Paris, Texas, I'm careful.

Chase looked at me like I was odd but answered the question nonetheless. "Yes, he's in Kansas the state."

"Can I ask you something?" I asked nervously.

"Yes, you can have more M&M's," he said graciously, and I felt shame flood through my body.

"No, thanks," I said, and then held up one of the notes. "Do you know who's sending these?"

His face suddenly closed down. "You got one, too?"

"Actually, I've gotten a couple. Who's sending them?"

His face went back to smiling. "Oh, you know. Stars always have fans who are a little extreme."

Huh? "This doesn't sound like a fan. The comments are pretty negative. They all say you're—"

He cut me off. "Look, it's pretty common for celebs to have

people leave them notes. And sometimes people go too far. But I'm not worried."

"Chase, do you know the person who's sending them?"

I left it gender neutral even though Grandma Sally had told me it was a man. I wanted to see what Chase knew.

He paused for just a second. Then, "No, I don't."

Why the pause? And why didn't he care about the nonstop negative comments coming into the theater? "I think we should find out. Who knows if this fan will turn violent?"

He laughed. "Believe me, he won't."

He?

"Or she!" he quickly added.

Why so certain? "How do you know?"

Again a pause. "Just a feeling." Then another big smile. "Look, don't worry about him."

Aha!

"Or her."

Oh, brother.

He got up and walked toward the door. "I'm gonna go over my script now, so . . ."

He obviously wanted to end the conversation. I got the hint and walked out.

"The guy is harmless," he said as he closed the door.

I knew it!

The door opened and he popped his head out. "Or the girl!"

That did it. He definitely knew who was sending the notes. But he didn't want anyone else to know. Why?

I was just the busybody to find out!

Well, as the late afternoon wore on, my hopes for watching the whole show from start to finish faded away. They ran the same scene change again and again, trying to time out something called a "quick change" (that's when an actor changes costumes in seconds). Anike, the leading lady, was supposed to walk offstage while wearing a dowdy button-down shirt and jeans and then the lights and set onstage would shift to a sassy nightclub. She was then supposed to come back onstage in an evening gown and a new hairstyle. She only had around fifteen seconds to completely change her outfit, shoes, jewelry, and wig. Every time she reentered, something was wrong: the back of her dress wasn't zippered, her new wig wasn't pinned on, she was missing her purse and a shoe, et cetera.

I knew she had dressers backstage helping her make the change, but I couldn't understand how they were able to unbutton her shirt in fifteen seconds let alone give her a whole new outfit. Well, at one point, she asked Peter if she could run offstage in a blackout. When he asked her why, she said, "So I can save time and do *this* on my way offstage without the audience seeing," and at that moment she ripped open her shirt! First of all, I was shocked seeing her in just a bra (they say that being an actor means losing all modesty), but I was most shocked because her button-down shirt wasn't really a button-down. The front of it had buttons all the way down, but the opening was Velcroed together! Turns out, she didn't have to unbutton all of those buttons to open it; she just had to rip it apart. So cool! Doing it on her way offstage saved precious seconds, and after forty-five minutes, they finally got the quick change right ... and then the next tedium began. Suffice it to say, I had no problem leaving the theater at six when they were on their second hour trying to get the turntable onstage to stop on an exact beat in the music. I walked up to the front of the stage, waved goodbye to Chase, and walked to the uptown subway. Tomorrow would be different, because no matter what, the Gypsy run-through is happening at 6:00 p.m. and Chase invited me!

Oh yeah, let me explain: The term "Broadway Gypsy" refers to a singer/dancer who goes from show to show, traveling like a Gypsy. Before a Broadway show begins official previews, there's usually a final dress rehearsal on a day and time when most other Broadway shows aren't performing, so actors who are working can come and see the show. That's why it's called a Gypsy run-through. Tomorrow, the whole audience would be filled with Broadway insiders ... and me!

I left the theater excited about the upcoming dinner and decided to make a mental list of my goals as I traveled uptown. This was a really big deal and I didn't want to blow it. *Dear Self, tonight I will solidify my dating relationship with Devon and not bring up the splitting headache he caused me all day long by sending relentless idiotic texts in code. By the solidification, the closeness of our relationship will also serve to make Spencer jealous and his obvious jealousy will hopefully cause Scotty to break up with him. P.S.: It's not that I want Spencer back. I just don't necessarily want him dating someone.*

Back to my list: *I will also reconnect with Becky and, if neces-*

sary, ask her to help with my Spencer/Scotty breakup plan. Plus, I will use the smarts of Becky and Spencer (ignoring Scotty) to help with the Hubert/Phantom mystery. As well as figure out some way to stop Chase from giving the performance in public he's been doing in rehearsals.

Hmm . . . maybe I should be my own version of the Phantom and leave Chase a list of things he needs to *stop* doing. Number 1: Don't do half a scene while standing offstage. Number 2: Don't add a Spanish accent halfway through a serious song. "That's Why I Love You" ends with him singing, "Das a-why I luf . . . a-*jooooooo.*" Of course, when you hear it, it sounds like he loves a Jew. I know my rabbi will like it, but who else? As I was coming up with the list, I realized that eliminating those things wouldn't make him suddenly have a good voice or know how to act onstage. He may simply be one of those people who should never, ever be in a musical. No matter what, though, I was determined to see the first performance tomorrow. I just might have to watch the whole thing through a tiny hole between my fingers as I cover my face with my hands.

Back to my plan for tonight. I also emphatically reminded myself that as I tell Becky and Spencer the update, I *will not* admit the reason why Hubert has a hold over me. They've already called me selfish. I don't need to give them any new ammunition.

I arrived at Becky's cousin's apartment with four chocolate chip cookies from Levain Bakery. I had bought five, but something happened to one of them on the way over. Something that involved chewing and swallowing.

We had made plans for seven-thirty, but I wound up getting there a little early. Dare I go up and face Becky alone? The last time we spoke was a nightmare. It was too cold to wait downstairs, so I took a deep breath and buzzed her apartment. Soon a buzz answered me back. I took the elevator up to the twelfth floor and rang the bell, and Becky opened the door.

Not surprisingly, she looked beautiful. She had her hair in a French braid and was wearing just enough makeup to bring out her gorgeous features but not enough to look like she was wearing any makeup. She definitely picked up some high-fashion tips at GlitZ because she was not only in a gorgeous baby blue wool skirt with a white sweater, but she was also wearing super-high heels. I guess when you work with models, you gotta dress like them. Although GlitZ only has male models. Is there a drag department? Weird. I guess she just wanted to get dressed up tonight for some reason.

She stared at me.

I stared at her.

Could we be friends again?

I was about to find out.

Our staring lasted five seconds and then she broke into an enormous smile and grabbed me for a hug. We both said, "I'm sorry" at the exact same time. Wow! I didn't wait for her to say it first. Thanks, Chase!

I followed Becky into the apartment as she talked. "Justin! It's been so weird not calling you," she said as we walked down the hallway and entered the small kitchen.

"For me, too," I said. "If we have another fight, let's not do it when I'm also trying to solve a mystery."

"I know." Then she stopped. "Huh?"

"I'll explain it all over dinner," I said. I started walking around and smelling the various pots and pans that were simmering on the stove.

"Spencer cooked last night," Becky explained, "and I'm heating it all up."

"Where is he?" I asked.

"I'm not sure," she said while stirring something that looked like curry sauce. "But he knows when dinner is. He'll be here."

Yes, but will his precious boyfriend be here, too? I wanted to find out if Scotty was coming without being obvious.

"Is Scotty coming?" I asked.

Well, I tried.

"I guess . . . ," she said vaguely. "I mean, probably . . ." She turned away and opened the oven door, then closed it without checking anything. She turned and looked at me directly. "I mean, yes. Yes, he is coming."

She obviously felt in the middle and I didn't want to make her feel awkward.

But how dare Spencer be bringing Scotty? Just because I told him to?

Hmph. Two could play at that game.

"Well, the more the merrier," I said breezily. "That's why I invited my new boyfriend."

I expected her to run to me and scream with delight. But instead she looked sad. "Do you really have a new boyfriend?" What was she sad about? She's the one who helped Spencer nab Scotty.

"I certainly do!" I said haughtily. "And he's really, really cute." Perhaps I was laying it on a bit too thick.

She turned around and started stirring the saucepan again. "Well, tell me about Broadway! Is it everything we've dreamed of?"

Before I could answer, the buzzer rang. "Hold on," she said as she scurried out of the kitchen. I continued stirring the saucepan.

I soon heard a knock, so I gave the pan a few more stirs and left the kitchen. Standing in the living room was Devon.

Yay!

And Scotty.

Hmph.

It was weird seeing them together. The replacements. Well, we'll see how long Scotty lasts. It's not easy to put up with Spencer's nonstop social causes. You have to have a pretty strong resolve to even read a newspaper in front of Spencer and not feel guilty for destroying so many trees. I walked up to Devon and, waiting till Becky was looking, gave him a kiss. I couldn't wait for her to tell Spencer. Hopefully his seething jealousy will be so obvious that he and Scotty will break up before dessert. Not just to get rid of Scotty, but also because I saw the brownies Spencer baked and I want Scotty's portion.

But then, I thought, were the brownies the only reason I was so intent on getting Spencer to break up with Scotty? I did feel a little too obsessed, even for me. Why did it really matter?

I had a new boyfriend.

It's not like I wanted Spencer back.

I reminded myself that *I* was the one who wanted to break up. Well, break(ish) up. So, yes, Spencer went a little further than I intended, but as soon as he said it, I knew it was for the best. Spencer and I are just too different to date. Devon is just like me and it's perfect.

"Do you guys want anything to drink?" Becky asked.

"I'll just have some water," Devon said.

That's exactly what I was in the mood for! It's a sign! "Me too!" I said, way too enthusiastically.

"Me three," said Scotty. I glared at his attempt at humor.

He started following Becky. "I'll come help you get it in the kitchen."

Hmph. Of course Spencer found someone just as considerate as himself. Unfortunately, that made me start feeling guilty for lying to Big Noise Media. As a matter of fact, I just read on Playbill.com that they've disbanded. I'm not crazy enough to think that my interning for them would have saved an entire business, but maybe I could have helped keep them afloat a little longer.

Your guilt is eating away at you. Admit what you did, apologize, and you'll feel free.

Argh! Why is everyone always trying to make me apologize? I've already done it twice! Isn't that enough? I decided that silence from me is what makes Spencer's voice so loud in my head, so I turned toward Devon and plunged into telling him what I found out today about the Phantom messenger. I left out the info about Chase being gay because it seemed like he didn't want that to be public knowledge. And besides, it made me feel more like an insider keeping that to myself.

I then asked him for Hubert details.

"Well," he said, lowering his voice and looking over both shoulders like he was being spied upon, "as you know, I saw the perp at nine in the a.m."

My head immediately started to hurt from the bad cop/spy movie talk.

"Wait," I interrupted. "Is Hubert the perp? I thought he was the subject. Doesn't 'perp' mean *perpetrator*?"

"You are correct."

"But—" I began.

"Has he or has he not perpetrated rude behavior?" he asked me. Oy! That's the same kind of response I'd give Spencer when he'd try to rain on my parade. I gave a barely perceptible nod, which I based on the barely perceptible nods I'd get from Spencer when I pulled a verbal fast one. Devon ran his fingers through his hair (I couldn't help wondering if the dryness hurt his hands) and continued.

"I followed him all over town. As you know, I texted you the locales using a shorthand I developed."

He paused. I knew what he wanted.

"Nice job," I reluctantly said. This was wearing me out. *I* was used to being the needy one.

"At thirteen hundred hours, I sent you an email with a single subject line saying he was having lunch and he was not alone." Oh! That's what "Dining. N/A" meant. I thought it meant he was eating and was not having an appetizer.

"I, of course, took a photo of both subjects."

Wait! I remembered that red-mustached guy I saw with Hubert the one time I followed him. Was that the guy? Maybe Hubert really was cheating! I took out my phone, clicked on photos, and found the pic I took.

"Was this who Hubert was with?" I asked, holding up my phone in triumph.

"No, it wasn't," said Devon, smirking.

Was he happy that I had a photo of the wrong guy? He seems to have a deep need to be right. Even more than me.

"All right," I reluctantly said, "let me see the photo you took."

He blinked. "I emailed it to you."

"You did?"

I got so many moronic texts and emails from him throughout the day that it's very possible I missed one.

"Well, I don't remember seeing any email with a photo. Show it to me on your phone."

"I can't," he said matter-of-factly. "I deleted it."

"Why?" I asked.

"Because," he said, sounding annoyed, "what if the perp confiscated my phone? I didn't want any proof that I was tracking him."

I'd had it.

"The *perp*? Do you mean Hubert?"

"Yes, Justin, I answered that already," he said in measured tones. "You know I mean Hubert."

I was getting very irritated and started muttering as I scrolled through my emails. "I'll find it myself, then." I scrolled all the way back to yesterday and didn't see it. "What was the subject line of the email?" I asked.

"It was 'delete immediately.'"

"Wait, what?" I asked.

He let out a frustrated sigh. "I wanted you to look at it and then delete it immediately. In case the perp confiscated your phone."

"The *perp*?" I yelled. "Do you mean Hubert?"

"Yes!" he yelled back. "Stop asking!"

"Why the *hell* would you write *delete immediately* as a subject?"

"I told you why! What are you angry about?"

"Because I did what you told me and deleted the email immediately."

"So?" he asked.

"Without looking at it!"

"Why would you do that?"

"Because you wrote *delete immediately*! I thought it was a virus or something."

"Now what do we do?"

"We? You mean you! Look for it in your sent mail."

"I can't!"

"Why not?"

"Because I deleted the email account! I told you I wanted to clear any evidence in case the perp and/or accomplice confiscated my phone."

I had had it. "Perp! Accomplice! This isn't a spy movie!" I bellowed. "And if it were, you'd be fired from the agency for being a terrible, terrible spy."

"How dare you!"

Becky and Scotty came out of the kitchen.

I put on a big smile even though I knew they must have heard us yelling. I didn't want them to report anything to Spencer when he got here.

"We have to make a decision," Becky said. "Spencer can't come."

"Why?" I asked, completely thrown.

"He's at GlitZ."

"That makes no sense," I said. "His internship ended yesterday."

Becky pursed her lips and shook her head. "I know. But that's where he called me from. He's been there for the past few hours."

"Why?"

"You know him and commitments. He probably had some project he promised to finish."

"I understand," said Scotty.

Typical. "I completely understand as well," I quickly, and possibly desperately, added.

"So," Becky said to everyone, "should we all eat without Spencer?"

"But, Becky," I whined, "can't we wait for him to get back? I was so looking forward to catching up with you and Spencer."

Translation: What is the point of eating here with Devon if Spencer isn't here to get jealous?

"Look, why don't we all take a rain check?" Scotty asked.

"Great idea," Becky piped in.

A rain check? I planned out this whole evening!

I decided to suggest we continue with the dinner and Skype with Spencer. I knew I could position the computer at a perfect angle so he'd have a close-up of me giving Devon a big smackeroo. Before I could offer my idea, however, I saw Devon putting his coat on.

He was leaving? I guess I was a little harsh with the "terrible, terrible spy" comment. And everything else I said.

"Well . . . ," Devon said without making eye contact, "I should probably spend some time with my family tonight anyway." He should? His baby sister and cockney nanny? "Maybe a rain check is best." He looked at me. "I can see you're disappointed Spencer isn't here."

I guess I didn't hide it very well. But I just wanted Spencer here to throw Devon in his face.

"You and Scotty can come over to Spencer's house on Long Island next Sunday," Becky offered.

"Thanks, Becky," Devon said without committing to anything, and then left.

Ouch.

If Devon and I broke up, then I'd have no ammunition against Scotty. I gave him a once-over. *This isn't finished*, I thought.

"Are you looking at Scotty's outfit?" Becky asked. "Isn't it great?"

Uh-oh. Was I that obvious? "Yes! I love it! I want it! Where'd you get it?"

Scotty gave an embarrassed smile. "I get lots of my clothes made by a tailor in Italy. It's hard to find pants that fit because I have long legs but a really small waist."

"Me too," I said without thinking. Uh-oh. *Long legs and a really small waist?* "I mean 'me too' . . . as in I, too, find it hard to find pants that fit. But . . . for other reasons."

I knew all pairs of eyes were on my short legs and opposite-of-small waist.

"Well, if you'll excuse me," I said, slowly backing away from them, "I'm going to try to catch Devon." I grabbed my coat and fled into the hallway. I exited Becky's lobby into the cold night air and put my coat on as I neared the corner of Amsterdam Avenue.

So now what? None of my planning paid off. Devon and I were not getting along, to put it mildly, and we spent no time figuring out why Hubert lied about leaving New York. I was supposedly friends with Spencer again, but he didn't even care enough to come to dinner. Becky and I barely got a chance to talk because Spencer's new boyfriend was so busy sucking up to her. And Chase, the one person who's been nice to me consistently, was about to humiliate himself in public and I couldn't do anything to stop it.

I remembered that my stress level went down if I ate, so I made an emergency stop at Delicious Dairy and bought an everything bagel with cream cheese that I ate as I walked. I finally calmed down as I got nearer to Grandma Sally's. But then I felt my heart start racing again when I looked at the front door. There was something waiting for me. This time it wasn't a letter.

It was a package.

As soon as I opened the door to Grandma Sally's apartment, I heard, "I thought you were eating out. Don't expect any food."

Welcome home?

It didn't matter. I was eager to see what the Phantom sent me. "I don't need any food," I said.

"*You're* not hungry?" Grandma Sally sputtered while clutching her chest. "Are you trying to kill me? Thank goodness I already took my heart medication." She chuckled as she walked into her room and closed the door.

I ignored her comedy routine, went into my bedroom, and quickly opened the package. This time it didn't have a three-word note. It had a letter.

Dear Justin,

You don't know me. But I know who you are. I've seen your website, and I've seen the videos you've posted of yourself. You're a talented guy. Well, if he wanted me to like him, mission accomplished. *I also know you care about Chase.* So the notes *were* about Chase! *I saw your post last night. I've decided to leave this with you because, unlike people who work with him, you have nothing to gain from either his success or failure. It's apparent that you like him for him. Chase and I were once very close, but he hurt me and it made me very angry. I wanted to hurt him back. That's why I was leaving notes.* Wait! This must be referring to the friendship that Chase said was ruined. *I felt that I had been betrayed and I wanted people to know it. But when I saw what the gossip sites were writing about him yesterday, everything changed.* Oh. That must be why he didn't leave any notes today. *Yes, I had been angry, but I didn't want to destroy Chase. However, someone does. Everyone is saying Chase is a bad actor and can't sing. It's not true!* Yes, it is. *I know you're thinking, "Yes, it is."* Impressive. *But I'm including this DVD so you can see what he's really like. I'm trusting you to do something to help him. I don't know who else to reach out to. There are various reasons why I can't reveal myself. Watch this DVD and help Chase!*

I popped it into my laptop and pushed PLAY. It was a home video. The title came on: "Havenhurst High School Presents MAN OF LA MANCHA." A high school show? What did this have to do with Chase? I started watching. It was nothing special for the first few minutes. Then the guy playing Don Quixote, the leading role, came on the screen. It was Chase! He was a teenager, but I could easily recognize him. Shockingly, he wasn't whispering . . . and he wasn't facing away from the audience! His acting was really good. I had seen him be a good actor on *Vicious Tongues,* but this wasn't stupid TV soap opera acting. This was a real theater performance.

Then the first song began. It was a duet with him and Sancho Panza, who was played by a chubby guy who looked familiar.

I kept listening and all I could think was, *Wow!*

Chase had a GREAT voice! Where the hell has it been? I pushed STOP after his big note and thought about what I could do. Show this DVD to the entire company to prove that he had talent? But even if I did, what would it matter? Chase would still give a horrible performance. The question again is why? All the people posting on BroadwayBitchery.com were saying it was because he was a TV actor and therefore had no idea how to perform onstage, but this DVD proved that theory wrong. Tomorrow afternoon was the rest of the *Thousand-Watt Smile* tech and then tomorrow night Chase would be thrown to the wolves at the Gypsy run-through. I've read that a Broadway show has a few weeks of previews where it's performed for a paying audience but reviewers don't come until right before opening night. So, yes, the show wouldn't be officially reviewed for a while, but I think the result of tomorrow night's performance could be worse than a bad opening night review. The audience will not only be filled with fellow Broadway actors, but also with showbiz fans who got themselves an invitation and are just dying to post their opinion on every Internet gossip site. Sadly, those gossip sites are read a lot more than regular theater reviews. *People* magazine wouldn't necessarily do a piece on a Broadway show, but if it's being mentioned on all the hot Internet celebrity sites, it then becomes news. And what person is going to buy tickets to a show that everyone is saying has the worst performance ever seen on Broadway? The devastating word of mouth that will start this week could have the power to close the show before it even opens!

I have to do something before Chase ruins everything.

I woke up after 9:00 a.m. on top of my blanket, still wearing the same clothes as yesterday. I must have fallen asleep watching the DVD for the third time. I checked my phone and saw a text from Spencer asking me to call him right away. I had no interest in calling him back just to hear him ask, *How could you act so crazy in front of Scotty?* I didn't need to be reprimanded when I was dealing with the pressure of trying to save an entire Broadway show! I changed my shirt, put some de-Jewfro product in my hair, and left the apartment without waking Grandma Sally. I hoped the cold air would help me think of a plan. Within two blocks I was starving and immediately went to Zabar's for a muffin and coffee. Before I walked in, I checked to see if I had enough money. I reached for my wallet in my pants and when I took it out, all these business cards fell to the sidewalk. Oh no! I was supposed to scan them for Chase, but I forgot because I was so distracted last night from the

Phantom's DVD. I started picking them up and suddenly stopped and stared at one. It was for Upper West Side Realty and it featured a picture of Howard Brennan wearing a suit and a friendly smile. A smile with a mustache over it.

A red mustache.

And an entirely red head of hair.

What the—?

I took out my phone and compared photos.

Yes! It was the same guy who was walking around with Hubert that day I followed him!

I guess that wasn't necessarily significant because they could be friends.

Wait . . . that statement is based on the premise that Hubert *has* friends. There's no way that's true, so I'm sure their stroll together is an important piece of the puzzle.

I had to make a bold move. I dialed the number on the business card.

Ugh! It went right to voice mail. I was about to hang up when I heard his recorded voice suggest calling his cell phone if it was an emergency. I immediately dialed the cell number because it *was* an emergency. Chase's career was on the line!

"Hello? This is Howard," I heard after the third ring. There was lots of noise behind him. He was obviously walking in the street.

"Hi," I said. Then what? I hadn't really planned out what my scheme was. "Uh . . . this is . . ." A car honked. "Mr. Honky." *Oh no!* "Mr. Car . . . son Honky. Call me Carson."

"OK . . . ," he said.

"I'm working for Chase Hudson. And Hubert." What was his last name? I had no idea. I faked a laugh. "Good ol' Hubert."

"Yes?" he asked. "I'm about to go into the office. Can this wait until—"

"I'm sorry, it can't," I said quickly.

"Is it about the new apartment?" he asked.

"The Dakota?" I asked. That was hardly new. They'd been there for months.

"No," Howard said, already sounding annoyed. "The one Hubert just started renting."

Now it was getting interesting.

"Yes. Yes, it is," I answered.

"Hubert told me he was all moved in. Has there been a problem?"

"No . . . uh . . . not necessarily," I said, stalling. What did I want?

"Please don't tell me Hubert changed his mind. The lease is signed," Howard said. "Pardon me, but he's going to drive me crazy. I've never shown a client that many apartments."

"That's what I'm calling about," I said, trying to think through what I needed to find out. "He would like to have . . . you know, for his records, a list of the apartments you showed him."

"OK. I have that at the office."

"And actually, I have his calendar here. Let me just confirm some things. You started showing him apartments on . . ."

"Monday. Two weeks ago," he answered.

Aha! When I started interning! Coincidence? I don't think so!

"Right. On Monday and . . ."

"Every day after that."

"That's a lot of days," I remarked.

"Tell me about it. You know Hubert." He laughed a little. Not a *Hubert is so much fun* laugh but a *Hubert is so incredibly annoying* laugh. "He went from wanting a Victorian house in Westchester, to looking at Tudors on Long Island. Finally he insisted on an Upper West Side apartment but didn't like anything I showed him."

"Right, he told me that," I lied. "But then he *really* liked the one you showed him on . . ."

"Wednesday afternoon," Howard said, finishing my sentence.

I was leaving blanks at the end of my sentences, knowing that Howard was one of those New Yorkers who has no time for slow talkers.

"That's the one on . . ."

"Eighty-Second Street."

"And he signed the lease on . . ."

"Thursday morning."

"Yep. I have all that information." Meaning, I *now* have all that information.

"So, what's the problem? Did his stuff arrive?"

"Uh . . ." *What do I say? Yes? No?* I hesitated and Howard explained.

"He told me he had someone shopping for new furniture that whole time. Was it delivered?"

"Oh, *that* stuff." I decided to assume it worked out. "Yes, the delivery was fine. It happened on . . ."

When did it happen? I hoped he would give me the info.

"Hello?" He sounded annoyed. "Do we have a bad connection?"

I better say something. "The delivery happened like it was supposed to."

"Friday?"

Phew. "Exactly."

"So what's the problem? I got him the keys right away because he told me he'd have an assistant there to supervise delivery. Did the keys work?"

"Yes. They fit right into those locks." Too specific. "Or lock. I can't remember. That's not the issue, though. It's . . ." I trailed off, hoping he'd come up with something else.

"Yes?"

I guess the well had dried up.

"Oops," I said, "that's him beeping in. Gotta go! Thanks!" I hung up and stood in front of Zabar's, thinking about what I just learned.

First of all, Hubert had been apartment hunting for two weeks. *And* he apparently had someone shopping for him while he was doing it.

Wait a minute. *I* was the one shopping for him! Of course! I was constantly sending Hubert color swatches as well as taking photos of ottomans and leather sleeper sofas and expensive lamps for his new place! He claimed Chase was redecorating. Ha! Chase wasn't redecorating. Hubert was . . . what's the opposite of *redecorating*? I guess decorating.

But why? Are he and Chase planning on moving? Why would Hubert move in before Chase? And why wouldn't Chase mention it to me?

The answer is clear. Hubert got this apartment for himself and Chase has no idea.

But what Hubert doesn't know is that I have the address! I'm sure it's the one he texted me when he wanted me to wait for his "friend's stuff" to get delivered. *I* was the assistant who was going to be there on Friday. But when Chase foiled his plans by having me come to the theater, Hubert had to fake a trip to Kansas so he'd be there for the moving men.

I was off to Eighty-Second Street.

But first I had to get what I came for.

I downed two cups of delicious Zabar's coffee (so much cheaper than Starbucks!) and a yummy blueberry muffin (with butter) and went right to Hubert's new apartment. I was on to him and couldn't wait to tell him.

I giggled, imagining what his face would look like when he opened his apartment door and saw me standing there. Shock? Devastation? Defeat? I was so looking forward to spelling out everything I knew that he thought he'd been covering up so well. As I stormed over, I heard Spencer's voice come in loud and clear.

Shouldn't you take a moment and come up with a specific plan?

Typical. Always trying to stop me right when I was excited about doing something. Well, not literally trying to stop me, but always trying to make me "think things through." Well, there was one advantage to no longer talking to Spencer all the time; he couldn't hold me back when I was raring to go!

I approached Hubert's building, which was a beautifully restored brownstone and found the buzzer for 5R.

Dare I buzz? What if I was wrong and Hubert didn't live here? I looked closer and saw that right next to the buzzer was a handwritten label:

Hubert
Mykos

Found it!

I pushed the buzzer and soon heard his distinctive, annoying, and unfriendly voice. "Who is it?"

Uh-oh. Who was it?

"Delivery," I said. That seemed the most logical.

There was a pause. "From where?"

"Uh . . ." I then garbled a name that sounded like West Elm with Pottery Barn and a smattering of Crate and Barrel. I guess it worked because he buzzed me in.

I took the elevator up to the fifth floor, walked up to his door, rang the bell, and stood back, excited to see his expression when he realized that I'd tracked him down.

I heard footsteps approaching and then I heard him call something out from behind the door. "One minute, Justin."

What the—?

The door opened and I didn't get any of the facial expressions from him I had so anticipated. He simply commanded, "Close the door behind you," as he walked back into his living room.

"But," I muttered as I closed the door, "how did you know it was me?"

"I saw you on the video monitor when you rang. What do you want?" he asked, sounding bored. "I have to unpack."

Where was the panic? Where was the sputtering? Argh! I had to gain back the upper hand.

Not surprisingly, I saw all the things I had shopped for this week placed tastefully all around the room: the Jonathan Adler carpet, the Room and Board love seat, the Crate and Barrel media center. And I'm sure the bathroom had the two-hundred-thread-count bamboo towels, the modular wastepaper basket based on a design by Frank Lloyd Wright, and the teal-colored super-absorbent bath mat that were all bought under the guise of being destined for Chase's dressing room.

I was completely irritated by Hubert's calm demeanor and couldn't wait for it to turn into panic mixed with begging for leniency.

"Well, Hubert," I began, clasping my hands behind my back and taking long strides around the still-unpacked boxes everywhere. "I thought you'd be interested in knowing that everything you tried to keep secret has been figured out"—I whirled around—"by me!" He didn't look up. Rude.

I started listing everything. "I know you asked me to intern these two weeks so you'd be free to look at apartments. I know this is your apartment and it doesn't belong to your so-called friend."

He was now scraping a price tag off a paperweight. Annoying. What did I need to reveal to get the "How did you know?!" moment I so craved. I kept going.

"I also know you planned on me being here on Friday to help unpack for your 'friend' until Chase ruined your plans and I was called to the theater." Nothing. Well, there was more. "I therefore know *that's* why you pretended to go to Kansas . . . so you'd be free to unpack all weekend and settle in."

"Right," Hubert calmly said while taking bubble wrap off a beautiful green vase. "Do you also know that Big Noise Media was forced to close?"

Where was he going with that? "Yeah . . ."

"Perhaps they could have stayed afloat if they had more help these last two weeks. But they didn't." He stopped unwrapping the vase to look at me directly. "Because you lied about your grandmother."

That again?

"What's your point, Hubert? Everything you did is ten times worse. I don't even know the people at Big Noise. You're lying to your boyfriend."

He continued like I hadn't said anything. "And you lied about a school assignment. That would mean you'd automatically get no credit, I would think. And, even if not, I would think you wouldn't want your friends or your parents to know that you lied about a death just to help yourself."

I guess he had a point. A devastating, no-way-out point. "So . . ."

He went back to the bubble wrap. "So, everything you're saying is true."

Aha!

"But who cares?"

A-*huh?*

"Nothing I did is illegal. And if you tell anyone anything, I'll
tell *everyone* how you selfishly exploited the death of your grandmother just to help yourself."

Selfish. That's what Spencer called me at Starbucks.

"You did whatever you could to get what you wanted."

You'll do anything to get what you want. Becky's words echoed
in my head.

I didn't want to think about that. Especially now that we were
all finally friends again. I couldn't ever let them know how true
their words were.

Hubert went back to ignoring me, taking the vase he un-
wrapped and putting it on the windowsill. It was the perfect place
because when the sun hit it, the green glass sparkled.

I had no more ammunition to make Hubert keep his trap
shut.

Argh! This was all Spencer's fault! Because we're not speaking
to each other as often as we used to, he didn't prevent me from
coming here and revealing everything I knew to Hubert.

Hubert moved the vase a little to the right and then turned
around. "Are you done, Justin?"

"Yes," I said softly. "Yes, I am."

I didn't walk out with my tail between my legs, but that's only because I don't have one.

What was I thinking? Hubert warned me last week that he'd reveal my lie to everyone if I ever said anything bad about him.

I left his brownstone and headed down Eighty-Second Street toward Broadway. My cell phone rang.

Spencer!

Now he wants to warn me not to go to Hubert's apartment? Too little, too late. I pushed the IGNORE button so it would go straight to voice mail.

I then heard a *ding*.

It was a text from Devon.

Wowza! I think we were both out of control last night.

That was true. I wrote back, *I agree. I'm sorry.*

The apologizing thing was getting easier!

I read his next text as I walked toward the subway at Seventy-Ninth Street. *We never finished talking about the perp/subject/ Hubert. This sounds crazy, but I think he's living somewhere on Eighty-Second Street.*

Talk about too little, too late.

I didn't want him to feel bad, though, so I texted back, *Excellent spy work!!! Will fill you in on what develops today.*

Would anything develop? And even if it did, could I ever tell anyone?

I walked to the subway and took it to Times Square. I decided I would go to the theater, but not to watch tech. I just wanted to say goodbye to Chase. I couldn't bear to watch another horrible rehearsal. And I definitely didn't have the stomach to watch the first public performance tonight while surrounded by people just dying to write mean things about Chase all over the Internet. Yes, according to the DVD he has a lot of talent, but it's talent he's keeping completely hidden for some reason. No matter how many times I tried to think of a plan, I realized I had no way of making him perform well tonight. If the director couldn't do it, how could I?

I was done with Chase and with *Thousand-Watt Smile*. If it's painful and frustrating to watch his moronic acting/singing choices in rehearsal, it will be ten times worse watching it in front of an ever increasingly hostile/mirthful audience tonight.

I got in the stage door, held my breath, and walked past Cigar Face. Right next to the call-board was a stack of brand-new Playbills. They must have just been printed and I couldn't resist taking one and putting it in my backpack for reading later. I walked farther into the theater, passing some actors going to their dressing rooms and some just arriving. Rehearsal wouldn't officially begin for another hour, but I knew Chase always arrived early to warm up. I walked to his dressing room but stopped in front of it. The door was closed for some reason. That's weird. Chase always keeps his door open. Was he not here yet? Hmm . . . maybe he decided to sleep in today to rest up for tonight's Gypsy run-through.

I knocked a few times and was about to walk away when I heard a soft "Come in."

Why so soft?

I slowly opened the door and poked my head in, but Chase wasn't there.

Was he in the bathroom?

"Chase?" I said tentatively.

I was right.

I heard the water running in the bathroom and then saw Chase come out wearing his Scene One cowboy costume.

But something seemed off.

How weird! He was actually wearing one of the cowboy costumes the boys in the chorus wear, yet he had on the Stetson hat he wears for the whole show.

Why would Chase wear his hat but someone else's costume?

Then I realized why.

It wasn't Chase.

20

I stood in Chase's dressing room and stared at the man in front of me, who I now recognized.

"Hi . . . ," I said to the man who I realized was Mickey Hendrix, one of the ensemble guys. In reality, he didn't look anything like Chase (black hair, dark eyes, and at least three inches taller), but seeing him in Chase's dressing room wearing a similar costume *and* Chase's hat made me think it was Chase.

"Hi, Justin," he said, holding out his hand. "I'm Mickey. I remember when Chase introduced you a few days ago."

"Right . . . ," I said, completely wigged out. He was so completely calm. Had he murdered Chase and was wearing his hat in triumph? Was Chase alive but tied up in the bathroom right now?

Mickey sat down at the makeup mirror.

I checked to make sure the door was open in case I needed to make a run for it.

"Oh, man! I'm scared," he said while powdering down his

face. "Well, excited and scared." Then he laughed. "That's a lyric by Sondheim."

Hmph. He didn't have to tell me that. I had at least three recordings of *Into the Woods*.

"Why?" I asked, nervous for what the answer could be. Was it "exciting" to kidnap Chase? But now he's "scared" of getting caught?

He kept powdering. "Today's dress rehearsal, buddy! It's both a dream and a nightmare."

He still wasn't making sense.

"*What* is?" I said, sounding impatient.

He stopped powdering and turned toward me. "I'm going on this afternoon! For Chase." Then he pointed to his hat. "That's why I'm dressed like this. I'm his understudy."

What?

Was Chase sick?

"What happened?" I asked nervously.

Mickey gave me an enormous smile. "Nothing happened. Our fearless director wanted to give Chase the afternoon off before his first big performance. I mean, the guy's been rehearsing nonstop. He must be exhausted."

Oh, I thought, *that's nice of Peter.*

He started putting on his cowboy boots. "It's so early in the run that they haven't made me my own official understudy costumes, so I'm wearing what I normally wear in the show and adding the Chase costume pieces that fit." He tipped his hat, or should

I say Chase's hat. "Like this . . . Thank goodness the swing is ready to go on for me." Then he started explaining even though I already knew what he meant. "A swing is another word for understudy. There's a female swing and a male swing and if anyone in the ensemble is out, the swing goes on for them. So Ned is on for me this afternoon."

I know all about understudies and swings, but things started to not add up.

"Have a good rehearsal!" I said as I walked out of the dressing room. I needed a chance to think things through.

I stood in the wings of the stage and watched some dancers stretching out on the stage.

Hmm . . . Peter thought it was better for Chase to rest this afternoon?

I stared at the dancers and finally came to the conclusion that this understudy situation was indeed bizarre. And as I stared at one particular dancer with his shirt off, I also came to the conclusion that I have to cut out carbs entirely. But back to Peter giving Chase an afternoon free. They must have ju-u-u-ust finished teching Act Two last night. That means that this afternoon would have been Chase's only chance to run the whole show before his first public performance. In other words, the very first time he'll perform *Thousand-Watt Smile* from start to finish will be in front of an actual audience.

It made no sense. Who cares if he's a little tired? His (probably awful) performance tonight will definitely suffer because he hasn't had a chance to experience how the scenes and songs will flow together while in costume with the orchestra and with all the backstage quick costume changes he has to make.

Well, there was nothing I could do about it. I couldn't ask Peter why he was making such a dumb choice. And I couldn't make Chase give a better performance.

I took one last look at the stage and walked away. I then breathed deeply, held it in, and walked past tobacco alley and out the stage door.

It was a sunny but cold day and I waited for the M104 bus to take me to Grandma Sally's.

There was no one I could really talk to about this. I didn't want to hang out with Becky until she had time to forget how crazy I acted last night. And I spent the morning avoiding Spencer's calls and texts (he left another message, which I deleted without listening to), because I didn't want him to give me a lecture about last night's crazy behavior. And even though Devon and I apologized to each other, I was still feeling distant toward him. The whole boyfriend thing with him seemed forced. He has so many personality traits that are annoying. Personality traits that I guess I also have, but they're kind of adorable on me. Or at least, Spencer thought they were. I knew I should probably say goodbye to Chase face to face, but I wasn't feeling up to hanging out all day in the city just for that. Especially because he'd ask why I wasn't staying for the Gypsy run-through. How would I answer? "Because I actually like you and I can't bear to watch you become a laughingstock?"

Sunday is the worst time to take a bus because they run on a much slower schedule. My ears started to freeze because the wind was picking up. Wait a minute. My ears were freezing because I forgot my hat in Chase/Mickey's dressing room.

Argh!

I turned around and walked back to the theater.

I did my signature breath holding as I walked past the stage doorman literally mid-spit, and I knocked on Chase/Mickey's door.

He opened it and smiled when he saw me.

"Hey there, Justin. Did you come back to wish me luck?"

"Sure did!" I said with a smile. "I also came back because I forgot my hat and it's freezing outside."

He handed it to me with a sad face. "You're not leaving, are you? It would be nice to have someone in the audience who's not taking notes."

I knew what he meant. It's hard to give a great performance when everyone watching is somehow involved with the show. No one is there to enjoy it. They're there to work on it and see the problems that need fixing.

"I can't," I began, "I need to get back to my—"

"Oh, come on," he interrupted. "At least stay for the first act."

Well . . . as loyal as I felt to Chase, I was curious to see Mickey go on. First of all, it's always cool when I see a new actor play a role I've seen before because I love to compare and contrast performances. So far I've seen three different guys play the Phantom and it's great seeing the variations in how they play the part. Secondly, I had to be honest: Chase was brutally terrible in the part. A part of me wanted to see what the show would be like with a real Broadway pro playing the lead.

I decided to stay. At least for a little bit.

"You convinced me, Mickey," I said, taking off my coat. "Have a great time. I'll make sure to laugh and clap extra loud."

I took the backstage door that led to the audience. I could hear the orchestra tuning up. I could also hear Peter talking with the staff behind the table.

"The conductor has all the new cues," said Gary, passing out sheets of paper.

"And the cast?" said Peter, pronouncing it "cahst."

"Yes," said Gary, sounding exasperated. "I told you they were all emailed last night."

Ooh! There were changes! I was excited to see some new stuff.

"I just want to make sure everyone knows what's different," said the ever-nervous Peter, mopping sweat from his forehead with his scarf. I kept expecting the scarf to be stained black from the copious amount of dye he must slather in his hairdo.

"Why are y'all acting like it's a bushel of new stuff?" said Jim Bob.

I shook my head and thought, *Why do Southern people always find a way to put "y'all" in a sentence? He easily could have said "you both."* Anyway, back to eavesdropping.

"Ain't nothin' hard about it. It's just my original script. They memorized it once. It'll all come back to them lickety-split."

Excellent! It seems like the changes Chase made were being changed back. I was so relieved he finally agreed! Hmm . . . maybe tonight wouldn't be a catastrophe after all. Chase would get an afternoon to rest up and those unfunny jokes and bizarre lines he added would be out. Of course, his singing and staging would still be a travesty, but at least the actual lines he said wouldn't invoke the world's first ever entire-theater-eye-roll.

The staff stopped talking as the lights in the audience dimmed. I rushed up to the third row for a better view and the orchestra began playing the opening. After a few measures, Mickey walked onstage. He looked great. Handsome and really confident. He began singing the opening and for the first time, I was able to hear the melody and the lyrics. Wow! It was a great song. It's too bad the audience tonight wouldn't be able to hear it.

I sat there watching the show and got more and more frustrated. Mickey was fine in the role, but if Chase put in the same effort to play this part as he did to play Don Quixote, he'd be amazing. First of all, Chase is much more suited to the role because when he's in costume he really looks like a Wild West gangster. For whatever reason, Mickey looks like a skinny, fit dancer who's playing a gangster. Plus, Mickey can sing all right but he sounds like a guy with a pleasant voice. On that *Man of La Mancha* video, I could hear that Chase's voice was unique. Strong but with a tone that added a sweet vulnerability.

I thought I would enjoy the run-through, but it actually put me in a worse mood. Mickey knew the lines and the songs, but that's all he was. Someone saying the lines and singing the songs. The whole time I was aware that I was watching an actor. I never once thought he was a gangster with a heart of gold. Thankfully, intermission came and I decided to leave. I walked up the aisle to exit, but when I passed the staff table, I slowed down because I heard Jim Bob's loud voice and I couldn't resist a final chance to eavesdrop. I did the ol' sit-two-rows-behind-to-listen routine.

"I told you!" said Jim Bob, sounding ecstatic. "He'll be fantastic tonight!"

Who'll be fantastic tonight?

Gary spoke next in a much lower voice. "I've spoken to costumes and they're confident it'll be fine if he wears his own costumes. He's got Chase's hat, which looks great."

"Sure does," said Jim Bob. "And whatever looks bad, no one will care about. It's the first week of previews!"

"But—" Peter began.

Gary held up a finger and kept talking. "The good news is, by the end of the week's performances, we'll be able to alter the rest of Chase's costumes so they'll fit him."

Holy crap! They weren't putting Mickey on this afternoon to give Chase a rest. They were rehearsing Mickey to take over the role!

Chase is being fired! I had to do something.

I ran into Gary while I was walking up the aisle.

"So," he asked me, "what do you think of Mickey?"

"He's fine," I said. "But . . ."

He looked around. "I know. He's not right."

"Is he going on tonight?" I brazenly asked.

Gary looked surprised. "Did you talk to Chase?" he asked me.

"A little . . ." That answer meant nothing, but apparently it relaxed Gary enough to spill everything.

"I'm sure he's upset, but if he went on tonight, we'd close before we even opened. Yes, the show needs a big name, but the producer thinks we'll get a ton of publicity because an understudy is taking over for a star. We'll probably be able to run a couple of months instead of having to close in a week."

"But," I said a little desperately, "the show is good. And having a celebrity in the lead role would guarantee a long run."

"Who?" Gary asked. "It's too late. The show has so much bad press attached to it that no star would wanna touch it. This is really the best solution."

And with that I heard the stage manager call, "Places."

I thought about it. It's one thing for Chase to give horrible performances and for the show to close. He could always say the show was bad and he did the best he could. Even if people write about how terrible he was, he could always blame it on bad direction.

But being fired would be a deep public embarrassment.

I definitely couldn't stay to watch Act Two.

I had to find Chase and figure out a way to save him and this musical!

21

As soon as I got outside, I started walking toward Eighth Avenue and got out my phone. I was so thankful Chase had given me his number so I didn't have to go through evil Hubert.

Ah! The battery was red! I must have forgotten to plug it in last night because I was so distracted from watching that DVD. Well, all I needed was enough power to make one phone call.

He answered after the first ring. "Hello?"

"Chase? It's Justin."

"Hey, Justin," he said, sounding somber.

I decided to play dumb. "Where are you?" I asked. I needed to speak to him face to face.

"Well, it's a long story, but I'm not at rehearsal. I'm actually in my apartment and—"

"I'll see you in five minutes," I interrupted. "My phone's almost out of juice and I need to see you!" I hung up and hailed a cab that was barreling up Eighth.

I didn't want Chase to tell me not to come and he seems too polite to not let me in once I showed up.

Of course, I'm assuming Hubert isn't with him. That one would have no problem barring my entry.

I got out of the cab, approached the doorman kiosk, and told him my name.

The doorman got on his phone and after a minute, he told me the apartment number and pointed me in the direction of the elevators. Yes! I had hoped that I'd see the inside of the Dakota when I began this internship and it was finally happening.

The elevators opened into a very wide hallway and I walked to apartment 8F.

As I knocked, the door swung open on its own. I leaned my head in.

Wow.

The apartment was beautiful. Open and airy. Hardwood floors. Sparingly but beautifully decorated. And gorgeous views of the park.

I pushed the door all the way open. "Knock, knock," I said as I walked in. Argh! When will my mom stop making appearances through my mouth?

"Come in, Justin." Chase was sitting on a long white leather couch. He was wearing sweatpants and a ratty T-shirt.

"Sorry I'm all sweaty. You know how it is after you hit the gym."

I nodded, which was my way of pretending I'd ever been to a gym.

"Listen, Chase, I hate to barge in here, but I stopped by rehearsal and—"

"Justin. They fired me."

So he knew.

"Oh, Chase, I'm so sorry," I said, sitting down at the other end of the couch. Just because I felt sympathy didn't mean I wanted to be in the radius of his gym sweat. P.U.

"I can't believe it," he said. "There was no warning. Nothing. The director was always friendly to me."

"How'd you find out?" I asked.

"They called Hubert this morning. He's also my manager, you know"—*WHY?!*—"and he broke the news to me over the phone."

"Oh?" I said, wondering if Chase suspected anything. "Where is he now?"

"He's flying here. He got the first flight out."

They have flights from Eighty-Second to Seventy-Second Street?

Chase looked out the window. "Hubert was in such a rage. He's going to do everything he can to fight it."

Well, that's one good thing about Hubert being so devious. He of all people could probably figure out some way to get Chase hired again.

"You know Hubert," he said with a laugh. "I could very well be performing tonight. When he wants his way, he gets it." Then he looked away and muttered to himself. "He warned me not to trust anyone on that show."

Typical. That seems to be Hubert's method in any situation.

He's made Chase distrust everyone so he'll only rely on Hubert. If I stayed longer than a couple of weeks, I'm sure Hubert would poison Chase's mind against me.

Chase took another swig of VitaminWater. "Even if he gets my job back, though, I'm missing all of today's rehearsal. I'd be scared to go on tonight."

"Look, Chase. I agree it'd be really helpful to have a run-through with the orchestra and costumes and everything, but it's not like you couldn't go on without it."

He sighed. "I guess you're right. But I hate not being at rehearsal. I thought I'd have today to run through all my lines and songs. I'd actually be nervous going on tonight without doing it at least once."

If I were him, I wouldn't be nervous about that. I'd be nervous about my horrible singing/acting choices.

And yet . . . I know that he really can sing. And act!

Hmm . . .

Shouldn't I at least try?

"Chase, do you have sheet music for your songs and the original script you had at the beginning of rehearsals?"

"Yeah . . . ," he said tentatively. "Why?"

I got up.

"Because *I'm* going to run the show with you." I spoke fast because I was excited. "I'll read all the other lines and play piano for your songs. For all we know, you may be going on tonight. You should have a rehearsal if you want one."

"But . . ." He trailed off.

I had to convince him. He helped me so much with Spencer. Now it was my turn to help him.

"Listen, Chase, if our roles were reversed, would you let me sit around my apartment being depressed? Get dressed and let's start!"

And how do I politely implore him to take a shower first?

Luckily, he didn't need me to ask. He excused himself and went into the bathroom. Within a few minutes, I heard the shower. Ahhhh.

I texted Devon an update. *Chase was fired! Out of nowhere! BUT Hubert's working to get him his job back. Will keep you updated.*

Devon wrote back, *OMG*.

A half hour later, Chase was standing near the huge windows and I was behind the piano. I played the opening music, and he strode forward and started singing. Or whatever you call whispering with a slight melody attached.

I stopped playing.

I decided to be bold. "Chase, you have to sing out."

He shook his head. "That's what Peter said."

"Well, Peter's the director. He wants what's best for the show."

"Well, who says he knows what's best? After all, he's only done plays."

"Chase! It's not some obscure idea that a song in a musical needs to be heard! Why sing it that way?"

"Well, Hubert told me—"

"Hubert?!?!" I yelled. I should have known he was behind this!

But I had to play it cool. "I mean," I said with controlled calm, "what did Hubert tell you?"

"He said there are a lot of people who get to Broadway and don't know what they're doing." Unfortunately, that is true. "And he said I really should listen to only one person."

"And that person is him."

"Yes!" he said, sounding slightly defensive. "I told you. He's really been there for me."

"I remember you telling me . . ." *That he took advantage of you being in mourning for your mom to totally take over your life.* "So, throughout rehearsal he's been helping you?"

He smiled. "Yeah. He's really dedicated himself to this show. He told me very specific advice on how to sing and act and also gave me a lot of line changes as well. He was either at rehearsal or available whenever I called him."

So that's it. Every time Chase took a break, he'd call Hubert, who would give him another idiotic change.

Was Hubert's taste really that bad?

I couldn't mull this over with Chase because he would start defending Hubert and start lumping me in with people he can't trust.

How do I play this?

"Chase, just because Hubert has been a tremendous support to you—"

"He has!" Chase interrupted.

"I know. But it doesn't mean his expertise is in musicals." Or anything. I better say something nice. "He's an expert in television." I saw Chase smile. "He may be giving you what he thinks are great artistic choices for TV, but I can tell you they're not working on-stage."

"Look, Justin," Chase said, starting to parrot back Hubert's babbling, "he thinks I should just try it and then see how it goes, so—"

"Chase!" I said, cutting him off. "Don't you remember how you performed Don Quixote in high school?"

He seemed taken aback. "How'd you know I played that role?"

I had a DVD dropped off last night courtesy of your Phantom note writer.

No! Think!

"I read it somewhere . . . ," I said, avoiding his eyes. "You must have said it in an interview."

"No. I never mention that show," he said suspiciously.

Uh-oh. "Hubert must have told me." I kept talking so he couldn't quiz me. "Regardless, I have no idea how you played that role." A lie. "But think back to that time." I started rattling off his bizarre performance habits. "Did you ever whisper a song? Or get rid of a laugh line? Or turn your back to the audience?"

"No . . . but that was high school. Broadway's different."

"Is it? I don't really think so." I'd better use his hero. "You know Stephen Sondheim once said . . ." I had to make up something that would convince him. "The only difference between a high school audience and a Broadway audience . . . is the proximity to the cafetorium." Wow! That was quick thinking on my part!

"Really? Sondheim said that?"

"Many, many times." First rule of lying is—commit!

I could tell he was considering making some changes. I had to strike now.

"Chase, listen to me do the opening number."

I went to the piano and launched into the song with Chase's whisper-singing. After a few bars, I stopped.

"Now listen to this." I sang it full out and I'm not too shy to say I sounded great.

I finished and looked him in the eye. "If you were in the audience, which version would you rather hear?"

He looked torn. "Well . . ."

"Come on, Chase. The second one. It's not even a toss-up."

"I hear what you're saying, but . . ." He sounded frustrated.

He was so used to leaving decisions to Hubert that he couldn't trust his own opinions. I'd have to invoke Hubert somehow to hook him.

"Look, I totally agree with what Hubert says."

He perked up. "You do?"

"Yes. About trying things and then if they don't work, trying something new."

"Great!"

"So, you've been trying it Hubert's way and no one has liked it, so try it a new way tonight. *My* way."

He immediately shook his head. "Justin, I've never given his way a chance. Hubert told me the reaction could be completely different when we have a full audience."

Argh! Hubert keeps foiling my plans, even from afar.

"Look, Chase, I'm hoping Hubert will get your job back and

you'll have lots of performances to try new things, but"—I put on a sad face—"tonight is the last night of my internship and the only time I'll be able to see the show. For a really long time."

"Why?"

Uh-oh. Why?

"Because . . ." Quick! Think of a lie! "I go back to school tomorrow. It'll be hard for me to get back to the city." Perfect!

Wait. That wasn't a lie. *And* he looked like he was almost convinced. Hmm . . . I have to use the truth more often.

How about being truthful all the time?

Don't push it, Spencer.

"I hear what you're saying, Justin . . . but . . ."

Ah! I needed to appeal to the older brother feelings he had for me.

"Come on, Chase. I'm having the internship you always wanted when you were a kid. Imagine if you met a big star when you were sixteen and he took your advice. What a thrilling way for me to end my internship." I put on my "I'm just an eager student" face. "It'll be something I'll always remember."

He flashed his big "I used to be a model" smile. "OK, Justin! I'll do it! I can always go back to Hubert's way next week."

Hopefully never. "Yay! Let's go."

We started running the show. And every time we got to a song, I played it and he sang. Really sang. And he sounded great! I told him that they rehearsed today with all the old lines and he'd have to do it that way tonight if he went on. I told him he could always change them to Hubert's lines for the first preview, which wasn't until Tuesday.

He had such great instincts and his performance was really working. At one point, though, we were doing a scene and he said a really funny one-liner that fell flat.

He looked at me fearfully. "I know I should be able to do this, but . . . I don't know how to get a laugh on that," he admitted.

"That's OK," I said soothingly. "I'm pretty certain that your line is not getting a laugh because you're walking while you say it."

"What do you mean?" he asked, looking less scared.

"I've studied a lot of comedy," I said, "and I know audiences get distracted with aimless wandering."

"But on *Vicious Tongues,* I can cross the room and zing someone."

"Yes! But the camera is following your face, isn't it?"

"Oh . . . you're right," he admitted.

"Chase, when you're onstage, it's better to plant it and say the line straight out."

I know I sounded bossy, but I also knew I was right.

"Watch me," I said as I stood center and delivered the line. Yes, only Chase laughed, but I know it would have brought the house down.

"That was hilarious," Chase said. Then he looked nervous. "But what if it doesn't work for me? What if I'm just not that funny?"

Gorgeous, talented people aren't confident all the time? Who knew?

"Chase! Try it. You can do it." I felt like I was my mom when she was teaching me to ride a two-wheeler.

Chase delivered the line and, not surprisingly, it was funny.

"I'll do it your way tonight!" Chase said with a wink. Then, "While we're at it, can we go over the beginning of the opening number? I think it's too high for me."

That couldn't be. I heard him sing higher as Don Quixote.

"No, it isn't too high, Chase. You're not breathing. You can't hit that high note without taking a big breath first."

We ran the song, he took a breath like I told him, and he nailed it.

We had just finished Act Two and were sitting on the floor, going over some of the line changes Chase would have to remember if he went on tonight, when the door flew open.

"I got here as fast as I could," Hubert said. Then he saw me and gave me a look that I knew meant *Don't say a thing or else.*

"Hubert!" Chase said, and ran to him. I hated seeing that Chase liked him so much. I stayed seated on the floor and watched them hug and kiss. Well, I finally figured out a way to easily lose my appetite.

"What's the update?" Chase asked, looking concerned.

"Not great," Hubert said, putting down his (probably empty) suitcase. I had to hand it to him for using props to keep up the lie. "The bad news is," he said while taking off his coat, "I can't get you back into *Thousand-Watt Smile.*"

Oh no! I could see the sadness on Chase's face. I felt like sinking to the floor in disappointment, but I was already there, so I just let my shoulders collapse. However, I realized how that position really highlighted my stomach hanging over my pants, so I immediately sat upright.

"But," Hubert said with his version of a smile, "there is a silver lining." Hubert sat on the couch and took out his laptop.

"This is what I was doing during my flight," he said as he started typing in a Web address.

Flight? "Wow, Hubert!" I said as I walked to the back of the couch. "Usually short flights don't have Internet."

He glared at me over his shoulder. "How's your grandmother, Justin?" Touché.

"Chase," he said with a big smile, "I spoke to the studio and . . . your part hasn't been recast!"

"For what?" asked Chase, sitting down next to Hubert.

"Look!" Hubert said, pointing to his laptop. On the screen was EntertainmentWeekly.com, with a headline that read, "Chase Hudson leaves Broadway to do *Wicked Words.*"

Hubert leaned back in triumph. "Look at that! Now people will think it was all your doing."

Chase was still looking at the screen, not speaking, so I piped up.

"Chase . . . I thought you didn't want to do the *Vicious Tongues* spin-off?"

"Of course he does," Hubert said, whipping his head toward me. "Chase knows TV is where the real money is."

"Maybe he doesn't care about money," I said.

"Justin," Hubert said, calmly getting up and walking over to me, "your internship officially ended Friday." Then he stared at me. "I think it's time for you to leave."

"Chase?" I asked, hoping to be saved.

"Yeah, Justin," Chase said, sounding defeated. "I guess there's no more Broadway here for you. You might as well go home." He gave me what looked like a brave smile. "You should rest up for school tomorrow."

Hubert seemed so satisfied I couldn't help thinking he knew more than he was saying.

"When does it start filming?" I asked.

Hubert turned to me as if I were an annoying mosquito who buzzed by. Thankfully, Chase answered. "In around two months."

"Actually," Hubert said, "they've pushed up the filming. It begins at the end of the week."

It all seemed too convenient.

I looked over to Hubert, who had the epitome of a smug smile on his face. He was so sure of himself about everything. And didn't seem to care that Chase was so sad. I didn't believe that everyone would think Chase left on purpose. The Broadway community is small and loves gossip. I'm sure ThousandWattInsider had already posted about him being fired and then the word would spread. I decided I needed to see what was being written on the BroadwayBitchery message board. If ThousandWattInsider wrote about how his lack of talent led to his firing, I could at least counteract it by telling everyone how amazing he was this afternoon. I'm pretty much the only one who can save his Broadway reputation.

I went to enter the site on my phone and saw a black screen. No battery!

I had to get online as soon as possible so there'd be another insider telling the truth.

Aha! I saw the answer sitting in front of me.

"You're right, Chase," I said, starting to gather my things. "I probably should go."

Hubert looked surprised that I gave up without a fight. But he also looked pleased with himself.

I checked my watch. "I need to find when the next train leaves for Long Island." I turned toward Hubert. "Can I look it up on your computer? I'd love to get the very next one."

"I'd love that for you, too," Hubert said enthusiastically, while gesturing at his computer.

I'm sure he was happy that I didn't blow his cover and wanted me out of Chase's life as soon as possible.

"So, is my role exactly the same? Just a little older?" Chase asked, sounding depressed.

"Let's get something to drink and talk about it," Hubert said as he led Chase into the kitchen. I could hear him begin to give Chase details and I knew they would both be distracted and not see me log onto BroadwayBitchery.com. When I got to the home screen and went to enter my screen name, my hands froze above the keyboard.

There was a screen name already saved.

Hubert was ThousandWattInsider.

22

I quickly closed out of the site.

That was all the proof I needed. Hubert was trying to destroy Chase!

But I couldn't let Hubert know I was planning on saying or doing anything because he wouldn't hesitate to reveal my version of the truth. P.S.: I decided to use some Republican double-talk to myself to see if it made me feel less guilty. For example:

Man-made global warming = climate change

Me lying about my grandma dying = version of truth

Hubert and Chase walked out of the kitchen, each holding a can of diet soda.

"Well, I'm sorry about how this turned out," Hubert said to him, obviously lying, "but we can talk about it later. Right now I have some important shopping to do." He meant he had some unpacking to finish. He took a long swig of soda and placed it on the counter.

"What time is the flight tomorrow?" Chase asked as Hubert was putting on his coat.

"Ten a.m. We get into L.A. at one."

So soon? I bet Hubert wanted Chase out of New York as soon as possible to prevent him from finding anything out.

I started getting my things together while thinking of a way I could get some alone time with Chase. I had to help him!

Hubert and I walked to the door of the apartment. He could tell I was trying to linger.

"Stop dawdling, Justin. I need to leave ASAP."

Chase walked down the hallway and pushed the button for the elevator. We all stood there in silence till the doors finally opened. Hubert and I both got in the elevator and right before the door closed, I called to Chase. "Wait! I'm going straight back to Long Island and it's a long trip. Can I use your bathroom?"

"Sure," Chase said before Hubert could say no.

I ran out of the elevator and down the hallway as I heard Chase say goodbye and the elevator door close. Ha-ha, Hubert! Next time don't say you need to leave "ASAP" if you don't want it to backfire. As a matter of fact, stop saying ASAP. It's annoying!

Now I'd be alone with Chase. But what could I tell him?

Nothing.

Hubert would find out about everything I revealed, and he would spill the beans about me, which would end up in a full-semester grounding from my parents. And no internship credit. *And* Spencer's judgment.

I used the bathroom and walked back into the living room

to see Chase standing in front of one of the enormous windows. Silence. He had put on an "It's all for the best" attitude in front of Hubert, but he was obviously devastated. So was I.

Finally I stated the obvious. "I thought you didn't want to do *Wicked Words.*"

He kept looking out the window. "I don't, but it's much better than being unemployed. It's a lot of money to turn down."

"But it's not Broadway," I said.

"Well," he said, turning around, "the good news is Hubert is working on getting me back on Broadway during my hiatus."

"He is?"

"While we were in the kitchen, he told me he's working on a couple of different possibilities and will be flying back and forth to New York to negotiate."

Hmm, everything Hubert says had an ulterior motive, but it took hard thinking to figure out.

However, I knew I had to do something about this situation first.

But what?

I needed time.

"Chase," I said, "turns out my train doesn't come for a little while. Could I hang out here and charge my phone?"

"Sure, Justin. I'm going to take a long shower and try to steam away my stress. I'll come out and say goodbye before you leave."

And with that he entered his bedroom and closed the door.

I was at a complete loss. Chase was fired. Hubert had won.

I tried to focus my brain on getting his job back, but even I couldn't see a way.

What now? Go back to Grandma Sally's and really take the next train home?

That was depressing.

I decided to do what I always do when I'm depressed. Distract myself.

I went to my backpack and took out the Playbill for *Thousand-Watt Smile* I had snatched from backstage. I thought I could lose myself for a while by looking at actors' headshots and reading their bios. I sat on the white leather couch and opened it.

There was Chase's name, right above the title.

I sighed.

In three hours, Mickey would be playing that part.

As sad as it was for Chase, I knew it must be an incredibly exciting time for Mickey. I wondered if he had ever had a big role on Broadway before this. I started looking for his name in the Playbill to see his credits and soon began reading all of the actors' bios.

I stopped when I got to Cristopher Mykos.

Cristopher Mykos.

Where had I heard that name before?

Then I remembered! It's also Hubert's last name. I saw it on his apartment buzzer. Was his brother in the show? Was that somehow part of his scheme?

Chase came out of the bedroom in jeans and a blue button-down shirt. His hair was wet and it looked like he just shaved.

"Chase, is Hubert's brother in *Thousand-Watt Smile*?"

"His brother? Why? Do you think someone in the cast looks like him?"

"No," I said, "I just saw that someone else had the same last name."

"Huh?" Chase furrowed his brow. "Hubert is like Madonna. He doesn't use a last name."

Oy vey. How much more pretentious can Hubert be?

"He's simply *Oo-bare.*"

No last name? Then why did it say Hubert Mykos next to his buzzer?

Unless . . . it was two different names for two different people who were living in the same apartment!

"Who is Cristopher Mykos?"

"He's that curly-haired dancer in the ensemble," Chase said as he walked to the beautiful marble-countertopped kitchen. He started to pour himself some sparkling apple cider. "Isn't he great?"

"Yeah . . . ," I said, even though I never really noticed him. "Has he done a lot of shows?"

"Funny you should ask. He had just graduated from a musical theater school when Hubert met him on a flight. Since Hubert's a big supporter of young talent"—*He is?*—"he pulled a couple of strings and got him in the chorus. He's a really good dancer."

That's not all he is. He's now Hubert's roommate.

Wait a minute, "roommate"? If my detective abilities are as accurate as they always are, he's also Hubert's secret boyfriend! Why else would Hubert have signed a lease for a secret apartment? I'll tell you why! So they could live together without Chase knowing!

Although, with Chase being fired, the whole thing seems like a waste. Chase and Hubert are going back to California, so Hubert won't be able to use the New York apartment after all. I guess even Hubert's plans can get foiled.

Wait! Of course he's going to be using that apartment! *That's* why he claimed he's going to have to start taking a lot of trips to New York! He won't be traveling to Manhattan to negotiate Chase's supposed next Broadway show; he'll be flying here to visit his boyfriend in their new luxury apartment!

Chase needs to know!

And yet, I can't tell him any of it.

He sat down on the couch. "I wanna tell you something, Justin."

Uh-oh. The last time I heard a comment like that was right before Spencer broke up with me.

"Yeah?" I said nervously.

He leaned back and looked toward Central Park. Then he turned back. "You know, this whole experience was not great for me. I hadn't performed since high school and I was really nervous about doing musical theater again. But because I was the star, I felt I had to act confident. Hubert told me not to trust anyone on the staff and that worked for me because it meant I didn't have to tell anyone I was scared." He took a sip of his sparkling cider. "But rehearsing with you this afternoon . . . it was amazing. I didn't have to know everything."

Chase just said rehearsing with me was amazing! I sat there with a big smile on my face.

"I want to thank you," he said, holding out his hand, and I shook it. "It felt, I don't know . . . liberating to be able to ask for help. It was OK that I wasn't perfect."

"I had a great time, too," I said, and thought about how much fun it was to run scenes with him and give him advice and watch him get better.

"Well," he said, standing up and looking at his watch, "I guess you better go. I hope we see each other again."

I stood up, too. "I hope so, too. And," I added, "I hope you're on Broadway really soon. You deserve it."

I unplugged my phone, which had finally charged, and put on my coat. When I got to the door of his apartment, he gave me a hug.

"Take care, Justin. You're a great kid."

I took the elevator down with a smile on my face but a sad feeling inside.

It was over.

I left the Dakota and started walking toward Grandma Sally's apartment.

My cell phone rang and I picked it up without looking to see who it was.

It was Spencer.

And everything changed.

23

I spoke with Spencer for around fifteen minutes without going inside. I was freezing on the street but too riveted by the conversation to move my body. All I could do was talk.

As soon as I hung up, I called Devon. Well, first I hightailed it inside the Starbucks on Seventy-Third and Columbus for a venti coffee to help my teeth stop chattering. Then I dialed him because I knew I needed as much help as I could get.

As soon as he answered, he apologized again for last night.

"Devon, it's OK. I was acting crazy."

"*I* was acting crazy."

"It's just—"

"It's just—"

"Sometimes I need a lot of attention," we both said, and then laughed.

He really was a nice guy. But I had been thinking about him

off and on throughout the day. I forced myself to admit that I was mainly using him to get over Spencer. After our first date, it didn't feel right, but I kept it going just to make Spencer jealous.

"Devon," I said nervously, "are we too similar to date?"

"Justin," he said, sounding relieved, "I was thinking the same thing."

Wow. That was easy!

"But I want to be friends," I told him. Then, just to clarify, I added, "And I'm not lying when I say that."

He laughed. "I want to be friends, too. And more important, I want to solve this whole Chase mystery with you!"

How great was that! I was able to end a relationship that wasn't working but keep the parts that were. I took a minute to congratulate myself and then got back to business and texted him a photo I found online of Cristopher Mykos.

"Devon, is that the guy who was at lunch with Hubert?"

"Yes!" Devon said, excited. "How'd you know?"

I immediately launched into everything that had happened that day.

In the middle of the story, Devon interrupted. "He was fired with no warning at all?"

Warning, shmarning. I hate when the flow of one of my stories is interrupted.

"Yes," I said, using the interruption to take a quick bite of a cake pop. Delish! "That's one of the reasons he was so upset."

"That's also the reason it's illegal," Devon said.

"*What?*" I blurted out, causing cake pop crumbs to fly everywhere.

"Justin, you know I'm obsessed with Broadway. I know all the union rules. An actor can't get fired unless he gets warned. It's called 'just cause.'"

"Or what?"

"Or Chase could sue them and they'd have to pay him his whole year's salary. I'm betting that would be hundreds of thousands of dollars."

"Devon! You're amazing. This is exactly what I was looking for. I'll call you back," I said, and hung up.

I was giddy with excitement. They wouldn't want to pay him all that money just to not perform tonight. No matter what, Chase is going on!

Now I just had to get him to the theater without Hubert finding out.

And before any of that, I had to finish my cake pops. That's right, *pops*. They have three flavors and it's too difficult to choose just one.

I enjoyed them all, then headed right back to the Dakota.

I went up to Chase's apartment and told him I was taking a later train home because I needed his help.

"With what?"

"Come shopping with me!"

"Why do I—"

I saw his coat lying on a chair and handed it to him. "Chase, no one knows Hubert better than you do and I want to thank him for the internship by getting him a bi-i-i-ig surprise." Which isn't a lie. When Hubert finds out what's going on, he'll definitely be surprised.

I knew using Hubert as a lure would make Chase follow me and soon we hopped in a cab and arrived at the theater at six-thirty.

"Why are we here, Justin?" Chase asked as we got out. "I thought you said we were shopping for Hubert."

I turned around and looked him in the eye. "Chase, this is for you. You deserve it."

"What? No! I don't want to go in there."

"Trust me, Chase." I reached up and put my hands on both of his shoulders. "Like you did this afternoon."

He looked indecisive. Then he gave me a little smile and walked with me.

As soon as we entered the stage door, I held my breath as usual. To my right was an extra-large pile of wet tobacco in the garbage and to my left was Peter, the director, taping up a good luck card on the call-board. Standing next to him was Gary, putting up next week's schedule.

"Hi, guys . . . ," Gary said, sounding very confused.

"Justin! Chase, old chap!" Peter said as if caught wearing only underwear.

"Listen up!" I said, standing with my hands on my hips and trying to sound like an adult. I was basing my stance on how the lead detective from *Law & Order* stands when he's telling off a judge. The voice I used was my version of Bea Arthur from *Golden Girls* having a stern talk with her mother.

"Peter. Gary. The three of us know it's against union rules to fire an actor without three warnings."

"Justin!" Chase said, sounding surprised and irritated.

Peter looked back and forth from Chase and then to me.

"Justin, you are correct, my boy," Peter said, somewhat condescendingly. "But what you may not know is that when both parties decide it's best for an actor to leave, it's called a mutual agreement and no one owes anyone anything."

"Well, Chase doesn't agree."

"Justin," said Gary, "it's sweet that you're trying to save the day, but Hubert already agreed for Chase."

"Yeah? Well, nothing was signed." Hopefully. "And I've spoken to Hubert and he said you completely misunderstood him."

"What do you mean?" Gary asked, sounding slightly panicked.

"Chase never got three warnings and his lawyer will sue the pants off this show unless Chase performs tonight."

Peter took out his handkerchief and patted his forehead. Then he looked angry. "He wants three warnings? He'll get them for the next three performances. And be fired by the end of the week."

"That's fine," I said, knowing that the only important thing is that he went on tonight.

Nobody moved. Finally I barked, "Gary!" He looked at me in shock. "Don't you have an announcement to make to the cast?"

Gary looked at me, then at Peter. Peter took a moment and

then slightly nodded. Gary ran to the stage manager's office and his voice suddenly came out of the backstage speakers.

"Attention, cast. At tonight's performance, Mickey Hendrix will go on for his regular part in the ensemble. The role usually played by Chase Hudson will be played by . . . Chase Hudson."

We heard a flurry of conversation floating down from the dressing rooms and soon saw a confused Mickey walk from Chase's dressing room area up the stairs. I turned and grabbed Chase's arm.

"Let's go."

We left Peter in a daze and as we walked into his dressing room, Chase started laughing. "You're amazing! This day has had some ups and downs!"

"I know," I said.

"But"—Chase turned to me—"why would Hubert mutually agree to have them fire me?"

"He didn't," I lied. "That's why he sent me here to clarify it."

"Then why would he tell me we're flying to L.A. tomorrow if he thought I'd get my job back?"

Oy. So many questions. "Um . . . why don't you send him a quick text?"

"I will. There's a lot that doesn't make sense." He took out his phone.

"Hey!" I said before he texted anything. "Don't forget to sign in! You don't want to give them *any* reason to fire you." Just as I hoped, he put his phone down and quickly left.

I did what I needed to do and exited his dressing room. "Bye,

Chase!" I said when I saw him at the call-board. "I'll come back and wish you luck before you go on."

And with that I ran out of the theater and waited under the marquee.

I texted Hubert that Chase was going on and within seconds, I knew he was calling Chase frantically. By the way, it wasn't a psychic feeling. I knew because I had Chase's cell phone in my pocket. When he went to the call-board, I'd pocketed it. I didn't want them talking till I could tell Hubert what I knew.

Just as I suspected, a cab pulled up fifteen minutes later.

As Hubert stepped out, I walked over.

"Out of my way, Justin," he said, and began to walk toward the stage door.

"I'd wait if I were you," I said in a clear and stern voice.

Hubert paused momentarily.

I stood in front of the stage door. "I know you were sabotaging Chase's performance. I know you moved into your new apartment with your boyfriend."

"Justin, I'm so bored with your reveals. Yes, I wanted Chase out of this show. There's no money on Broadway. I made sure his performance would be horrible enough to close the show in a few weeks so he could begin filming the *Vicious Tongues* sequel." *That's* why he wanted him to stink! "But when they pushed up the filming date, I had to figure out a way to get him to Los Angeles quickly." Meaning tomorrow. "So, as I'm sure you guessed, I told the producers to release him from his *Thousand-Watt Smile* contract and there would be no consequences to them." He raised one eyebrow.

"Why didn't you let them fire him weeks ago?"

Hubert looked away for a second. "If you must know, I . . . I was enjoying attending rehearsals."

I glared. "You mean you were enjoying having a reason to be around Cristopher all day! You got him the job and then you spent weeks manipulating him to be your new boyfriend behind Chase's back!"

Hubert shrugged. "I didn't have to manipulate him. He's impressed by me."

Gross! "Well, I'm not!" I yelled. I realized I needed to keep my voice so I lowered it to an angry whisper. "You're not only a cheater, but you also ruined Chase's Broadway career!"

Hubert sighed. "You may not think so, but I did that for his own good."

What a liar! He did it for *his* own good. His cut of Chase's TV salary is far more than his cut of Chase's Broadway salary.

"He's staying in *Thousand-Watt Smile*," I said sternly.

Hubert's eyes narrowed. "No, he's not. And if you try anything, I will tell your little secret to everybody and you will fail your internship."

A few actors walked past us and I moved out of the way to let them into the stage door. Hubert went to follow them. "Hubert, I wouldn't. Or else *your* little secret will be told to everybody." He kept walking. "Your little secret about *GlitZ*."

Hubert stopped with his hand still clutching the handle of the stage door.

He turned around slowly. "What are you referring to?"

I smiled. A big, wide smile.

"Hubert," I said, coming right up to him. "My friend Spencer works in the accounting department of GlitZ. Need I say more?"

He actually looked down. And for the first time in my entire experience with him, he was silent!

"So, yes," I continued, "what you're threatening to tell about me is not pretty, but what I did is not against the law."

Pause.

"You're bluffing," he finally said.

"Try me."

We stood and stared at each other.

I decided to take the soft approach. Better for him to think I'm weak. "Besides," I said, "all I want is for Chase to have a chance to do the show tonight." Then, just to make sure he'd agree, I added, "We both know he's gonna bomb, anyway."

He answered in a very soft voice. "All right."

"Oh!" I said quickly. "One more thing. I need a ticket for myself and four more for my friends. And my grandmother. Why don't you get yourself to the box office and handle that for me?"

Pause.

I couldn't resist . . . "ASAP!"

Hmm . . . that actually felt good. I may add it to my vocabulary after all.

And then . . . he actually did it! I waited on the street for a few minutes and soon Hubert returned and handed me the tickets.

He started walking toward the stage door.

"I'm going to come with you, if you don't mind," I said, not trusting him.

We both went into Chase's dressing room.

"Hubert!" Chase said, and gave him a kiss.

Thankfully I only heard the sound because I was able to turn my head and block out the visual.

"Sorry I haven't called," Chase said. "I can't find my phone anywhere."

"It's right there," I said, pointing to his couch.

Chase looked. "That's so weird. I'm sure it wasn't there a minute ago."

"Anyway," I said, moving on, "we're just here to wish you luck. Right, Hubert?" I said, staring him down.

"That's right, Chase," Hubert said. "We'll talk after the show about . . . what's next."

"Let's go!" I said, putting my arm through Hubert's. "There's only an hour till the show!"

Hubert and I left the dressing room like best friends. As soon as we turned the corner, we broke apart and walked in silence to the stage door. We exited to the street and turned in opposite directions. He was probably going to get something to eat before the show. Or cry. I turned back around and watched him walk down the street. He seemed alone. All of his scheming and trickery couldn't save him in the long run.

I wondered if he'd always been like that. He probably started out a nice guy, but as he began to perfect his lying and scheming abilities, they became his only way of life.

Then I had a horrific thought.

Scheming? Trickery? Lies?

Am I on my way to becoming like him one day?

Is there a way for me to stop it?

I thought about what Chase said after rehearsal.

I thought about what Spencer would say.

Oh no.

I realized what I had to do.

I walked to the Starbucks on Forty-Seventh and Broadway and logged on to my website.

I sat in the audience as the lights came down for the beginning of Act One. I gave Devon the aisle seat and sat to the right of him. Spencer sat next to me, then Scotty (!) and Becky. As soon as Chase came onstage, I was positive I heard some snickers from the audience. But then he started to sing and I heard gasps.

Good gasps!

The audience was prepared for a nightmarish performance, and instead they saw the birth of a Broadway star. As the song went on, I watched the stage 50 percent of the time and looked at the audience the other 50 percent. It seemed like every mouth I saw was agape. When the opening number ended, the applause seemed to last as long as the song. One person wasn't applauding. I watched Hubert's face go from glaring to simply depressed. It was almost as thrilling as seeing Chase be brilliant. One of the best parts was watching Grandma Sally. She loved it! I got her the seat right next to Hubert and whenever something funny happened onstage, she'd hit him on the arm and say, "Hot damn!"

The only hard thing for me was having Scotty in the same row. I was very proud of myself for telling Spencer to invite him, but when I looked around the audience to see people's reactions, I made a point of not looking anywhere near him. Yes, I had wanted a break from Spencer, but who was I kidding? An hour was enough. I wanted him back!

At intermission, I asked him to come outside with me. Thankfully, he didn't ask Scotty to come with us.

"Justin!" he said, giving me a hug. "I'm so proud of you. Chase is doing such a great job."

"Thank you, Spencer," I said, while tons of people jockeyed around us to have a quick smoke. I'm always shocked that people still smoke in this day and age. Do they not know the progression is usually smelly clothes to yellow teeth to hacking cough to worse? And by "worse" I mean not being able to hit high notes, as well as death!

"Spencer, this is not really the place, but . . . can we give us another try?"

I was hoping for a big "Of course we can" and an enormous hug. Instead, he looked serious.

"Justin . . . ," Spencer began.

I didn't want him to tell me no, so I kept talking. "Listen, I tried to date someone else and he had everything I thought I wanted, but it was like dating another me." I grabbed his hands. "Spencer, I don't want another me. I want another you." Huh? That made no sense. Why did reconciliation scenes always sound so great in movies? I should have written out a rough draft in advance. "No, not another you. I want *you!*" I looked into his eyes. Well, I looked through the cigarette smoke that swirled around us and tried to zero in on his eyes. "You're the voice of reason. You're the one who tells me when I'm out of control. Spencer . . ." This was hard to say, so I took a deep breath. While I coughed I said, "I need you."

"That's very sweet, Justin—"

Ah! He's going to say no! "I promise I'll change. I won't scheme. I won't exaggerate—"

"Justin!" he said firmly. "Stop right there. I don't want you to change."

"You don't?" Well, he certainly did before. "Then why did you break up with me?"

"Because you wanted it!" *Huh?* "I could tell for months that you were drifting away from me. You wanted out."

Ouch. He was right. I couldn't wait to come to New York and date someone just like me.

"I knew it was just a matter of time before you broke up with me, so I mentally prepared myself for it." Wow. He was as logical as I was emotional. "You probably didn't notice, but I took anything you did that mildly irritated me and I used it to build a separation between us."

Didn't notice? If he rolled his eyes any more at lunch, I would have gotten him seizure medication.

Spencer kept talking. "If I constantly felt irritated with you, I knew that would make it easier when we ended it."

So, I brought about the breakup with Spencer. And yet . . . I don't regret what happened. Dating a version of me for just a few days made me realize what a saint Spencer is. And how much I love him exactly the way he is. *And* seeing him all dressed up for the show tonight reminded me how cute he is!

"I missed you, Justin. I never realized how boring my life would be without you."

"I missed you, Spencer. I never realized how much I need you to rein me in." I thought about what it had been like being with another me. "Quite frankly, I'm annoying."

"No, you're not," Spencer said with a sweet smile. "You're the best."

We kissed right there on the smoke-filled sidewalk in front of the theater.

"I broke up with Devon this afternoon, by the way," I said, waiting for him to tell me he was going to break up with Scotty.

"I hoped so!" he said.

Then silence.

The lights started flashing, indicating Act Two was about to begin. Thankfully, the cigarettes were being put out and the air was clearing.

Finally I spoke. "Spencer . . . what about Scotty?"

"What about him?"

I had to spell it out? Certainly he was going to break up with him!

Wasn't he?

"What's the deal with him?"

"Um . . . I can't talk about that." Again he was hauling out that nonstatement?

"Why can you not talk about it?"

"Because," Becky said, suddenly appearing next to us, "I made him promise to keep his mouth shut."

Where did she come from? And what did she mean? "Keep his mouth shut that they're dating each other?" I asked.

"No, you moron," Becky said, laughing. "Keep his mouth shut that *I'm* dating him."

I then realized that Scotty was standing there as well. And he and Becky were holding hands.

"What? Why? Huh?" I was flabbergasted.

"Didn't you see us holding hands the whole first act?" she asked.

No! I had completely avoided looking at what I thought was my competition.

But, wait . . . it didn't make sense.

"Aren't you gay?" I asked Scotty.

Scotty laughed. "No."

"But—"

"Wait a minute," he said. "Did you think I was because I did a campaign against gay bullying?"

"Um . . ."

"Justin!" Becky said playfully. "Don't you think straight people can stand up for what's right, even if it doesn't affect them directly?"

Of course I did. I just . . . as usual, made an assumption that was completely wrong. Hmph. I blame this on not having Spencer around. Besides, I solved so many mysteries in the last few hours that I refused to feel embarrassed. "OK, OK," I conceded. "I'm busted. But the question is"—I pointed my finger at her—"why didn't you tell me?"

Becky looked down and then back at me. "Because I thought about what you said at Starbucks."

That was a bad memory. "Becky, I'm sorry. I—"

"It's OK, Justin. You had a point. I do let other people do things for me." Scotty put his arm around her. "I knew if I told you I liked Scotty, or wanted to start dating him, you'd figure out some scheme to get him. Then it would be yet another thing you've done for me."

She was right. But was that so wrong? "Becky, I only do those things because I care about you."

"I know, Justin." She gave me one of her smiles that make you wonder why she's not on the cover of *Seventeen*. "But you're not always going to be right next to me. I have to learn to do things on my own. That was my goal for this internship." Scotty gave her a kiss. With two S's!

"What the *hell* are you all doing out there? Act Two is about to start." Not surprisingly, Grandma Sally ruined the intimacy of the moment and we all headed back to our seats.

Act Two was even better than Act One, and when Chase came out for his bow, he got a full-house standing ovation. Yes, I started it, but everyone else joined in. I was so proud of him!

I bid Grandma Sally a quick goodbye and headed backstage, trailed by my friends. I told them it was important that they check my website and then meet me backstage in ten minutes. I was able to grab my stuff and run, and I was thankful Hubert had checked his coat because it would delay his appearance by a few minutes.

As soon as I got to the backstage area, Peter picked me up in his arms. "Justin, my boy! I don't know what you did, but you got Chase to give one of the best Broadway debuts I've ever seen."

He put me down and immediately leaned over to catch his breath. I'm short, but I'm not so light.

"Thanks for letting him go on."

"Let him?" he said. "Let's not mince words. You forced my hand. But bravo, boy!"

He soon got distracted by Gary walking by, and I went to Chase's dressing room. The door was open.

I stood in the doorway and saw Chase sitting on his couch with a huge smile.

"Justin! Come here right now!"

I ran over to him and he got up and hugged me.

"Well, the student taught the teacher," he said as we sat on his couch. "I listened to you and you were right."

I blushed. "Well, I'm glad you trusted me. I was so happy for you as you took your final bow."

"I got a standing O!" he said. "And," he added with a wink, "I saw you start it."

"You deserved it, Chase," I said.

He walked over to the door and closed it.

"Justin," he said, turning around, "this whole day has been so topsy-turvy. I feel like I had a mask over my eyes and I can finally see."

"Hubert?" I dared to ask.

"Hubert," he thankfully responded as he walked back and sat on the couch. "I was in denial that he was giving me horrible advice. And I was in denial about how mean he was to everyone around me. He hurt a lot of people."

Oy! He sounded so guilty. "Chase! You were in a bad place when you first met Hubert and he took advantage of it."

"When I heard you arguing with Peter to get my job back, I didn't believe at first that Hubert had agreed to have me fired. But of course it's true. He sold me out."

I nodded. "He did. And, I'm sorry to say, he did a whole lot more."

He gave a sad smile. "I've known about his affair with Cristopher. He thinks I'm an idiot, but of course I knew."

Phew! I did not want to have to break that news. I had something else to tell him that I knew would hurt.

"Chase, that's not all Hubert's done."

The door flew open. There stood Hubert. Standing behind him were Becky, Spencer, and Scotty. And Grandma Sally.

"Hello, Chase. Hello, Justin," he said, sounding like a villain in a James Bond film.

"Come in," said Chase, trying to be friendly but clearly uncomfortable.

"Before you say any more, Justin, I want to say a few things."

My friends crowded by the door, but Hubert walked over to the couch with a confident stride.

"Chase," he said with a sickening smile, "I have spoken to *Wicked Words* and they are willing to start filming two weeks after you open *Thousand-Watt Smile*. In other words, you will open the show, but you will utilize the clause in your contract that lets you leave if you get the lead in a TV show."

"First of all, Hubert, we're through," said Chase calmly.

"Yes, I can see our personal relationship is over. But since I negotiated your *Wicked Words* contract, I will continue to get fifteen percent of your salary."

"Forget it, Hubert," Chase said, sounding weary. "I'm not leaving this job."

Hubert stayed relaxed. "I thought this might happen and I am prepared to tell you that you will indeed leave."

"You can't make him!" I said, standing up.

"Justin," Hubert said, turning toward me, "I know you think you have the upper hand, but I had all of Acts One and Two to consider my options. And I have a few."

He bent down to stare me in the eye. "For some inexplicable reason, Chase seems to care about you." He looked like he tasted something sour. "And your well-being. And, I would assume, your reputation. That has given me the upper hand." He stood up straight and moved across the room, away from all of us. It was as if he were center stage and we were the audience. "So, I bring this back to you, Chase. If you refuse to take the fabulous TV job you've been offered, I will be forced to reveal something about Justin that will embarrass and shame him. To his parents, to his school, and to the friends and family that stand here now."

Chase looked stricken and lowered his voice. "Is that true, Justin? Does he know something about you?"

"Yes, it is, Chase, but—"

"And is it something you're ashamed of?"

I looked down at my feet. "Yes, I am ashamed." I looked up again. "But—"

"Enough, Justin. I'm not going to let you get hurt," he said, sounding like my dad. He looked up at Hubert with a defeated look in his eye. He sighed. "OK, Hubert. You win."

Hubert smiled and had the nerve to take a little bow.

I stood up.

"Oh no, you haven't, Hubert." I purposefully pronounced it the non-French way!

Hubert was obviously taken aback. I didn't give him a chance to say anything. "Everybody already knows the truth. Except Chase."

Hubert blinked a few times. "What?"

"Exactly what I said." Then I turned toward Chase. "You see, I wanted this internship so badly that I quit the other one at the last minute. I made up a lie to get out of it. I said that my grandmother had died and that I had to spend time mourning with my family." I let out a deep breath and looked at everybody. "I am embarrassed and ashamed to admit I did something like that."

Hubert regained his composure. "Big deal. Your friends know now. However, I'm sure you won't want your school hearing about this."

I shrugged. "I'm sure they'll find out the same way my friends did." I sat back down next to Chase. "Chase, when you told me how liberating it was to admit that you weren't perfect, I thought about what I had done. It was a not-nice thing to do, but you made me realize it would probably feel better to admit it and deal with the consequences." Chase smiled and gave me a pat on the back. "So I wrote all about it on my website."

"It was very well written, FYI," said Spencer.

Good ol' Spencer.

"I'm prepared to deal with the fallout. From my school. From my parents. From my friends."

"Justin," said Becky, coming over, "yeah, you lied, but we understand. You've always been obsessed with Broadway and this was an amazing opportunity."

"I would have done the same thing," added Devon.

"Me too," added Scotty.

"As long as you didn't say *I* died," Grandma Sally piped in, "I don't give a crap."

"So, Hubert," I said, standing up again, "as I've mentioned, I am prepared to deal with all the consequences." I could see he was starting to get nervous. There was a thin sheen of sweat above his lip making his overtanned, orange skin glisten.

"But," I continued, circling the room, "are you prepared to deal with the consequences from"—I whirled around dramatically and faced him—"the police?"

Everyone looked at him. His eyes were wide as he looked around the room frantically.

Chase stood up. "What is he talking about, Hubert?"

I waited for Hubert to say something.

"Justin?" asked Chase.

"Why don't I let Spencer speak," I said, gesturing to him.

"Well, Mr. Hudson," he said, stepping forward, "by the way, great performance tonight!"

"Thank you," said Chase, flashing him one of his model smiles.

"Anyway," Spencer continued, "I ran into Justin a few nights ago and he made a passing comment about how you don't model anymore."

"I don't," Chase interjected.

"Right. He also said you mentioned that you miss getting the modeling checks more than the modeling itself."

"I do . . . ," said Chase, sounding like he didn't understand where Spencer was going with this.

"Well, Mr. Hudson," said Spencer, "you actually *have* been getting checks."

"What?" Chase asked, and looked from me to Spencer to Hubert and then back again.

"I can explain," said Hubert. "Calm down."

"Actually," said Spencer, holding up his finger to silence Hubert, "I can explain better and I wouldn't calm down, Mr. Hudson. You see, GlitZ still has lots of photos of you. Photos that are being used in ads all over Europe. Ads that pay a good amount of money."

"What photos?" Chase asked.

"Photos from when you were a teen model. As a matter of fact, Hubert asked Justin to bring over another batch this week."

"Oh!" said Scotty. "That's when I first met you." I didn't quite make eye contact because the memory of Becky escorting me out was best left forgotten.

"So," I said, picking up the story, "my genius ex-but-now-current boyfriend thought it was strange when I told him that you missed getting checks when he had seen checks for you in the accounting department."

"Correct. My internship kept me too busy to do any investigating. But I got permission to go into GlitZ on Saturday," Spencer said.

"Late into the evening," Becky remarked proudly.

I smiled.

"Missing our dinner," Scotty clarified.

I nodded.

"And missing Justin acting crazy," added Devon.

I glared.

"And," Spencer picked up again, "I traced the checks and found that they were all being deposited"—he paused for effect; I was glad to see my dramatic line readings had rubbed off on him— "into an account owned by a Mr. Hubert Weatherbee."

Hubert recoiled from his own last name.

Ha-ha!

"I kept trying to reach Justin all day today."

"But my phone charge ran out." Sort of true.

"He finally answered his phone a few hours ago and I filled him in on what I discovered."

"I told Hubert what Spencer told me and that's why he didn't fight you going on tonight."

Everyone had fanned out around the sides of the room. Hubert stood in the middle.

"Chase . . . ," he started to say.

Chase held up his hand. "Don't say anything more, please."

"But . . ."

"Just leave now."

"I have a very good—"

"All contact with me from now on should only be through my lawyer."

Hubert opened his mouth to speak and then closed it.

He knew he was beat.

He started to walk out and right before he left, he turned around. I expected him to say, "I'll be back!" But he actually looked quite sad.

"Goodbye, Chase," he said, and left.

I guess he did have feelings. Again, I saw the need to have people like Spencer, Becky, and Chase around me so I don't turn into Hubert. I grabbed Spencer's hand tight.

"Don't ever let me change my name to something stupid," I begged him in a whisper.

"OK," he said, and gave me a kiss.

There were a lot of emotions on Chase's face. Sadness. Confusion. Betrayal. Relief.

No one spoke.

Until . . .

"Are those for visitors?" Grandma Sally said, and grabbed a big handful of chocolates.

I glared at her.

And then took two for myself. Yum!

Chase was sitting on the couch. "The funny part is, I don't even have a lawyer of my own. Hubert and I use the same one."

Ooh! I had a great idea!

"Chase! The owner of Big Noise Media began her career as an entertainment lawyer. Give her a call. I know her dad and I'm sure she'll work super hard because she needs a gig!"

As I was writing down the number for Chase, I heard Becky audibly gasp.

Standing in the doorway was Mitchell Flynn!

He's not only a big Broadway star, but he's also one of Becky's favorites. He's as handsome as Chase, but with shoulder-length sandy-blond hair and shoulders almost as broad as the door frame.

"Chase," he said, walking in.

Chase stood up. "Mitchell."

They looked at each other.

Were they friends? Rivals?

"I just came to—"

"Come here!" Chase said, and wrapped him in a big hug.

Suddenly they began talking a mile a minute.

"Chase! I was an idiot. Will you ever forgive me?"

"I was the idiot, Mitchell."

"We both were."

Was this a nighttime soap? I was loving it!

Chase hugged him again. "I listened to Hubert. It's like he

brainwashed me against you. Against everyone." He put his hands on Mitchell's shoulders and looked right in his eyes. "I'm sorry."

"I get it, Chase. He took advantage of your sadness. It was a bad time for you."

"But I never wanted to lose you!"

They hugged and then Chase started laughing.

"We're acting like we're alone! I have to introduce you to everybody."

Mitchell waved at us.

"Everybody!" Chase said, clapping his hands to get our attention. "This is Mitchell Flynn. Now he's a Broadway star, but I knew him as Mitchell Fleishbaum, theater geek!"

Mitchell laughed. "We went to high school together and starred in all the musicals!"

"Correction," said Chase, giving him a punch on the arm. "*I* starred in all the musicals. You were always my sidekick."

"What? Sancho Panza is a big part!"

"Not as big as Don Quixote!"

AH!!!!!! I can't believe I didn't recognize him on the *Man of La Mancha* video!

Mitchell was the Phantom!

Wow. He was able to lose all that weight as he got older. Hmm . . . maybe I won't always be one waist size away from stretch pants.

Chase introduced everybody and when Mitchell shook my hand, he winked and whispered, "You can keep the DVD."

"Thanks," I said.

We all stood there and I suddenly realized there was a lot of unfinished business between them. They needed some severe private time.

"Uh ... why don't you two catch up?" I asked, while backing everybody else out of the room.

"Justin! Call me tomorrow after school!" Chase yelled as we left.

We were almost out the stage door when I realized I forgot someone.

I ran back to the dressing room and saw Grandma Sally putting the remaining chocolate in her purse. "He said it's for guests," she muttered defensively as I ushered her out.

Since it wasn't that late, we all decided to get something to eat.

"Why go out?" asked Grandma Sally. "I still have tons of food at the apartment that I bought for you." She got quiet. "And you'll be gone soon."

It almost sounded like she was going to miss me. Grandma Sally is expressing warm feelings?

Wow. I guess everybody can mature, no matter what stage of life they're in.

I looked at her warmly. Instead of looking back at me, she scanned my friends and gave them a wink. "That means tomorrow I won't have to guard my plate from the human vacuum cleaner anymore!"

And some people stay the same.

EPILOGUE

It's been a few weeks since *Thousand-Watt Smile*'s first preview and I've only heard great things about the show. Chase has started doing the morning talk shows, and all the hosts introduce him by saying he's the leading contender for this year's Tony Award! Who would have thought that when I first heard him whisper-sing at that tech rehearsal?

Right now it's snowing out, but I'm firmly ensconced in my house. I will, in fact, be firmly ensconced here for the next few weeks as well. When my parents found out that I lied about my grandma dying, they grounded me. Which I was prepared for. The good news is, they're proud of me for admitting what I did, so they're allowing me to do the spring musical! Mrs. Hall chose Stephen Sondheim's *Company* and I got the lead! Since we have one performance on a Monday, Chase told me he's coming to see it. Becky got cast, too, and she's freaking out that Chase is bringing Mitchell. And the best news is, even though I'm grounded for two more weeks, my parents are letting me out to go to the *Thousand-Watt Smile* opening night! Spencer and I are renting tuxedos and Chase is getting us tickets to the after-party!

OK, here's everything that's happened since the Gypsy run-through. Chase got in touch with Mr. Perlman's daughter, Sofia, who used to run Big Noise Media. They hit it off right away and now she's his lawyer. As a matter of fact, she introduced Chase to her other partners and he liked them so much he hired them as his full-time staff! So, getting rid of Hubert has paid off in many ways.

Speaking of which, when Cristopher found out Hubert was also dating Chase, he moved out that night. I don't know how Hubert thought he was going to continue keeping that a secret, but he had a lot of confidence about hiding things. I mean, he was filching money from Chase for months *and* secretly negotiating with *Wicked Words* the whole time Chase was rehearsing *Thousand-Watt Smile.* Hubert gave Chase all of his GlitZ money back and Chase decided not to press charges. Hubert tried for a while to get another job in entertainment, but everybody in Hollywood and New York knows what happened and no one will hire him. Chase found out that he's teaching television production at the very fancy prep school he graduated from. At first I was annoyed Hubert wasn't being punished, but then I heard that it's a very strict school where the kids wear uniforms and the principal won't allow Hubert to be called by his first name. I decided that having teenagers call him Mr. Weatherbee all day long is punishment enough.

Turns out, Mitchell and Chase weren't just high school acting partners; they were also high school sweethearts and kept dating even as their careers took off on different coasts—Chase on TV and Mitchell on Broadway. They were about to come out as a couple right when Chase's mom died and he met Hubert. Hubert convinced him not to come out, claiming it would be "career suicide," and soon he manipulated Chase into firing his entire staff. Mitchell confronted Chase about his reliance on Hubert, which led to a huge fight and a subsequent messy breakup. Mitchell thought he was over it, but when Chase moved to New York, he snapped. He decided to leave a note at a *Thousand-Watt Smile* rehearsal so the cast would know that Chase was living a lie. He was only going to do it once, but once he started, he couldn't stop.

I want to think his behavior was something I'd never do, but I understand the desire. I mean, a little part of me had planned to go to GlitZ and tell everybody that Spencer still slept with a teddy bear! Mitchell had Chase's name on a Google alert, and one day my website came up because I had started writing about my internship. On my first day in New York, I put up that picture of myself standing on Grandma Sally's stoop. Little did I know that the address of the building was clearly visible behind me. Mitchell saw it and dropped off his first note that night. He told me he wore that mask because it protected him from the freezing weather and prevented any Broadway fans from recognizing him. Yes, his behavior was creepy, but it was harmless. And the truth is, if he hadn't dropped off that *Man of La Mancha* DVD, I never would have known Chase had so much talent. The great news is, they went to couples counseling and are back together again. And last week, on Chase's day off, they flew to L.A. and came out on *Ellen*. Yay!

Of course, Spencer and I see each other all the time and, since tonight is Sunday, we're hanging out with Becky. I'm still grounded, so the get-together is at my house, but I'm extra excited because the whole gang is coming. Devon, whom I email and text with every day, is taking the train out with Scotty. And the most fun part is, tonight is the unveiling of the New Year's Eve Monopoly game we never got to play! My original version was dedicated to JobSkill, but that was before any of us knew what it would be like. I've since redone the game to reflect what really went on.

First, all the playing pieces represent everyone who's playing: me, Spencer, Becky, Devon, and Scotty. There's also a Phantom mask that fits over all the pieces so anyone can elect to be the Phantom for a while. It comes with index cards because being the Phantom means that if you land on someone's property, you have to leave them a bizarre note. Boardwalk and Park Place are now Broadway (my fave place) and the Dakota (the most beautiful place). Instead of Go to Jail cards, I made cards that say "Intern at GlitZ." And the Chance and Community Chest cards are Grandma Sally insults. They don't help you advance in the game, but I know everyone's still going to clamor for a chance to read one out loud. It took me hours, but I wrote a long list and had them all printed out, from "You're wearing *that*?" to "You eat like you're starving, but you don't look it."

On my first day back at school, I went right to Ms. Horvath's office and told her that I lied about my grandma's death. Ms. Horvath is also known as E.R. because there's always some part of her body that is on the way *to* and/or just came *from* an emergency room. When I walked into her room, I was confused because she was in a wheelchair, but her arm was in a sling. I guess she could have injured both her arm and her leg, but twice during our meeting she saw someone in the hall she needed to talk to and ran down the hallway to catch them.

The first time she walked back into the room, she gave me her version of an explanation. "Sometimes when you sprain you arm, you can compensate by putting too much pressure on your legs." *You can?* "I'm using the wheelchair as a precaution." She made no sense, but I wasn't surprised when she told me she'd have to take away my credit for JobSkill because I didn't do the internship I was supposed to do. She asked me how I spent my two weeks and I told her that I interned for Chase Hudson. Suddenly, everything changed.

"Chase? Chase Hudson?" she sputtered. She started panting and I didn't know if it was her notorious high blood pressure or something else.

"You've . . . you've met him?" she asked with her eyes fluttering.

Wait a minute. Panting?

Eyes fluttering?

This wasn't one of her signature made-up sicknesses.

No.

E.R. is a *Vicious Tongues* superfan!

Yes! Maybe this could play to my advantage!

"Well, I guess you can say I've met him," I said, trying to be modest. "Many times. In fact, we hung out a *lot.*"

Her cheeks began to turn red and her hands flew to her face.

I'm sure she knew I was on to her because she quickly said, "I must be having an allergic reaction. Those two crackers I had at lunch gave me *quite* a dose of gluten!"

How can two crackers give you quite a dose of anything?

I nodded like I understood and decided to start leaving to see if she'd stop me. I was halfway out the door when she called to me.

"Wait!" she yelled, and bolted out of her wheelchair. She led me back into the room with her good arm. "Do you know why Chase isn't doing *Wicked Words*? Also, is he still dating Zoe Swenson?" I started to answer, but she kept talking. "And will the fourth season of *Vicious Tongues* ever come out on DVD? I'm hoping the special features will have some more hilarious bloopers like the first three seasons." Yet again, I started to answer, but she cut me off. "I'm just curious, you know . . . for academic reasons."

"Of course," I said. Then I sighed heavily. "I would love to stay and tell you everything, and boy do I know a lot, but I have to try to figure out some way to make up for the JobSkill credit I lost."

Her eyes darted back and forth incredibly quickly and at first I thought she was having one of her vertigo attacks that always seem to happen at school assemblies for maximum attention, but then I realized she was frantically thinking.

"How about," she said slowly, "you do a writing assignment about how you spent JobSkill and we'll see if you can get credit that way? Wouldn't that be nice?"

She looked at me needily.

"Wow!" I said. "That would be great."

"And spare no detail." She ripped her arm out of her sling and grabbed both of my hands. Hard. "Write down *everything*."

I left her room excited at the prospect of making up my credit, but then I became overwhelmed. There was so much to write. And some of the things that happened were embarrassing!

And a few were my own fault. Possibly more than a few.

But whether or not 91% can be considered "more than a few," I will always remember those two weeks in Manhattan. And the most amazing part is, Spencer, Becky, and I all got exactly what we hoped we'd get.

It's true! Becky wanted to do something completely on her own. And she did. *And* she and Scotty are still seeing each other with no help from me!

Except at lunch when I offer free, unsolicited advice, she still acts like I'm driving her crazy. But I noticed she did ask Scotty to the Spring Fling even though she first told me a big TV star would find it too babyish.

Spencer had told us on that fateful night in Starbucks that he was disappointed because he had hoped to use math to help the world. Well, because he was in the accounting department, he discovered that those GlitZ checks weren't being cashed by Chase and it did indeed "help the world" by preventing Hubert from ruining Chase's life.

And I had the magical experience of seeing Chase give that brilliant first performance. I dreamed of seeing myself on Broadway and even though I wasn't physically onstage, I achieved my goal. Chase and I rehearsed for hours on Sunday and there were so many moments I helped him with. Yes, Chase was doing the actual performing, but every time he nailed a laugh or remembered to breathe before a high note, it was like seeing myself on that stage.

Writing the report wasn't as hard as I thought. After all, I've had plenty of time to write since I've been stuck in this house every night.

I finished it today and it's almost twenty pages! I took out the really personal stuff about Chase but left in anything about *Vicious Tongues,* plus an extended description of how he looked wearing his gym outfit. I just have to run spell-check and I'm done.

It's perfect timing because any minute Spencer will arrive with the food, Becky with a DVD, and Scotty and Devon with two bags of Levain cookies.

Tomorrow I hand it in. And just to make sure E.R. gives me full credit, I'm having a friend drop it off with me. That's right, Chase is coming to the school to personally hand it to E.R. Hopefully she'll have her signature smelling salts in her purse so she can be revived after she faints.

And yes, Spencer approves of my plan. Even he thinks a little scheming once in a while is fine, as long as I run it by him first.

Speaking of Spencer, I think I hear the doorbell. And voices.

Yes! It's Spencer, Devon, Scotty, and Becky.

This theater geek may have fallen a few times (more than a few), but I have a feeling he's about to rise again.

ASAP!

ACKNOWLEDGMENTS

My agent, Eric Myers, who took me on as a client after reading just a little bit of my first book, *Broadway Nights*. Thank you for believing in me and dealing with my mind-boggling procrastination.

My mom for constantly recommending great books for me to read and keeping my love of reading alive.

My sister Beth for reading and complimenting my Playbill.com column each week and therefore giving me confidence in my writing. As well as "downloading" (aka printing) it for Mom every week. (Our mom thinks when something has been printed, it's been downloaded. She literally doesn't know what the word means.)

My sister Nancy for loving my books and begging me to get someone in Hollywood to turn them into a film.

My dad for taking me to the library all the time after my piano lesson, where I learned to love young adult novels.

My wonderful family: my husband for an immeasureable amount of support and love, and our kid, Juli, for recommending my books to all of her friends (and for letting me read this to her as a bedtime story, aka using her as a human guinea pig to tell me if the book is good or not).

The whole team at Random House, especially Michelle Nagler. You make me feel like an important author.

To my friend Jack Plotnick, who was able to calmly deal with my calling him in the middle of the night and telling him I couldn't finish the story. And for helping me figure out the mystery of Hubert and the Phantom.

And, most importantly, to Schuyler Hooke. Without his guidance, editing, pushing, and, quite frankly, the initial idea of my writing a young adult novel, this book *never* would have happened.

ABOUT THE AUTHOR

SETH RUDETSKY is the Broadway host, seven days a week, on Sirius Satellite Radio. As a pianist, Seth has played for more than a dozen Broadway shows, including *Ragtime, Les Miz,* and *Phantom.* He was the artistic producer and music director for the first five annual Actors Fund Fall Concerts, including *Dreamgirls* with Audra McDonald and *Hair* with Jennifer Hudson. In 2007 he made his Broadway acting debut in *The Ritz* and has also appeared on TV in *Law & Order: Criminal Intent.* As an author, he penned the books *The Q Guide to Broadway,* now in its third printing, and *Broadway Nights,* which was also released as an audiobook featuring the voices of Andrea Martin, Jonathan Groff, and Kristin Chenoweth. He also writes a weekly column on Playbill.com.